DAWN OF MIST

DAWN OF MIST

THE OREMERE CHRONICLES PREQUEL COLLECTION

HELEN SCHEUERER

TALEM PRESS

Published by Talem Press, 2020

An imprint of Writer's Edit Press

www.talempress.com

First printing, 2020

Print ISBN 978-0-6486731-1-8

Ebook ISBN 978-0-6486731-0-1

Cover design by Alissa Dinallo

CONTENTS

ALSO BY HELEN SCHEUERER

The Oremere Chronicles

Heart of Mist (Book I, 2017)
Reign of Mist (Book II, 2018)
War of Mist (Book III, 2019)

This one's for the mist dwellers ...

AUTHOR'S NOTE

I started writing these prequel stories long before my novel, *Heart of Mist,* came out in 2017. They were a method I used in order to get to know my characters better, to make sure their stories didn't simply spring into being upon opening a book, or cease upon turning the last page.

Originally, I never intended to share them with anyone. They were a technique I employed to build well-rounded characters and nothing more. There was something intensely rewarding about working on these stories and plotting characters' lives just for me. But soon, I had the idea to send them to my email subscribers, as bonus material for those who were loyally following the progress of *Heart of Mist* before its release.

And then, a funny thing happened. I kept writing them.

The more of these stories I wrote, the more I enjoyed writing them, and my readers it seemed, liked them too. The prequels provided an escape for me, just as the *Oremere* books did. This time: an escape from the stress of book production and marketing. An escape from the deadlines and the enormity of the series' overarching plots. They gave me the space and the freedom to enjoy my characters again.

In April 2017, I sent the first ever prequel, 'Break', to my subscribers. Between now and then, in addition to the *Oremere* books, I've published around three prequels each year.

In this collection, you'll find those original nine prequels (edited), but you'll also find seven new prequels, completely exclusive to this book. Each one of these stories takes place *before* the events in *Heart of Mist*. For the most part, the narratives focus on three of the four main point-of-view characters in *The Oremere Chronicles*: Bleak, Swinton and Henri, for the simple reason that our friend Dash hadn't actually been born yet for much of this period. The prequels themselves are standalone, but are presented in this book chronologically for each character, so I'd suggest reading cover-to-cover.

Amidst these pages, you will find breadcrumbs from the series explored in depth; you'll learn the secrets we never truly get the answers to in the series; and potentially most important of all, you'll come to understand the characters you love more fully. Or so I hope.

Whether this venture into the mist is your first, your millionth or your last, I wish you happy reading, folks …

— Helen Scheuerer

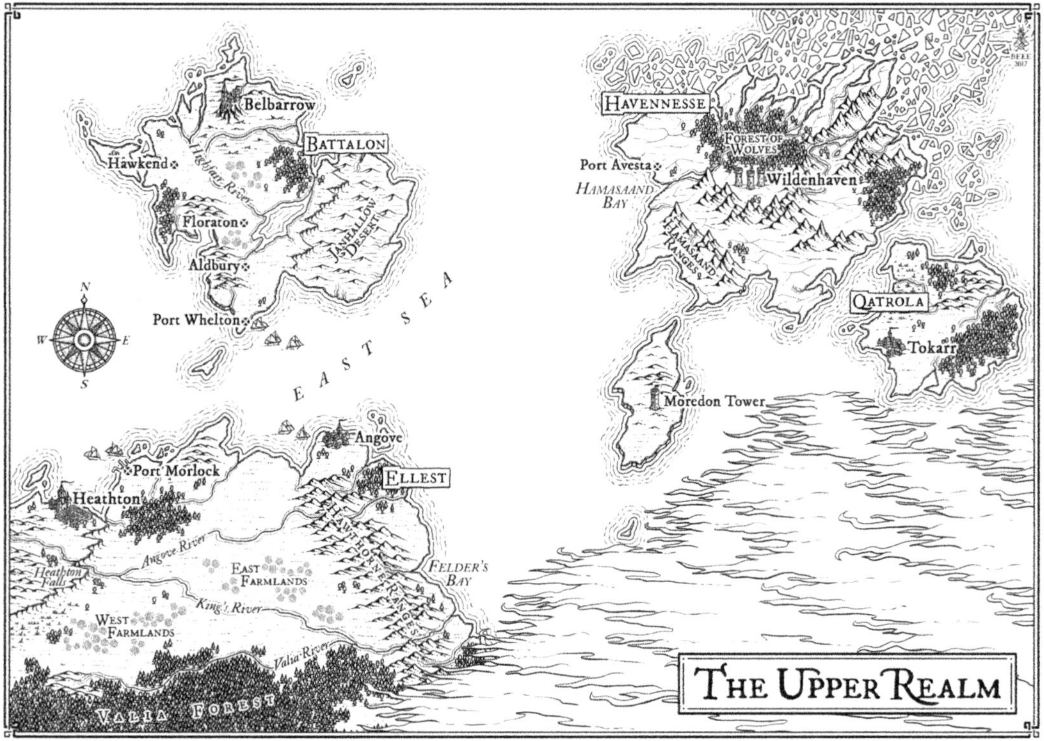
The Upper Realm
Havennesse
Forest of Wolves
Wildenhaven
Port Avesta
Hamasaand Bay
Hamasaand Ranges
Qatrola
Tokarr
Moredon Tower
Battalon
Belbarrow
Hawkend
Highfair River
Floraton
Aldbury
Janhallow Desert
Port Whelton
East Sea
N
E
S
W
Angove
Ellest
Port Morlock
Heathton
Hawthorne Ranges
Felder's Bay
Angove River
Heathton Falls
East Farmlands
King's River
West Farmlands
Valia River
Valia Forest

BREAK

Waves slapped against the side of the ship, and Bleak inhaled the briny sea air as they dipped up and down with the current. The coast of Ellest had disappeared an hour ago, and now there was no land in sight, only the flat expanse of water in every direction. Bren and Senior were checking the fishing nets while Bleak manned the wheel. She watched the two figures, teenager and man, wrangle with the pulleys and chat quietly between themselves. Bren's fair hair had fallen into his eyes and he tucked it behind his ear. She did the same, absentmindedly, tucking loose wisps of her own ash-blonde hair into the knot atop her head.

'How's it faring up there, Half-Pint?' Senior called out, squinting through the sun's glare as he looped a rope around his elbow.

'Better than down there with you and Butter Fingers,' she replied, grinning.

Senior had called her 'Half-Pint' ever since she could remember. At first, it had been her scrawny frame that earned her the nickname, but more recently she'd taken to having half a pint of ale with dinner. A hot meal and a drink with Senior was one of her favourite pastimes. It felt like family.

'Enough cheek outta ya,' Senior said, hanging the rope in its place and making his way toward the helm. 'At least Bren knows how to respect his elders,' he added, messing up her hair when he reached her.

She swatted his hand away and moved aside for him.

Senior's weathered hands gripped the wheel. He glanced at her, his kind brown eyes meeting her own odd-coloured irises. She didn't look away as she usually did with people. Her odd eyes had always been a source of anguish for her; people all over the realm saw them as a defection, a sign of dark magic that had once crawled across the continents. But Senior … Senior had said different was *good*, different was *better*. He'd said the same thing about her magic.

'There aren't many Ashai folk like you left,' he'd say. 'Your magic is a *gift*.'

Now, she turned back to the seas before them. 'Nets full yet?' she asked.

'Not full enough. Give it a few hours and we'll head inland.'

'Battalonian trout?'

'Mostly. Reckon I can see some bream in there too.'

Bleak nodded and lifted her face to the sun, closing her eyes. The warm rays soaked into her skin, and contentment settled over her. This was where she was meant to be, out on the water with Senior and Bren. She watched her friend adjust the sails. His white shirt was near-transparent with sweat and clung to his muscular back. He fumbled with one of the pulleys.

Butter Fingers, Bleak mused, and raised a brow at Senior. Senior shook his head in mock disdain.

'Check the mainsail, will ya? The lad's good for heavy lifting, but them ropes need an expert touch, eh?' He winked.

Bleak laughed and slid down the rail to the main deck, elbowing Bren out of the way before he made a real mess of things.

Bren rolled his eyes and rubbed his ribs, resigned. 'Senior sent ya to supervise, then?'

'More like take over.'

'If I don't do it right, bloody show me how, will ya?'

'I *have*.'

'So show me again.'

Bleak tried to hide her smile, but Bren's own grin told her she'd failed. She took the rope from his hands and held it out in front of her.

'For the four hundredth time,' she said, 'it's called a hammerhead knot.' She threaded the damp rope through the ring of the sail, and felt his gaze settle on her, not the knot she was tying.

'Watching?'

'Yep.'

She glanced up at him and frowned. He burst out laughing, and she punched his arm.

'Hey! Yer s'posed to be teaching me!'

'Then quit mucking around.'

Bren raised his hands in surrender. 'Sorry, sorry!' he said, staring pointedly at the rope in her hands.

She glared at him and wove the length between her fingers, looping it around and pulling it tight. 'See?'

He nodded, the laughter gone. 'Let me try?'

She held the rope out to him, and his calloused fingers touched her own as he took it from her. Bleak pulled her hand away, panic surging as his mind opened to hers. She took a step back.

Mind whisperer. That's what her kind were called. Ever since she'd met Senior as a child, she had heard things. *Voices*. The thoughts of those around her. It came and went, but with Bren ... When their skin touched, she heard the whisperings of his mind, clear as day, as though he were speaking inside her head.

Gift? She didn't think so. She needed to find another healer in Heathton. There *had* to be someone there who could help her.

'Like this?' Bren was saying, showing her the new knot. His voice brought her back, and she examined his handiwork, careful not to touch him when she took it from his hands.

'Tighter,' she said. 'Like *this*.'

'Right.' His brow furrowed as he watched her work the rope. When she'd secured it to the mainsail, she wiped her hands on her pants and went to the starboard side. She rested her elbows on the railing and leaned forward into the lowering sun's warm rays. She loved the feeling of the heat sinking into her skin as the wind tried to pull her hair from its tie. Here, she could forget about what she was. Here, she could just *be*.

Bren joined her, nudging her gently so there was room for his muscled arms. The silence between them was comfortable: laced with familiarity, and the same deep appreciation for the rocking sea below them. Bren and his two eldest brothers were the only ones of the seven Clayton boys who worked out on the water. The rest of them preferred the stability of firm ground beneath their boots. Mrs Clayton preferred it that way too, and was always fussing upon Bren's return.

Bleak snuck a glance in Bren's direction. He'd grown a lot in the past few months or so. He'd always been tall, but now he towered over her, and his previously lanky frame had bulked out with muscle thanks to Senior's delegation of heavy lifting. The arm of his shirt billowed in the breeze. He smelled faintly of rose soap.

'Half-Pint, Butter Fingers! Quit yer daydreaming

and check the nets. Sun's going down,' Senior called from the helm.

Bleak smiled. 'Come on,' she said to Bren.

They went to the stern, and Bleak saw the nets brimming with Battalonian trout and bream.

'Looking good here, Senior,' she called up to her carer.

He nodded. 'We'll head straight on to Heathton then. I've got a few men in the docks there. We'll keep the catch fresh.'

Hope swelled in Bleak's chest. Heading on to Heathton meant she'd have another chance at finding a healer. Perhaps there was a cure for her magic she hadn't found yet. Continuing to the capital also meant they'd stay out on the seas overnight. She slept far better out at sea, as though the current rocked her to sleep like an infant. The route they'd take in the morning was also more exciting, more challenging. She knew these waters better than she knew herself now, and was always thirsting for a real test of her expertise.

Bleak watched as Bren speared three trout in the dragging net and brought them up onto the deck. She licked her lips. There was nothing more delicious than the day's catch grilling on the fire.

'Half-Pint,' Senior said, grasping her shoulder, 'give an old man a hand taking in the sails, will ya? Can't run this beauty all on me own.'

Together, they lowered the heavy sails while Bren sat hunched over with his fillet knife, descaling the rainbow fish. He worked meticulously, at the same time stoking the flames of the small cooking fire, placing their grilling tray on top.

'He might be a butter fingers, Half-Pint, but the lad knows how to gut a trout, I'll say that,' Senior said.

The sun dipped below the horizon, the air turning cool. The moon's reflection shimmered across the top of the black water, and thousands of stars winked down at them. After they'd dropped anchor, they brought a small table up on deck from the cabin below and sat around it, eating the grilled fish with their fingers. The meat was tender – Bren had flavoured it with Battalonian spices. Like Senior always said, dinner tasted better after you'd earned it. Bleak ate her fish, and then picked at Bren's leftovers until he slapped her hand away. She leaned back, hand on her belly, suddenly sleepy.

'I'll take first watch,' said Bren, patting her knee.

She wasn't going to argue. Her lids were heavy and the cot below deck was calling her name. She left Bren and Senior to clear up and staggered down the stairs into the cosy cabin, where she lit a lamp and pushed off her boots.

There were two cot beds, hers and Senior's. It had only been in the last six months that Bren had started to join them on their intermittent trips without the whole crew. At first, Bleak had resented the addition. She relished the time she had just with Senior. But Bren was her friend, and Senior loved him like a son. And they *had* had some adventures together.

Bleak eased herself into her cot. Her body sank down into the straw mattress and she tugged the blankets up to her chin. Yes, she quite liked having Bren Clayton around, especially when he cooked dinner.

The rocking sea was like a lullaby, soothing her, somehow keeping all her worries at bay. She nestled further into the blankets, heard Senior bid Bren goodnight in the distance and enter the cabin. Sleep pulled her under.

She dreamed of a faraway place. A place of grey, a place of mist. Long fronds of soft grass tickled her palms as she walked through them. It was familiar to her.

What is this place? When was I here before?

She arrived at a pair of wrought-iron gates that towered above her, embellished with flourishes ending in sharp spikes. She'd seen these gates swing open before, many times, but where? It certainly hadn't been like this – shrouded in mist, coated in an eeriness that would break the focus of even the strongest warrior. And she was no warrior.

Goosebumps rushed across her skin as she stepped through the open gates, the town that lay before her now all too familiar. Bleak felt a hot breath in her ear and jumped, stifling a yelp of terror.

She whirled around. There was no one there. She was completely alone.

Am I losing my mind?

Hands trembling by her sides, Bleak stepped tentatively onto the main road, slowly making her way towards the village square she somehow *knew* was beyond the mist. The damp air settled on her skin. Nothing moved here. It was a ghost town, filled with strange whisperings and a resounding sadness that clutched at Bleak's chest. Around her, the steps of the townhouses opened up onto the street she was on, but there were no lanterns lit within. She could only see the mist before her by the light of the moon, high and brilliant, almost silver against the inky night.

'Bleak,' someone called in the distance. She clapped a hand over her mouth, muffling a scream. Trying to quieten her racing thoughts, she focused, straining to hear the voice. Her name sounded familiar on the stranger's lips, wherever they were.

Unsteady on her feet, she stumbled suddenly, catching herself just before she landed on the rough dirt. *'Bleak!'*

She started. The voice was closer this time, and urgent. She knew that voice.

'Bleak, help.'

The panic tore shreds from her, jolting her right to the core.

. . .

Bleak was ripped from her dream and shot bolt upright in her cot. Slick with sweat, her chest heaved as she tried to catch her breath.

Just a dream, she told herself, *a nightmare.* She wiped her brow on the sleeve of her shirt, still reeling.

'Bleak!'

She jumped again. The voice was clear as crystal in her mind now, and she knew who it belonged to. *Bren.*

Bleak flung herself at the ladder and scrambled up on deck. Outside, rain hammered down and she slipped on the soaked timber as she scrambled to find Bren, landing painfully on her hip. The sea battered the side of the ship, a vicious wave breaking across the deck like a rabid dog foaming at the mouth.

'Bren!' she cried out, squinting through the downpour, unable to see him. 'Bren!'

A fist of fear clenched around Bleak's heart. The ship free-fell hard into the next swell, more icy salt water spraying across the main deck.

'Bleak!'

'Where *are* you?' Bleak screamed into the wind. She looked around wildly, searching for his muscular figure, possibly fallen and injured. But the ship was empty, and her voice was lost amidst the roar of the waves.

He's not here – not on the ship, she realised.

She bolted to the port side and gripped the railing

for dear life, scanning the sea. There was nothing but giant black waves sucking at the hull.

'Bleak —'

The voice came from the starboard side. Bleak launched herself in its direction, snatching up a rope from one of the hooks. As she ran, she looped it around her waist, tying it tight. When she reached the railing, she searched the churning swell desperately.

He's here, he has *to be.*

With expert hands she tied the other end of the rope to the railing in a blur and crawled over the other side, clutching the railing as the ship lurched into the crushing force of the water below.

There was a flash of white amidst the dark swell. *Bren's shirt,* Bleak realised, and she jumped.

The drop took forever, and Bleak braced herself for the icy impact. But when she broke the water's surface, nothing could have prepared her for the shattering pain, the bone-splitting cold. She plunged deep into the sea, her lungs already screaming for air, her body already threatening to shut down.

Swim, Bleak urged herself, *swim to Bren.* She broke the sea's surface with a desperate gasp for air. A wave pummelled into her, sending her spiralling into the depths of the water once more. She had to *fight.* With all the strength she had, she kicked and flailed and pushed herself through the churning waves. Her boots were blocks of iron. She was dragged under as she struggled to kick them free.

The rope! she remembered, gripping the length tied around her waist and following it up to air.

There was a flash of white again. Bleak had no idea what she'd do when she reached Bren, or *if* she'd reach him, but she had to try, or she'd die with him. Bren and Senior were all she had – she wouldn't go back to Angove without one of them. But it was the face of Mrs Clayton that appeared in her mind then: how she'd look when they told her she'd lost her son. It was her face that forced Bleak to find that strength, that power inside her, and forge on through the pounding sea.

When she reached Bren, he was face down.

'Bren,' Bleak screamed, turning him over, floating him on his back. 'Bren!'

She struggled to hold him against her, his shoulder blades pressed to her chest as the waves continued to slap against them and drag them under.

'I'm here now, Bren, I'm here,' she said into his ear, gripping the rope around her waist with her free hand.

What now? We'll drown here. Bleak cursed herself for not waking Senior, but there had been no time. She turned back to Bren's motionless form. How could she get them *both* back up on deck?

Is he even breathing? Bleak tried to feel his breath, but she was so frozen she couldn't feel *anything*, not even her own limbs. Her teeth were chattering so hard she could barely think.

It doesn't end like this, she told herself. *It can't end like this.*

She eyed the swollen fishing nets at the hull.

That's it.

With everything she had, Bleak dragged Bren through the current, near-drowning as his heavy frame tugged her under. She choked and spluttered, water filling her nose and lungs and stinging her eyes, but she kept going, kicking and gasping for air. At last she reached the nets, which were brimming with fish. Her limbs were like rocks and her energy was sapped. Sobbing, she worked Bren's limp body into the nets with the fish, deliberately tangling his arm so that his drooping head remained above water. He had to survive – *they* had to survive.

Bleak took a deep breath. Her lungs rattled with fluid and her heart hammered against her frozen core. This either worked, or they died. It was simple.

The only thing simple in our time is life and death. Senior's words came back to her as she gripped the rope tied to her middle and began the climb. Her muscles screamed. She tried to use her feet to redistribute some of her body weight, but she couldn't feel her feet, and the length of rope below flapped about wildly. Bleak hauled herself up, inch by inch, pain lancing through her body as the wind chilled her skin and her bones. The effort tore through her biceps. But she kept going. She didn't know how high she'd climbed, only that the railing of the ship was now in sight. In one final surge of energy, she threw herself up over the railing, gasping. But it wasn't over.

Bleak scrambled to her feet, unsteady as a newborn filly, but it didn't matter. She had to get to the nets, to Bren.

Senior emerged from the cabin, his face draining of colour at the sight of her. She shoved past him, darting to the stern. Her fingers fumbled with the pulleys. *Butter Fingers*. The name filled her head and steadied her hands as she worked the ropes. Senior was there, unable to understand her but helping her anyway, realising that something was *terribly* wrong.

Together, they worked the pulleys. The bulging net rose up into the air, into the rain and wind, weighed down by hundreds of fish, and somewhere, Bren's unconscious body.

'Bren!' The broken voice was Senior's this time, shock and terror etched on his lined face as he spotted the boy's pale arm sticking through the ropes and fish.

The net swung over onto the deck and landed with a thump on the timber, flapping fish spilling from its confines. There was Bren, amidst the glimmering rainbow scales. Bleak rushed towards him, shoving the netting aside and hauling Bren's head into her lap. His lips were blue, his tanned skin deathly pale. Bleak slapped the side of his face.

'Bren,' she said and slapped him again. 'Bren!' Her voice cracked and her breaths came in quick, short bursts.

Senior rubbed Bren's chest, heating the skin over his heart. 'Come on, Butter Fingers,' he murmured, rain dripping from his nose as he leaned over the unconscious boy.

'Lie him flat,' Senior said suddenly, and Bleak obeyed, shifting Bren from her lap, placing his head gently on the wet timber planks.

Senior knelt beside Bren's body and lay his hands on Bren's chest, one on top of the other. He started to pump Bren's heart from the outside.

'Please, Bren,' Bleak whispered, gripping his shoulder hard. She couldn't feel the cold anymore, or the pain. All she felt was desperation for him to live, for him to be alright.

Senior pressed on Bren's chest again and again, his jaw clenched, his eyes focused.

'I will not bring a body back to your ma, Butter Fingers,' he ground out.

Suddenly Bren's eyes flew open and his chest heaved. There was a rattling gasp for air as he fought to breathe. Bleak's heart leaped, and she rolled him onto his side. What seemed like half the sea emptied from Bren as he vomited and spluttered, rasping for breath.

Relief. Utter relief flooded Bleak, warming her chilled bones. Her body sagged. She was so, *so* heavy. But she was fine, better than fine, Bren was alive.

Bleak felt herself slide as everything went black, and her head hit the timber deck

. . .

The smell of freshly baked damper filled Bleak's nostrils, and she realised that she was no longer cold. Eyes still closed, she wriggled her toes and joy rushed through her; she could *feel* her toes again.

'Ya could'a died,' growled Senior's voice from beside her.

Her eyes fluttered open.

'Damn fool, Half-Pint,' he said, a warm hand closing around her arm.

The cabin was filled with soft light from the portholes. Bleak squinted up at Senior.

'Bren?' she croaked.

'The lad's fine. A little battered, with a bruised ego, but fine. Thanks to *you*.'

Bleak exhaled a shaky breath. 'What … what happened?'

'Says the storm hit suddenly. Thought he could handle it. Got thrown overboard, hit his head on the way down.'

'But he's alright?'

'Butter Fingers is *fine*. He's up there making breakfast, if ya got the strength.'

Bleak pushed herself up into a sitting position, every muscle protesting. She winced and leaned back into the cushions.

'I dunno know how ya did it,' Senior muttered, gazing at her in wonder. 'I dunno know how ya got there in time, or how ya managed to survive in that, let alone bring him back with ya. I don't understand any of it.'

Bleak shook her head. There was only one thing she understood. 'I heard him,' she said.

'But Bleak —' Understanding spread across Senior's face. He touched her temple with two fingers. 'You heard him, up here?'

She nodded.

It was Senior's turn to shake his head. 'I told ya it was a *gift*, Half-Pint. An absolute gift.'

Senior helped her out of the cot, put her arm around his shoulder. Together, they shuffled to the ladder.

'You sure you're up for this?' he said.

She nodded. By the looks of the cabin and the clothes, plates and mugs strewn about, she'd already spent a lot of time down here.

The ladder was harder to climb than she imagined – her legs were agony. But she made it out into the daylight. At the cooker stood Bren, turning golden loaves of damper over the grill, yellow rays of sun catching in his fair hair. He looked up and saw her there.

Bleak froze. What now? Had something changed between them? What would she say? She nearly buckled under the the weight of all her questions, and the recollection of the terror that had filled her at the thought of losing him. Bren must have seen each feeling pass through her, because he didn't rush to her, didn't splutter an emotional thanks. Instead, he grinned.

'Finally gracing us with yer presence?' he said.

'Ungrateful oaf,' she retorted, moving towards him and swiping a piece of damper from his plate.

Senior's knees cracked as he sat down by Bren and rolled his eyes.

'What happened to the catch?' Bleak said, suddenly remembering the hundreds of fish spilling across the deck.

'The rain helped there,' said Senior. 'We salvaged most of it, and whatever we lost we'll re-catch on the way to Heathton.'

'So you're not making us go back?' Hope flickered.

'I wanted to turn back to Angove,' the old fisherman said, glancing up from his food, 'but Butter Fingers here insisted that you'd want to continue on to the capital.'

Bleak couldn't hide her surprise.

Bren shrugged in her direction. 'I know there's something you want in Heathton.'

Her eyes widened.

But Bren just smiled. 'Whatever it is, I want to help you find it.'

Bleak looked from Bren to Senior, and nodded slowly. 'Yes,' she said. 'I want to go to Heathton.'

VIPER'S KISS

'Pull back!' Commander Dimitri Swinton bellowed over the rain of arrows. 'Pull back!'

The hot sand shifted beneath his boots as he slid down the other side of the crest they'd returned fire from. The skirmish was *not* going to plan. The desert rebels weren't the foolish commonfolk King Roswall of Battalon had claimed them to be.

An arrow skimmed across Swinton's armoured shoulder. 'Pull back,' he yelled again.

His men were scattered, not faring well in the foreign terrain. The village they'd attacked had been transformed into a military stronghold, one that Swinton's forces were yet to breach.

'Fi,' he called, spotting his bulky Battalonian friend knocking a lone rebel fighter to the ground. 'Tell the men to retreat.'

Captain Murphadias nodded and signalled to his

band of men. Swinton did the same. Divided, the Ellestian forces withdrew to the temporary barracks they'd built on the outskirts of the village. They hadn't expected to be here for long, and now, the camp offered little to no shelter. Swinton gritted his teeth as he helped his men. Arrows stuck out from more than one soldier, sweat and blood coated exposed flesh, and the muffled moans of pain became a chorus. Swinton dragged Stefan towards cover. The young squire, who shouldn't have been out in the field at all, now had an arrow protruding from his shoulder.

'Come on, Stefan,' Swinton muttered. 'It's only a flesh wound.'

'It's worse.' Fi came up beside them, lifting Stefan's other arm around his shoulder. 'We need to remove the arrow and wash the wound out, fast,' he said. 'These have been tipped with viper venom.'

Swinton swore. 'Lennox,' he called to the nearest able soldier. 'Anyone who's got an arrow wound is to be brought to the medic tent immediately.'

'Yes, Commander.'

The medic tent offered no reprieve from the heat or the stench. Swinton and Fi pushed Stefan onto a cot and held him down as a healer eased the arrow from the wound. Stefan cried and clawed at Swinton's arm, but Swinton held him steady.

'Serves you damn right for disobeying orders,' he snapped.

Fi grimaced. 'Maybe wait until he survives before you start on the lectures, eh, old friend?'

Swinton glowered as the tent filled with over a dozen men nursing arrow wounds. 'The village is impenetrable with the force we have,' he hissed at Fi. 'We need to change tactics.'

'Agreed.'

'Meet me in my tent in ten minutes.'

Swinton left Fi to direct the healers. He had to *think*. But the desert muddled his mind. He hated this place. He hated the blazing heat that pressed down on his armour. He hated the fountain grass that concealed deadly serpents. And he hated the way the sand constantly shifted beneath his boots, making him unsteady on his feet. But what he hated *most* of all was being dragged into a neighbouring king's fight.

King Roswall had raised taxes for agriculture outside of the capital, and as a result, two of the desert clans had rebelled against the crown. So far, the rebels had killed three separate Battalonian units who had come to bring them the king's justice. They knew the desert better than any city soldiers, and used the elements and terrain to their advantage. At his wits' end, King Roswall had sought the aid of King Arden, who had sent Swinton and his men to deal with the rebels.

Now, Swinton trudged heavily across the sand, ignoring the stench of unwashed bodies and festering wounds. War camps just about anywhere left much to be desired; war camps in the desert were foul on another level entirely.

Wiping the sweat from his brow with a rag, he entered his tent. He removed his breastplate, the cotton shirt beneath sticking to his skin. The armour had left a red indent on his sternum. Rubbing the welt mindlessly, he went to the table and surveyed the strategy sketches he'd made the night before.

Useless. Utterly useless. The rebels had fortified their walls to withstand just about anything, and from what Fi had said, they had supplies to last months. Swinton massaged the bridge of his nose. As the newly appointed commander of the Ellestian army, he needed to end this quickly and quietly, before he lost too many men. Before his chance at knighthood slipped away.

'Don't look so defeated, old friend,' Fi said, striding into the tent.

'Well, it's not looking promising. How are these rebels so organised?'

Fi shrugged. 'Never underestimate the hardiness of those who live in the Janhallow Desert. It takes a certain kind of people to flourish out here.'

'I'll keep that in mind,' Swinton muttered. 'How's Stefan?'

'He'll live.'

'Good. Your king didn't see fit to warn us of the viper venom, then?'

'It's unusual that a clan would have it …'

Swinton exhaled a heavy breath. 'If you hadn't

been here ... we would have lost those men. Would have lost Stefan.'

'Good thing I'm here, then.'

'Indeed ...' Swinton paced the tent. 'You say it's unusual for a desert clan to have a store of viper venom?'

Fi nodded. 'A large store, yes. Which they clearly have.'

'Which means they can pick us off with arrows every time we charge. Even a shallow graze could be fatal ...'

'We need to breach their walls. In close quarters, we could defeat them – they're not skilled warriors. They have good archers, but other than that ...'

Swinton stopped. 'Where do they get the venom from?'

'Judging by the stores they have ... they'd need dozens of vipers. Maybe more. Only a small amount can be milked from the fangs at a time. They would have a farm.'

Suppressing a shudder, Swinton continued to pace, while Fiore sat down and poured them both drinks.

The Battalonian took a long swig from his cup and looked to Swinton. 'They wouldn't keep the farm in the village ...' he said slowly.

'No?'

Fi shook his head. 'Too dangerous to keep that many vipers so close.'

'So ...?'

'It'll be around here somewhere, still within range for them to top up their stores.'

'So we cut off their supply?'

Fi stood and pressed a cup into Swinton's hand. 'We can do better than that …'

They waited until nightfall, when the desert transformed from a sweltering red plain into a dark, cold abyss. Swinton and Fi rode out alone, their horses whinnying anxiously, as though they sensed what lay at the end of their search. Swinton himself still wasn't convinced it was a plausible plan, and the idea of playing with a bunch of vipers didn't exactly set his mind at ease.

'It has to be within riding range of the stronghold,' Fiore said over the soft thud of their horses' hooves. 'But it will be guarded.'

'Heavily?'

'I doubt it. They don't have the men to spare.'

Swinton nodded, urging his horse to keep up with Fi's. In the pale moonlight, the desert looked like one big blanket of dust to Swinton, but Fiore knew the lay of the land well, and led them across its vast plains with ease.

'You smell that?' Fi asked, halting his mount.

Swinton inhaled. 'Lantern oil.'

'We're close. Take it on foot from here. We want to see them before they see us, old friend.'

They left their horses. As Swinton unsheathed his

battleaxes, he said a silent prayer that the mounts would be there upon their return. He could think of nothing worse than being stranded out in the Janhallow Desert.

'Quick, quiet deaths,' he said. 'Under no circumstance can an alarm be sounded.'

Fiore palmed his fighting knives and said nothing.

Up ahead, peering over the crest of a dune, the pair spotted half a dozen lanterns illuminating a single building, and three sentries.

'I don't mind those odds,' Fi said. 'Wait here.'

'What?' Swinton hissed, watching in disbelief as Fi removed his jerkin embroidered with the Ellestian royal sigil.

'It's better this way,' he said. 'Trust me, old friend.' He left Swinton in the shadows, watching on, bewildered.

Fiore approached the trio with open arms. Swinton couldn't hear exactly what he was saying in his native Battalonian tongue. But the sentries appeared receptive. Before Fiore struck.

He had them out cold in an instant.

Out cold, Swinton noted. *Not dead.* He said as much upon approach.

'They are my brothers,' Fiore said. 'I cannot kill them in cold blood, Dimitri. They're only doing their job.'

Swinton bit back a retort. He couldn't ask his friend to slaughter his own people, but he knew …

One of these days … Fiore's sympathies would come back to haunt him.

'Let's just get a move on,' Swinton ground out, following Fi to the building.

He heard them before they opened the door. The low hissing, en masse. Swinton's skin crawled. He wasn't partial to any deadly creatures, least of all Battalonian desert vipers. Fi passed him a handful of hessian sacks.

'Gods, we're actually going ahead with this madness?'

'Unless you have a better idea, Commander?'

Swinton swore at Fi and wrenched open the door.

A deep pit greeted them. What slithered within was the stuff of nightmares. Over a hundred black vipers glided across one another, their hissing near deafening.

The men surveyed the equipment that lined the wall: pairs of long iron tongs, hooks and leather gloves.

'We don't have all night,' Fi said, reaching across and taking a giant hook from the wall.

Cursing, Swinton did the same and peered into the pit. Shiny black bodies writhed around, the larger ones striking viciously at their smaller counterparts.

'You've done this before?'

Fi raised a brow. 'Sure.'

'Liar.'

They fixed a hessian sack to one of the hooks and levered it into the pit.

'This better bloody work,' Swinton said through clenched teeth. He held the pole with the sack over the bed of vipers, while Fi used a giant pair of tongs to heave squirming snakes into it. The bag wriggled over the pit, but Swinton held it firm with the hook.

'Bring it in,' Fi said.

Cringing, Swinton did as his friend bid.

'Use the loop of the hook to seal the bag.' Fi stepped towards him. 'Here.'

He let Fi take the hook, and had to stop himself leaping back. Gods, he hated Battalon.

'They can't get out?'

'No. Not unless we let them out.'

'Good.'

'Come on, we don't have much time.'

They worked quickly, aware that the guards outside wouldn't remain unconscious forever. When they had filled two dozen hessian sacks, they loaded them onto a cart.

'Horses aren't going to like this much,' Fi muttered, frowning at the moving bags.

'Can't say I like it much either.'

Fi laughed. 'Come on.'

It was nearing dawn when they returned to the barracks, cart in tow. The camp was quiet, with many of the men cradling their wounds and their pride in the privacy of their own tents. But they were out of time. Swinton summoned the leaders of each unit to his quarters and laid out their strategy.

'This must be *his* plan,' Lennox said from one end of the table, narrowing his eyes at Fi. 'It reeks of Battalonian deception.'

Fi crossed his muscled arms over his chest, a silent challenge.

But Swinton had had it with Lennox's horseshit attitude towards Fi.

'You'll show your captain the respect his rank demands,' he snapped at the soldier. 'And in case you haven't noticed, *our* plan needs to adapt. Or we'll end up like the previous three units. We're lucky to have Captain Murphadias' insights.'

Lennox opened his mouth to protest.

Swinton shook his head. 'Another word and I'll have you on watch duty for a month.' He turned to the rest of his men. 'We surround the entire perimeter. I want the catapults at the ready. We take advantage of the rising sun. Got it?'

'Yes, Commander,' the men mumbled.

'Anyone so much as scratched by an arrow is to retreat to the nearest medic. I won't lose any men today. Understood?'

Murmurs of agreement sounded around the tent.

'Good. On my command, then.'

The sun crept over the horizon as Swinton's men surrounded the village stronghold. Swinton himself stood by one of the catapults; a sack of hissing vipers lay wriggling in the bucket. His hand twitched at his side. This *had* to work.

His men were restless, eyeing the hessian bags nervously. Swinton had to stop himself from doing the same.

Three short whistles sounded. Fi's signal.

Swinton whistled back.

The men hastily unsealed the bags, while Swinton took a lit torch from Stefan and waved it in each direction.

The catapults released with a groan. The hessian bags went flying across the pink sky, straight into the heart of the enemy's stronghold.

Silence.

Swinton waved his torch again and the men muttered curses as they placed more viper missiles into the catapult buckets.

They waited. Swinton glanced back at the horizon, where the sun stained the clouds with fiery red and burnt orange. He waved his torch once more.

The packages flung from the catapults, long black bodies flying towards their target. Swinton's men reloaded and fired again. And again. They heard the soft thuds on the other side.

Swinton held up a fist. Quiet lingered within the walls. Swinton's breath caught in his lungs. What if it didn't work? What if they couldn't –

A shriek pierced the silence. And the screaming began in earnest.

'Archers, draw!' Swinton ordered. The sun had risen behind them.

The sound of chaos broke out inside the stronghold. Glass shattered, cries of terror screeched and commands were drowned out. The thick gates groaned open and a wave of rebel fighters poured out in a panic, brandishing their weapons, shielding their eyes against the blinding light of the sun.

'Loose!' Swinton bellowed.

Ellestian archers rained arrows on them.

'Draw!' he shouted again. 'Loose!'

Shouts of pain echoed across the gap between the forces, and Swinton drew his battleaxes. The rebels were still pouring from the fortress, but they were panicked, unprepared for close-quarters combat. And the sun … The sun behind the Ellestian army dazed the enemy.

'Charge!' Swinton yelled. He launched himself at the nearest rebel, striking him down in a single blow. Swinton's axes were a mere extension of himself; he wielded them with breathtaking accuracy, sinking them into enemy flesh and bone again and again. He felt the blood spatter across his armour, across his skin.

Around him, his men outmanoeuvred the inexperienced rebels, parrying and feinting, driving their blades into unprotected flesh. Swinton dodged an incoming blow and swung his axe into another man's neck. He went down like a sack of grain.

Swinton panted as he brushed the sweaty loose

hair from his brow and surveyed the battlefield. *Where's Fi?* His friend was nowhere in sight. He cut his way through the fighting, scanning the perimeter for the familiar face, suddenly uneasy.

Out of nowhere, a rebel landed a blow across his back, and Swinton staggered forward, his palms stinging across the hot sand. He scrambled to his feet and faced his opponent.

The man was no ordinary rebel. His stance betrayed his previous position – a former Battalonian warrior. He twirled his ornate fighting knives, and Swinton lunged. The clang of steel meeting steel vibrated up Swinton's arms and through his armour. The Battalonian met Swinton's attack blow for blow, his strength overshadowing Swinton's own. He moved with the precision and ease of a trained champion.

Suddenly, Swinton's feet were knocked out from beneath him. He was on his back, pinned to the ground. A blade came driving towards him – his block was weak, and his axe was sent hurtling across the sand. The Battalonian blade sank into Swinton's face. The slice opened his flesh from cheek to chin; his blood ran hot down his neck.

There was a cry. The man above him toppled over, the point of a sword protruding from his middle.

A filthy hand grasped Swinton's and hauled him up.

'Good thing I disobey orders, Commander,' Stefan said with a roguish grin.

Swinton grimaced. 'Remind me to thank you later.'

Then, he spotted Fi, who wasn't where he should have been.

'Stefan, go see if Lennox needs assistance,' he said, pointing the squire in the opposite direction.

'Right away, Commander.'

Swinton made his way towards his captain, watching as he helped Battalonian rebels onto camels and into carts.

'What are you doing?' he hissed when he reached Fi.

Fiore whirled around, startled.

'Fiore, have you lost your —'

Fiore grabbed his arm and pulled him into the shadows of the stronghold wall. 'Dimi ... I have to help them.'

'Fi, it's treason —'

'They are my people.'

'*We* are your people —'

'I'll never forget where I come from, Dimi. Help me.'

Swinton looked around at the injured Battalonians. Many of them not rebels, but women and children ... And then to his friend, his warm, gold eyes desperate.

'Gods,' Swinton muttered. He lifted a little boy

onto the nearest cart and then turned back to Fi. 'No one can know,' he said.

The Ellestian army celebrated their victory deep into the night. The cool evening air was filled with bawdy tunes and the overpowering scent of sweet Battalonian wine.

Swinton left the medic tent with twenty-seven fresh stitches from cheek to chin. He'd been lucky, and no doubt he owed Stefan a promotion. He didn't join the festivities, though. Instead, he sought the quiet of his own tent, his mind still buzzing with the events of the day.

'Thought you'd come back here,' said Fi, lounging in one of the chairs by the table, drink in hand.

Swinton nodded. 'Wanted to clear my head.'

'Thought that'd be the case too.'

'Seems I've become predictable.'

Fiore stood and filled another cup, handing it to Swinton. The wine was cool and refreshing.

'I wanted to thank you,' Fi said.

Swinton drained his cup. 'I don't understand why...'

'That's *why* I want to thank you. You risked everything. Without understanding why, for me, for my people.'

'Fi, we're your people now. You can't —'

Fiore refilled his cup. 'Dimitri, I am proud to call you brother.'

Swinton studied his friend, wondering if he'd ever know the Battalonian's full story, wondering if it even mattered. He clinked his drink to Fi's.

'To brotherhood, then.'

Fi's face broke into a wide smile, his gold eyes bright. 'To brotherhood.'

THE VALIAN HEIR

Thirteen-year-old Henrietta loved the utter freedom she felt atop the living bridges of Valia. Up here in the golden light of dusk, the magic of her ancestors whispered against her skin, wrapped around her as though she were exactly where she ought to be. The breathtaking beauty of the twisting branches stretching across the canopy made her proud to be a kindred-in-training, proud to be the sister of the next warrior queen.

'Sahara,' she called out, spotting the midnight-black braid among the leaves ahead. 'Wait for me.'

Her twin paused, leaning against a trunk protruding through the bridge. 'Didn't realise how slow you were,' she teased, her graphite eyes dancing.

'We'll see who's left behind when it's time for the Crossing,' Henri retorted, folding her arms across her chest. Sahara's fear of heights was a weakness they needed to address in her training, but so far she had been incredibly stubborn about working on it with Henri.

Now, Sahara merely clicked her tongue in frustration and started across the next bridge. Henri, as always, followed. She'd follow her sister to the ends of the realm if she had to.

As the twins trekked across the vast canopies, Henri's mind wandered to the upcoming trials. In addition to their usual daily training and testing, formal trials were held four times a year to weed out the weaker fighters. Those who failed were sent to the outskirts of the forest, known as the Sticks, where they lived a very different life to that of the Valia kindred.

Henri honestly didn't know how anyone managed to fail. They had been training since they were six years old: swords, spears, hand-to-hand combat and everything in between. To be a Valian was to embody strength and power, to be better than any other warrior in the realm. Henri had always revelled in the challenges. She loved the physicality of preparing to be one of the elite.

The upcoming trials were the most important yet. In their thirteenth year, all trainees were required to complete the Crossing. To swing across a gaping gorge and the formidable falls that barrelled down into the King's River below. Deadly and beautiful, requiring immense strength and fearlessness to complete, the Crossing was what Valian legends were made of. To complete the Crossing meant handing over one's black training leathers for the official forest-green leathers of the Valian kindred.

Henri and Sahara had crossed before, but never in front of their mother and queen, Allehra, and her elite kindred. With an audience like that, there was no higher honour at their age, and no greater risk to their reputation. Those who crossed with the most agility and abandon were selected for additional training in Havennesse, and would likely go on to become the heir's own force of elite kindred. There was no way Henri was going to miss out on that.

Sahara cleared her throat. 'You're thinking about the damn trials again.'

Henri gave a sheepish grin. 'Aren't you?'

'Not in the same way you are.'

Henri frowned. 'What do you mean?'

Sahara paused for a moment before shaking her head. 'Nothing. Come on. We're already late.'

Henri pushed aside her urge to press her sister as they arrived at the training circuit.

'There you are!' Petra exclaimed as they stepped onto the platform amidst the treetops.

'Henri's a little unfit,' Sahara taunted, waving a hand in her direction.

'Am not —'

But her sister cut her off. 'Where are the others?'

Petra gestured vaguely to the forest floor below. 'Tilly said something about the armoury. Marvel's still eating.'

'She's always eating,' Sahara laughed.

'Her ma's convinced her that the more food, the better when it comes to trials.'

'What about Athene?' Henri heard herself ask.

'On her way.' Petra repositioned one of the straw dummies.

Relief flooded through Henri. She always trained better when Athene was there.

She set about helping Petra with the dummies. There were a number of new drills she wanted to work through today. Her left side needed strengthening.

Petra nudged Sahara. 'And how's our future queen today?'

'Wish you wouldn't call me that,' Sahara muttered.

'Don't tell me you're still worried about your magic not coming through yet?' said a new voice from one of the ladders. Tilly appeared at the edge of the platform, her braid dishevelled and her face smudged with dirt.

'Wouldn't you be, if you were me?'

'Ashai or no, you'll be our queen,' Henri said.

'Exactly,' Tilly said, brushing her hands on her leathers.

Sahara sighed and waved a hand in Tilly's direction. 'What happened to you, anyway? Look at the state of you.'

Tilly grinned. 'Had to show some youngsters how to disarm properly.'

A pair of boots landed deftly beside Henri. 'Looks

like they showed you, more like.' Athene released the vine she'd used and bumped her hip against Henri's. 'Don't you think?'

Henri laughed.

Sahara cleared her throat. 'Can we get on with this? I'd like to get at least four hours' sleep before these damn trials.'

'The trials are important,' Athene said.

Sahara's eyes flashed. 'Obviously. Which is why I want to be well rested. This isn't even a scheduled training session. So let's begin.'

Henri was already at the weapons table, selecting her favourite pair of katars. 'Who's first?'

Athene stepped forward, unsheathing her sword. 'Do your worst.'

The kindred-in-training performed drill after drill and round after round of combat, until Henri had to wipe the sweat from her eyes and roll her aching shoulders. She'd bested Athene twice, and Marvel, who'd arrived late, as usual, with gravy still on her face. Night had well and truly settled around them when Sahara announced the end of their session.

While the others trudged off to wash before supper, Henri lingered. While her body was exhausted, her magic still fluttered within, full of life.

'Do you mind if I stay?' she asked her sister.

Sahara frowned. 'Why would I? Do what you want, Henri.' She sat down on a nearby bench and tipped her face to the stars.

'Is everything alright?' Henri said.

Sahara didn't look away from the sky. 'Everything is fine.'

'Are you nervous? About tomorrow?'

Another sigh. 'I don't care about tomorrow.'

'Good. You *should* be confident. I don't care about it either.'

Sahara snorted. 'We both know that's not true.'

Satisfied her sister was feeling positive about the upcoming trials, Henri flung a hand out. With her magic, she sent a dagger shooting through the air, embedding it straight into a straw dummy's heart. She felt Sahara's eyes on her, but she kept her focus on her power, the fluid magic that pulsed within and demanded to breach the surface.

Henri sent weapon after weapon soaring across the platform, guiding her power with simple hand gestures. Allehra had assured her that one day she wouldn't even need to use her hands – that when she was older, her magic would answer to the command of her mind alone. But Allehra had also said that Sahara's magic would announce itself soon. She'd been saying it for years, and yet …

Henri glanced at her sister. As though Sahara had read her mind, her hands went to her ankle, where the leg of her leathers had been pushed up to reveal the marking that wrapped around her skin there. An unusual tattoo Allehra had bestowed on her, to encourage her magic to present itself. So far, it had proved unsuccessful.

Catching her eye, Sahara adjusted her leathers and stood. 'Enough for tonight, Henri. I'm starving.'

The night went slowly for Henri. Waiting for the trials felt much like waiting for the morning of her name day to come when she was a child. She was restless with anticipation, still awake well into the dark, early hours. She could hear Sahara tossing in the bed above. It seemed her twin was just as eager for daybreak.

At last, morning was upon them and the first gong sounded. Henri dressed in her training leathers quickly and rebraided her midnight hair down one side, as was Valian custom. Sahara was watching her, her expression unreadable. Reluctantly, she swung down from her bed and readied herself in silence.

The quiet hung between them as they headed down to the main keep on the forest floor, where a crowd of Valians had already gathered. The sisters stood towards the front, as was tradition for the daughters of the reigning queen, but Allehra flashed them a glare.

'If you're not early, you're late' was one of her favoured sayings. Expectations were high for the Valian heir and her first-in-command.

Now, Allehra turned to the crowd. Dozens of kindred-in-training and their mothers and mentors waited eagerly for her address, their faces etched with awe and admiration.

'My kindred,' Allehra said, clasping her hands together. 'Welcome to one of the most important days in our year – the trials. The series of tests our trainees are about to embark upon has a rich history of honing the most powerful warriors in this realm, and eliminating those who are not worthy. Today, our candidates will partake in three rounds: weapons, hand-to-hand combat, and of course, the Crossing.'

Allehra scanned the faces of the kindred-in-training before her. 'To our trainees, I say this: *do not hold back.* Do not compromise. Demonstrate your strength at its fullest. This is your chance to show us your dedication to the Valian Way. A life in the Sticks awaits those who do not have what it takes. The first round begins in thirty minutes in Circuit One.'

At her final words, the crowd surged. There was a massive push to leave the keep and get to the circuit.

'Ready, girls?' Petra grinned, grasping Henri's shoulder.

'Henri was born ready,' Tilly quipped.

The twins followed the rest of the trainees through the forest. Excitement buzzed through Henri. None of the others were showcasing their skills with katars, so she knew she already had an edge.

She was going over her drills in her mind as they reached Circuit One. It was a small clearing in the forest, with a raised platform at one end. Allehra and her two best elite kindred made their way there and sat down, looking out onto the circuit.

'Names will be drawn at random,' Allehra said, reaching into a leather pouch. She selected two torn pieces of parchment. 'Tilly and Rayner. You're first.'

Tilly palmed her fighting knives and grinned as Rayner entered the circuit, drawing her sword.

Allehra's voice was soft as she said: 'Begin.'

The sharp scrape of metal sounded as blade met blade. But immediately, Henri saw that Tilly was simply indulging Rayner. Tilly's movements were effortless and Henri's chest swelled with pride as her friend whirled her knives and blocked Rayner's incoming swings. Even with Tilly's additional dramatic flourishes, the round was over before it began, with Tilly disarming her opponent, the edge of her blade to Rayner's throat. Allehra gave a single nod, signalling the victory, and both trainees bowed low to their queen before shaking hands and exiting the circuit.

'You think she'll be sent to the Sticks?' Petra asked from behind Henri.

Henri shook her head. 'She won't make the elite, though.'

'You're right about that.'

Henri watched the next round impatiently. Two trainees sparred with spears. It was a fair fight; the two were evenly matched. Henri winced as one girl took a blow to the side of the head and stumbled. She'd left herself open to that – a beginner's mistake. She should have known better. And sure enough, her opponent took advantage of her dizziness to deliver the winning strike.

Henri and Sahara watched round after round. Every time Allehra's hand disappeared into the bag, Henri held her breath. Waiting for her turn – and Sahara's – was agony. Though, looking around at the trainees who were left, Henri couldn't help but feel confident.

Marvel's name was called, and she bested her competition in mere moments. One of Allehra's elites actually applauded as Marvel helped her opponent up.

'Athene. Petra,' Allehra's voice called.

Henri's breath caught. She'd been so concerned with herself and Sahara, she'd forgotten to worry about Athene. Not that she needed to worry. Athene was one of the best in their group. But so was Petra …

Swords clashed and Petra's warrior cry sounded. Henri couldn't tear her eyes away as the two girls struck and parried in a blur of steel. Their fight was a class above the rest. It was silent but for the clang of blades and the scuff of boots in dirt. Athene advanced, hammering Petra with blow after blow, but Petra met every one with a sturdy block and an answering strike. They covered the ground of the entire circuit, forcing one another back and forth before Allehra and her elites.

'They're evenly matched,' Sahara muttered to Henri. 'This will go on forever.'

'Someone is always the stronger warrior,' Henri replied, still not taking her eyes from Athene.

'Depends on your definition of strong, Henri.'

'What —?'

But Petra feinted right, and in her arrogance, Athene fell for it. With a precise kick, Petra swept Athene's legs out from beneath her and held her sword at Athene's throat.

The entire crowd burst into applause. Smiling widely, Petra helped Athene to her feet and the girls embraced with a laugh. They knew it didn't matter who had claimed victory; both had proven themselves worthy Valian kindred.

Henri clapped along with the rest of them, still not sure whom she'd expected to emerge victorious from that round ...

'Sahara and Henrietta.'

The applause died and the crowd fell silent.

Henri's gaze shot to Sahara's, but her twin merely shrugged and entered the circuit. She turned and waited. Henri's heart was suddenly pounding. This was *not* how it was supposed to go —

'Henrietta.' Allehra's voice was cold and stern.

There was nothing for it. Henri unsheathed her katars as she stepped into the clearing to face her sister.

Sahara unsheathed her sword.

'Begin,' their mother commanded.

Sahara lunged. Henri was taken by surprise at the venom in her sister's attack, but she blocked the blow easily, her training kicking in immediately. She moved like water, sidestepping and dodging Sahara's strikes with little effort. And yet, something was stopping her from advancing herself. It didn't feel right. As much as she longed to impress her mother, their queen ... She was sparring with her own future ruler.

She blocked another blow, the impact of Sahara's blade against the sharp edge of her katar reverberating up her arm.

'What are you doing?' Sahara hissed in her ear as she swung again. 'Fight me.'

'I ...' From the corner of Henri's eye, she could see their mother's unreadable expression, but her hands gripped the sides of her chair so hard her knuckles had gone bone-white.

'Henri,' Sahara hissed again, delivering a kick to the back of her legs, sending her stumbling. Finding her footing, Henri nodded and faced her sister. This had to be done the Valian Way. The only way. She palmed her katars and advanced.

Relief seemed to flood Sahara's eyes, but Henri ignored it. She drove forward, holding nothing back. Sister or not, heir or not, the Valian Way meant strength against strength.

Henri's katars were a mere extension of herself and she relished every impact, every blow. The thrill of the fight coursed through her. But as Henri saw an opening to disarm Sahara, she realised something.

Her twin was lagging, in a way that she usually didn't. Surely she wasn't tired already?

Henri spun on her heel and leaped forward, coming at Sahara with not one but two precise strikes. Her sister fell, and Henri had her.

A smattering of applause sounded, but it was clear the Valians didn't know how loud to cheer for the trainee who'd defeated their heir. Sahara accepted Henri's hand up with a brief smile and they took their places back in the crowd.

'What was that about?' Henri muttered to her.

Sahara scowled at her and said nothing.

Henri turned back to the circuit. Allehra's eyes were like a brand on her.

No one was banished to the Sticks after the weapons round, which Henri found unusual. More often than not, a handful of trainees were sent away with each passing trial. Perhaps they had a stronger cohort this year. She didn't question it. There was no doubt that the next tests would divide them, though she was quietly confident in her own unit. She, Sahara, Tilly, Marvel, Athene and Petra had been training together forever.

Without a break, they made their way to the living bridges, where the next trial would take place: hand-to-hand combat while facing the towering heights of the canopies. Henri grit her teeth. Hand-to-hand combat always yielded more injuries than the other trials. The year before, she'd watched one girl get her nose shattered. There was a brutality to using bare fists, something animalistic that had her wringing her hands as she waited for her turn.

The rounds began all along the living bridges, pair after pair brawling before the fully fledged kindred and Allehra's elite. There were shouts of pain, and thuds and screams as girls hit branches on their fall to the forest floor.

Henri watched the organised chaos in awe. This was how Valia raised the most efficient warriors in the realm. Discipline. Pain. Endurance. These were her people. The girls who got through the trials today would be the women who became her fellow kindred, the elite who would watch her sister's back when she was queen.

Taking a measured breath, Henri took in the sight of the greenery above, golden beams of sunlight breaking through the leaves and branches. Again, she relished the whisper of magic against her skin. She wasn't allowed to use her powers in the trials – Allehra had made that abundantly clear. *Like I'd need them*, Henri thought.

'Henrietta,' Allehra's voice now called. 'You're with Priya.'

Henri felt a stab of pity for her opponent as she stepped out onto the living bridge. Priya paled at the very sight of her. Henri had seen the girl in passing, had seen her train every now and then over the years. She knew in her heart that this trial would send her to the Sticks if Henri fought in her usual style. But perhaps ... perhaps she could make it look like –

'Do not hold back. Do not compromise. Demonstrate your strength at its fullest.' Allehra's words rang in Henri's ears.

She locked eyes with Priya, took a deep breath and mouthed: *I'm sorry.*

It was late afternoon when Henri and the others began the trek to the Crossing. Henri's body was still singing with the adrenaline from the fight, her knuckles grazed and stinging. She said nothing of Priya, who, lip bloodied and quivering, had been forced to hand over her training leathers in exchange for a simple cotton tunic and pants. Athene's opponent had been sent to the Sticks as well. But they didn't speak of it.

Allehra had announced that eight trainees hadn't passed the trial. *Eight.* But the Valian queen said no more than that. There had always been a silent agreement among the kindred that no further shame should be brought to those who failed by discussing their shortcomings.

Sahara had won her trial, as had the rest of their unit. Their family was intact. As they wove through the canopies that stretched north, up into the Hawthorne Ranges, Henri pretended that it was just the six of them. She imagined they were on sentry duty or border patrol. All her life she'd waited for these trials, and now they were here ... she wasn't sure they were what she had expected.

'Nearly there.' Athene appeared beside her. Her braid had come loose; fiery red tendrils framed her face, and Henri had to stop herself from reaching out and tucking them behind her friend's ears.

'Nearly there,' she said instead.

It was a long trek, and Henri couldn't help glancing at Sahara, whom she knew would be growing increasingly nervous as the falls drew nearer. How her sister had obtained a fear of heights living in Valia Forest was beyond Henri. But Sahara would be fine. She always was.

Henri heard the falls before they came into view – the thunderous roar of thousands of gallons of water pummelling down into the King's River below. The sight of the Crossing itself always took Henri's breath away. A deadly abyss between two ends of the living bridges; a death sentence to anyone who fell. The sheer force of the falls thrilled Henri. Ancient magic coursed through the water, magic that called out to her and her alone.

Allehra took up a vine and, without a word, launched herself across the chasm. Her swing was graceful and confident; she sailed across without effort, landing deftly on the other side. She waited.

It was a race to see who could follow their queen first. Henri hung back with her unit and Sahara, who was noticeably paler. It was tradition for the heir to complete the Crossing last.

'You'll be fine,' she whispered to her sister, squeezing her arm, but careful not to draw attention towards them.

'Of course I'll be fine,' Sahara snapped.

Henri frowned. *What's wrong with her?* She didn't offer further comfort or reassurance. Instead, she watched their peers hurtle themselves across the void.

The first few made it, though not as gracefully as Allehra. The fourth girl, however, faltered as she leaped from the bridge and failed to gain enough momentum. Her vine didn't reach far enough across the other side, so she swung like a weak pendulum in the middle. She began to scream.

'Gods,' Petra managed, staring out at the poor girl. 'They can't just leave her —'

They didn't. Allehra herself swung across to the trainee and used her own magic to propel them to the other side.

'Another one for the Sticks,' Marvel said, chewing her bottom lip.

From afar, they watched their peer strip down and hand over her training leathers.

Four more followed in her wake.

The line had grown short, and soon, it was just Henri's unit left. Marvel went first with an exceptional swing, then Tilly, then Petra, who let out her now infamous warrior cry as she soared through the air.

Henri watched as one of Allehra's elite pressed a new vine into Athene's hand.

Her friend winked. 'See you on the other side.'

Before Henri could answer, the red braid had whipped away and Athene was sailing across the falls.

Henri swallowed. It was finally her turn. She stopped herself from looking back at Sahara, and focused on the distance across the spray of water ahead. She'd done this countless times before. She loved the thrill of it. This moment was hers.

She accepted the vine and launched herself across the void.

Her swing was perfect. Henri knew it as the water misted her face and Allehra and the others came into sight. She landed soundlessly on her feet, where Athene and Tilly grinned and clapped her on the back. She'd won every round. A place aboard the ship to Havennesse was hers.

Now, there was one more to go. Henri could *just* make out Sahara on the other side, the vine in her hand. She started her run-up. Full of grace, Sahara soared towards them – the epitome of the Valian Way, one hand even skimming the falls as she glided past. She was incredible —

But something was wrong. Henri felt it in her bones and in her magic.

Sahara locked eyes with her for a split second, and Henri's heart stopped. She saw Sahara's grip slip —

No —

Henri threw her magic outwards. It shot towards

her twin with an intensity Henri had never experienced before. It was as though it channelled her ancestors' magic, held in the bridge upon which she stood. She sent it flying towards her sister, her future queen. Her power wrapped around Sahara and the vine she held, keeping the momentum of her swing going. Henri made sure her own movements were subtle, hopefully undetectable, as her magic brought her sister sailing towards them.

Sahara quickly masked the confusion on her face as she dropped gracefully onto the ground before Henri. There was a cheer from the other trainees.

Allehra narrowed her eyes at her heir, and then her gaze slid to Henri.

She knows.

Henri held her breath. She'd broken the rules of the trials. It was an offence punishable by banishment, or worse. She could feel Allehra's magic simmering with fury, but the Valian queen said nothing. Instead, she turned to the cohort of trainees.

'Congratulations,' she told them, her voice projecting to the far reaches of the bridges. 'You have survived the trials. Which means you are now officially kindred of this forest.'

Rowdy applause sounded. Beside Henri, Tilly put her fingers between her teeth and whistled loudly.

'After the feast this evening, you will be presented with your leathers,' Allehra continued. 'These signify your entry into the most powerful army of warriors this realm has to offer. You will wear them with pride.'

Athene elbowed Henri in the ribs. This was what they'd been training their whole lives for. Almost.

'What of the journey to Havennesse?' Henri called out.

Allehra's cold eyes met hers. 'Those chosen will be notified tonight.'

Henri and Sahara accepted their official kindred leathers before all the citizens of Valia. Cheers echoed through the forest. There was no greater sight than the heir and her first-in-command taking their rightful places among the kindred, and among those travelling to Havennesse for additional training.

Henri's gaze slid to Sahara. She needed to talk to her twin about what had happened at the falls. But there was no time.

Henri, Sahara, Marvel, Tilly, Petra and Athene had all made the cut for the upcoming journey. A thrill of excitement shot through Henri, leaving her thoughts of the Crossing behind. She turned to Sahara. 'We'll get to see Eydis,' she said.

Sahara smiled widely. 'And her dogs.'

Eydis was their childhood friend, as well as the crown princess of Havennesse. It had been two years since they'd seen her last and Henri missed her. Eydis was a strange girl. She towered above the Valian twins, but often hid her lanky frame with enormous men's clothes. Sahara and Henri usually joked that the winter princess preferred the company of her hounds to that of people, but whenever the three of them were together, their laughter echoed through the halls of Wildenhaven.

Henri felt a cool hand grip her arm. Allehra pulled her and Sahara aside.

'Let it be known, my daughters, that this trip to Havennesse will be no joyous voyage …'

Henri baulked. 'We know, we —'

'You don't know.' Allehra's voice was like ice. 'The journey, the training in the mountains … It will test the limits of even your endurance.' She glanced at Sahara, who flushed. 'You must be ready.'

'We're ready,' Henri argued.

Allehra took a deep breath, her graphite eyes meeting Henri's, then Sahara's.

'Are you?'

THE GIFT

Heathton's pleasure alleys teemed with fools who were careless with their coin. Drawstring purses dangled in plain sight, a hypnotic pendulum to a savvy fingersmith. Bleak sliced clean through a belt loop, closing her small hand around the purse before the silver within could jangle. Drunks, gamblers and pleasure-seekers made easy pickings for someone with her particular skillset. Bleak had no qualms about divesting them of their valuables – she had a cure to find. She ducked deeper into the crowd, her boots pattering on the wet cobblestones. She was anonymous here, just a reveller trawling the streets seeking one form of gratification or another.

It was mid-morning now, and she wouldn't be missed. Senior, Bren and the crew had docked the ship at Port Morlock in the wee hours and unloaded the catch. Afterwards, the crew had retired to one of the local taverns for pints of ale, and as much as she'd longed to join them, Bleak had donned her hooded cloak and slipped away. It was now or never.

It had been the one of the villagers, who'd told her of the healer months ago. 'She's the best in all of Ellest,' he'd said. 'Sometimes even the *king* seeks her counsel.'

The sky was dark with heavy clouds, casting shadows across the establishments either side of the street. Bleak wove her way through the heaving crowds in Heathton's slums, squeezing past a group of rowdy men lingering outside of Madame Joelle Marie's infamous brothel. She ignored their bawdy remarks and sidestepped them.

Off-duty castle guards, Bleak realised, noting the sigil on the left breast – two crossed axes in a crown of fire. *How I'd love to rob them,* she thought as she gained distance from the group. But it wasn't worth the risk.

It began to rain, a slight drizzle at first, then the skies opened up and released a downpour. Icy droplets hit Bleak's skin and she tugged her cloak tightly around her. She turned right, down a far narrower lane. The rain hammered down in earnest, creating muddy rivers rushing across the cobblestones and dirt paths, sweeping the city's grime up in its current. Bleak turned another corner and, squinting through the torrent, saw the sign she was looking for being battered by the wind. She banged on the door with her fist. No answer. She clenched her jaw to keep her teeth from chattering. Soaked to the bone and frustrated, she pounded the door again.

'What?' a voice within yelled, as the door opened.

'I'm looking for Healer Ethelda,' Bleak said, unable to see inside.

'She's not available.'

'Too bad,' Bleak said, forcing her way into the dim hallway. 'I've come a long way to see her.'

An exasperated sigh sounded from beside her, and an older woman pushed the door shut before crossing her arms over her chest.

'What d'you want?' she said, scrutinising Bleak's odd eyes.

Bleak had to stop herself from shrinking back. Most people believed odd-coloured irises were a sign of dark magic. They would often gasp at the sight and mutter a prayer to the gods, so they'd be protected from depravity. But now, Bleak held her ground.

'I told you, to see Healer Ethelda.'

'And now you've seen her.' The woman gestured to herself, an unimpressed brow raised.

She was not what Bleak had been expecting. Everything she'd heard about Heathton's famous healer had implied she was near-ancient, perhaps a witch who'd prolonged her life by illegal, magical means. Although her face was that of someone who had lived life hard, her eyes were bright and youthful.

'Well?' she said.

Bleak swallowed.

Healer Ethelda tutted and motioned for Bleak to follow.

Bleak shoved her hands in her pockets, her fingers closing around the spare length of rope Senior had given her for practising her knots. She found steadying comfort in the token as she trudged after Healer Ethelda, down the creaking hallway and into a small sitting room. There was no window. Half a dozen thick candles flickered light and shadows across the damp walls. Bleak's palms grew clammy.

'Well?' Healer Ethelda dropped into a wingback cane chair.

'I need your help.'

'Obviously. It's a gold coin upfront. Then we'll see if I can assist you.'

Bleak flicked a gold coin at Ethelda and sat down in the chair beside her. 'I hope you're as good as they say you are.'

'I'm better. What ails you?'

Bleak looked around the room, noticing the bookshelves that lined each wall and the thick, cracked spines of hundreds of volumes. On the far side, there was a simple wooden table covered in countless small glass phials, and on the stand beside Bleak sat a mortar and pestle, a fine white powder crushed within. She shifted uncomfortably and glanced at the door.

'You fear indiscretion,' Ethelda said, clasping her hands together and resting them on her knees.

'Can you blame me?'

'I can blame you for being a fool.'

'Bedside manner's a bit worse for wear, isn't it?'

Ethelda sighed and stood, beginning to pace the room. 'Look here, I wouldn't be in business if my clients could not count on confidentiality.'

'Right.'

Bleak suppressed the urge to back away as Ethelda surged forward and grabbed her hands. She rubbed warmth back into Bleak's cold fingers.

'There is no cure for what you have, girl,' the healer said, cupping Bleak's hands in hers, studying the lines of her palms as though they held the answer.

'And what is it that I have?' Bleak asked, pulling back from the craggy-faced woman.

'You're a mind whisperer, an Ashai. The magic in you is potent, passed down from your mother if I'm not mistaken.'

Bleak swallowed, hard. *How does she know what I am, just from touching me? No one knows except me and Senior ...*

She clenched her teeth. 'You *are* mistaken. My mother wasn't an Ashai.'

The candles around them flickered, and Bleak realised she was uncomfortably warm.

'Oh? Is that so.'

'Yes,' Bleak ground out. 'You going to tell me something worth that gold coin payment?'

'It wasn't your gold.'

'Not my fault folks are careless. Besides, gold is gold, and it can be yours by the end of this conversation.'

'It's already mine.'

Bleak wiggled the coin at the woman. She'd stolen it back moments after she'd handed it over. 'It's yours when I say it's yours.'

'Be careful who you threaten, girl. Ashai aren't as safe as they used to be, not now the great Casimir is dead.'

Bleak snorted. 'Casimir? He's been dead a long time. Some saviour he turned out to be.'

'Is that what you're looking for, girl? A saviour?'

'No such thing as saviours.'

'No?'

'No. Only time-wasters.' She made to leave.

'What of my gold?'

'You had no answers for me.'

'Just because it was an answer you didn't like, doesn't mean it wasn't an answer.' The healer glared at her. 'What is it you need to know?'

'How do I stop it?'

'You can't.'

'Control it, then? How can I manage it? So that I don't hear every person's thoughts as soon as they think them.'

Ethelda considered her, sitting down again and leaning back in her cane chair. 'It truly plagues you?'

'Yes.'

'And the drink, it helps?'

'It's the only thing that does.'

Ethelda nodded. 'I have no experience in managing Ashai affairs. I am a healer of flesh and bone, not of the intangible. Keep your gold, girl. You and your habits need it more than I.'

Bleak shoved her way back through the crowds, wet and pissed off.

'Stupid bitch,' she muttered to herself. She couldn't believe how much time she'd wasted tracking down Healer Ethelda, for *nothing*. She gritted her teeth and elbowed the dawdler in front of her – she wasn't in the mood to be held up. What she needed more than anything was a pint.

Even in the rain, the markets were packed, and Bleak cursed to herself as she was knocked about by inconsiderate idiots. Thoughts swarmed around her like a colony of buzzing insects. She had to stop herself cupping her hands tightly over her ears. *Focus*, she told herself, *focus on getting to the tavern*. It had only been in recent months that her condition became unmanageable. What had once been the occasional stranger's thoughts had grown to an erratic, overwhelming onslaught.

This isn't the right change. The panicked thought practically screamed at Bleak, and she whirled around. She spotted the girl immediately, her pale-blue dress and apron marking her as a palace servant.

Soft red curls were swept up into a bun at the back of her head with wisps escaping the scrap of fabric holding it in place. She clutched several cakes of soap in one hand.

'But sir, you still owe me three silvers,' she was saying, palm outstretched.

'Do not,' the man on the other side of the stall snapped. 'Royals get a different price.'

'But —' the girl spluttered. 'I'll be punished. They'll think I took the change.'

'Not my problem, is it?'

'Sir, I beg you —'

'Beg, eh? You must really like keeping those royal arses clean …'

The girl's face flushed.

Bleak found herself at the servant's side. 'What's going on?' she asked. Her voice sounded stronger than she felt.

'None of your business,' said the stall owner, sneering. And then he spotted her odd-coloured irises. 'Get away from my shop, don't be dragging your evil here,' he added.

The girl looked to Bleak. Her mouth fell open in surprise, but she didn't back away as others did when they first saw her.

'Away with you, street filth!' the man yelled. Bleak stepped back, subtly tugging on the girl's apron. She followed Bleak's lead. When they had fallen into the crowd, Bleak released her apron.

'What are you doing?' the servant said, no anger

in her voice, just defeat. 'I truly needed that change. I'll be punished.'

'No you won't,' Bleak said.

'I'm afraid you don't know my masters well,' she replied.

'You won't be punished,' Bleak repeated. She pressed a coin purse into the girl's hand.

'What's this?'

'His takings for the day.'

'How did you —'

Bleak shrugged. 'Light fingers.'

'I cannot —'

'You can. And you should. I imagine it's not the first time you've been ripped off in this godsforsaken place.'

'No, but … what about you?'

'What about me? I manage well enough.'

The girl's eyes widened. Clearly it had been a while since she'd known kindness. 'My name's Therese,' she said, offering her hand.

Bleak shook it. 'Bleak.'

Therese didn't question the unusual name, nor her actions. 'I cannot thank you enough.'

'It's nothing.'

'If you ever need anything in Heathton, go the castle cook and ask for me.'

'That's not necessary.'

'Even so.'

'Who's your master?'

'I'm a housemaid, I report to the housekeeper proper.'

'I see.'

'I've just been told that I'll be seeing to the Commander of the King's Army personally, though.'

'A promotion?'

Therese shrugged.

Bleak nodded, smiling grimly. 'If you want decent soap, head to the shop on Kemp Lane. They offer better prices and better wares.'

'I'm in your debt.'

'I don't believe in debts,' Bleak said, turning to leave.

'It was a pleasure to meet you, Bleak.'

'And you, Therese. Good luck with the promotion.'

Bleak let the crowd swallow her, deft fingers dipping into the pockets of those around her. Before long, she'd snagged plunder enough for more than a few pints.

From outside the tavern, she spotted Senior, Bren and the crew where she'd left them. Their group was spilt across multiple booths in the warm yellow light of the bar, surrounded by dozens of empty glasses, raucous laughter ringing. At the last minute, Bleak opted for solitude instead and headed down to the docks.

The rain had stopped now, though her clothes and hair were still damp. Bleak tucked her hands under her arms against the bitter chill. She wandered along the wharves, lingering in the spot where she'd last seen her parents, where Senior had found her all those years ago. It had been a game. Just a game. She'd only been tiny. Sometimes she could still hear her mother counting as she hid … But Ma's melodic voice faded, a stronger memory taking hold. Red, a deep, dark red. It had soaked the hem of Bleak's pastel-yellow gown.

'Thought I'd find ya here,' Senior's voice sounded from behind her.

'Did you?' She didn't turn around.

'Every trip to Heathton you end up here at some point. Be damned if I know where ya go the rest of the time, but I know that much.'

Bleak glanced at her surroundings. The docks never changed much. The cobblestone walkways were always slick with fish guts; the stench in the air was near-unbearable; and the men, they were the same as well – perhaps a little more sun-worn and lined than they had once been, but there they were, packing the empty crates back onto the ships.

'If ya want to talk about it —' Senior started.

'I don't.'

Senior looked her over, concern etched on his leathered face. 'Well, when ya do, Half-Pint, ya know where to find me.'

They were up before dawn the next day, loading the ship with supplies to take back to Angove. It was backbreaking work, and although Bleak was the only female on board, she was no exception. Bleak worked as hard as any man, harder, even – constantly having to prove herself. By sunrise, her muscles ached, and she paused to take in the glowing gold orb at the sea's horizon, its reflection shimmering across the flat expanse of water.

'Alright, Bleak?' Bren said, resting a large hand on her shoulder.

She braced herself for his thoughts to hit her, as they so often did when he touched her. They didn't.

'Fine,' she said. 'You?'

'Fine,' he said with a grin, taking the crate from her hands as though it were a box of feathers. 'It's a good day, eh?'

'Same as every other …'

'With a sunrise like that? Not a chance.'

Bleak couldn't help but smile at her friend's optimism. He saw the good in everything.

'Half-Pint!' Senior called from the ship's deck. 'Grab the spare ropes, will ya? Can't be leaving those behind.'

She waved him off and jumped down onto the wharf, striding towards the remaining gear. She heaved the lengths up onto her shoulder, struggling beneath the weight.

She froze.

A man in the shadows watched her.

'What are you looking at?' she snapped, taking in

his tattered clothes and the dark set of lashes framing his eyes.

He pushed off from the rail he'd been leaning on and smirked. 'You,' he said.

Bleak rolled her eyes and adjusted the rope on her shoulder, making to leave. The man fell into step beside her, his ragged clothes billowing.

'You can't be serious,' Bleak muttered.

'I'm always serious.'

'Piss off.'

'I've got something for you.'

'Doesn't everyone. Nothing comes without a price in this realm. I'm not interested.'

'First gift's free.'

'Sure, sure. Who the hell are you?'

'They call me the Tailor.'

'Oh, *they* do, do they?'

'Indeed. They call you Bleak.'

Bleak forced her legs to keep moving. The beggar knew her name, so what? Anyone who frequented the docks could figure that out in a second.

'What do you want?'

'I told you. To give you a gift.'

'Right. And what's that, then?'

'A warning.'

This time, Bleak stopped in her tracks. 'Oh?'

He locked eyes with her, all traces of fun gone.

'Your search. It draws attention. The wrong kind of attention. You need to stop.'

'What? What are you —'

'Told you,' he said, eyebrows raised. 'First one's free.'

She opened her mouth to argue, to deny, but as she did, the doors to the nearby temple swung open. Throngs of people flooded the street. The Tailor, whoever he was, had gone.

Back onboard the ship, Bleak hung the ropes up on their hook.

'New friend?' Bren quipped.

'Don't be stupid.'

'Looked like a serious conversation.'

'None of your business.'

Bren shrugged. 'Just looking out for ya.'

'Don't need you to.'

'Ya don't think I don't know that? Doesn't mean I'm not gonna do it.'

Bleak grinned. 'I know.'

Smiling, Bren shook his head, strands of his fair hair falling into his eyes. 'Reckon we've earned ourselves a break?' he said.

'A break? It's barely daylight. You met Senior?'

Bren laughed and pulled a silver flask from inside his shirt. 'A quick toast, then?'

'Oh? To what?'

'To new friends?'

Bleak laughed. 'How about to old ones?'

'Won't say no to that.' He took a swig from the flask and handed it to Bleak.

She saluted him, and took a long gulp. Whatever it was, it burned her insides, but she also felt the warmth of it settle over her mind and calm her anxieties. She sipped again and reluctantly passed it back.

'Ya find what ya were looking for?' Bren asked, making his way to the mainsail.

Bleak paused. She'd never told Bren *what* she was looking for, exactly. He didn't know of her ability, but he was no fool. He knew she was after *something*, badly.

'No,' she said finally. She readied herself to climb the rigging, while Bren did the same beside her.

He glanced at her sympathetically. 'There's always next time, Half-Pint.'

She gripped the ropes and began to haul herself up, finding her footing easily.

Bren kept up beside her, muscles rippling beneath his shirt. The higher they climbed, the stronger the wind. It cut through her cloak and shirt, like ice on her skin. Bleak looked out to the East Sea, and the route they would take back to Angove.

'Let her down, Half-Pint!' Senior yelled out from the deck below.

Bleak released the sail from its confinement. The enormous white canvas dropped and caught in the wind and the whole ship lurched forward.

She looked to Bren. 'I suppose you're right …'

''Bout what?' he said.

She turned back to the open expanse of water before them, bracing herself against the cold. 'There's always next time.'

THE KING'S TOURNAMENT

On the eve of the annual King's Tournament in Willowdale, Commander Swinton's men were particularly rowdy. He himself had nearly just choked on his mouthful of ale while laughing. Fiore slapped him heartily on the back, pushing another full mug towards him, foam spilling over its sides.

'Imagine that,' Fi wheezed. 'Surviving the Janhallow Desert rebellion only to die in Grayside Tavern, hey, old friend?'

'A belly full of food and ale doesn't seem like a bad way to go,' Swinton countered, touching the long, pink scar across his jaw.

It had been a fortnight of hard training with his squadron in Willowdale: a constant barrage of drills, duels and horseback riding. Swinton looked around. The exhaustion had ebbed away from the haggard faces; smiles had replaced scowls and grimaces of pain. He leaned back in his seat, content. The men had improved greatly since he'd been made commander. That was something to be proud of. They all deserved to celebrate their last day of training and the start of the King's Tournament tomorrow.

Stefan, one of the young squires, pulled up a stool alongside them and turned to Fi, clasping him on the shoulder.

'How does it feel to be the best friend of the man who's about to become the youngest knight in the history of Ellest?' he asked.

Fi laughed. 'Ease up on the ale, Stef.'

'I'm serious.'

'So am I.'

'But he'll be *the youngest* —'

Swinton watched the exchange with quiet joy. They had returned to Heathton as victors from the rebellion in Battalon. King Arden had held a ceremony to present Swinton, Fi and Lennox with medals of heroism – though they weren't quite sure how Lennox had wrangled that. Swinton's knighthood hadn't been formally announced yet, but King Arden had been hinting at it for some time.

'You have everything you need, Commander?' Jasper the barman hovered by their table.

'Yes, thank you.'

'I've had your room cleaned, so it's ready for you.'

'You're too kind.'

'Anything at all, Commander. You say the word.'

Fiore leaned in as Jasper walked away. 'Just you wait … He'll come crawling, asking for favours when you're a "Sir".'

'Don't I know it —' Swinton stopped abruptly as he caught sight of a glowering pair of eyes from the opposite side of the tavern. Siv Lennox. One of the best swordsmen under his command; also one of the most vile. His glare was one of utter loathing.

What in Rheyah's name is wrong with that man? Lennox had been a thorn in his side since they'd started out as squires. Things had only got worse once Fi had arrived in Heathton and outfought them all. Lennox hated that a foreigner had brought a new, effective style of fighting into their midst and bested them. Not to mention that Fiore had been made Captain. A Battalonian. Lennox's pride had never recovered, and he'd been itching to overthrow their leadership ever since.

Swinton turned to make a comment to his friend, but Fi wasn't beside him anymore. The muscular Battalonian was now leaning against the bar, talking to an olive-skinned beauty. She was laughing. Hardly a surprise when it came to Fi.

'Can't help it, can he?' Stefan quipped, following Swinton's gaze.

Swinton laughed. 'Not in the slightest. He thinks he's a romantic.'

'Maybe he is.'

Swinton raised a skeptical brow and Stefan snorted.

As the night wore on, the men continued to drink. They broke out into bawdy tunes and the odd scuffle over cards. Everyone was in good spirits, including Swinton. It was rare that he let his guard down, rare that he took the opportunity to sit among the men as a companion rather than a commander.

But sleep called to him sooner than he would have liked. The jugs of ale and the past fortnight of vigorous drills had him feeling heavy. He made for the stairs to retire.

Jasper had indeed got the room ready. A fire burned in the small hearth and a basin had been prepared with fresh water to wash. Swinton closed the door behind him, nearly tripping over Fi's pack, which had been discarded carelessly across the floor. His friend's bed was untouched, and by the looks of things down at the bar, Swinton doubted there would be need to remake it the following morning.

People loved Fiore Murphadias. He was a natural storyteller, a dreamer, and the type of person who put others at immediate ease. Swinton was far more reserved, which was but one of the things that made them such an odd pairing to others. The women of Ellest loved Fi too, and he loved them. He managed to strike up conversation without a care in the world, and though he had a reputation for being a charmer, Swinton was yet to ever see someone leave in tears.

The door creaked open. 'You're awake,' Fi said, surprised.

'Just came up myself. You staying?'

Fi shook his head with a grin and went to the basin. The Battalonian stripped his shirt off and wet the bar of soap sitting on the side.

'Can I ask you something?' Swinton heard himself say as Fi splashed water onto his face.

'Always, old friend.' Fi patted himself dry and went to his pack, pulling out a fresh, albeit wrinkled, shirt.

'Have you ever wanted just one woman?' Swinton asked, sitting on the end of his bed.

Fi looked up. 'Of course.'

Swinton's brows shot up.

Fi laughed. 'Don't look so shocked, Dimi.'

'But ...'

'But what?'

'But you didn't stay with her? This one woman?'

Fi laughed. 'It was *her* who didn't stay with me.'

'Oh,' Swinton said. He hadn't realised. 'I'm sorry.'

'Don't be,' Fi replied with a shrug. 'Such is life, old friend. It wasn't as the gods intended.'

'How ... how do you ...'

Fi pulled on his shirt and buttoned it. 'How do you make peace with that?'

Swinton nodded, his stomach twisting as he thought of the girl he'd last been with. Rosetta. She'd worked on his father's estate. They'd grown up together. He'd loved her. But he'd never known if it was the same sort of love that people wrote sonnets about. That sort of love ... Well, he had little experience with it.

Fiore crossed the room and took his cloak from the hook. 'I tell myself: it doesn't matter who you were with at the beginning. It matters who's standing there with you at the end.'

Throwing on his cloak, Fi gave a mock salute and left.

Swinton sat there a moment before going to his own basin to wash and prepare for bed. *Who's standing there with you at the end.* It was a nice sentiment.

Swinton woke to the burn of chemicals in his nostrils. His body convulsed, but he was pinned down, a damp cloth clamped over his mouth and nose. He gasped for air, but the room spun. Hooded figures surrounded him, their thick hands restraining his weakening struggles, his cry of outrage muffled by the poison-soaked fabric.

'Come on,' said a familiar voice. 'Get him out of here.'

Lennox, Swinton realised as a wave of nausea hit him. He couldn't feel his legs. Or his arms. Panic shot through him as the group of men lifted him off the bed and hauled him towards the door.

Where are they taking me? What do they want? He'd never felt so helpless in his life. He tried to call out again, but all that escaped was a raspy moan. He could do nothing but listen to the soft thud of his own bare feet being dragged down the tavern stairs.

Outside, they pulled a hessian sack over his head. Now, the night was nothing but darkness. He was flung roughly across the back of a horse, where the chemicals finally took hold of his consciousness. As they rode off into the night, Swinton blacked out.

A swift kick to the ribs and blooming pain woke Swinton for a second time. He groaned, still unable to move.

Someone spat on him. 'Not the hero everyone thinks you are, eh, Commander?'

The sack was tugged off Swinton's head, and he squinted at the half-dozen men surrounding him. Lennox and his lackeys. The men who consistently gave less but expected more.

Lennox crouched before Swinton and grabbed him by the throat. 'Let's see them give a knighthood to you now. The commander who snubbed the King's Tournament.'

Swinton cursed himself. He'd underestimated the pack mentality and jealousy of Lennox and his brutes. He should have known better. He'd seen Lennox in action before.

'Poor Sir Caleb. He'll be so ashamed …' the bastard sneered.

Swinton's stomach churned at the mention of his father. Sir Caleb was expected at the tournament tomorrow, and if Swinton didn't show … Well, it wasn't just *his* reputation and future on the line.

Someone dealt him another blow, this time to the abdomen. Pain ricocheted up his body and his eyes watered. He rasped, finally finding his voice.

'You …' he managed. 'You had to drug me. Had to bring five friends … to beat me?'

It earned him a kick in the side. 'End outcome's the same, isn't it?'

'Coward,' Swinton spluttered. He knew he should shut up. Knew he wasn't doing himself any favours. But this … this pathetic excuse for a man wasn't going to get away with this.

Lennox just laughed, before his fist slammed into Swinton's face, and all went black once more.

The soft glow of dawn warmed Swinton's chilled skin and he woke with a start. He was lying in the damp grass of a woodland area, hands bound behind him. With a moan, he sat up, his whole body searing with pain from his injuries. He could feel how swollen his face was, could taste blood on his tongue. He felt dizzy – it was as though there was a fog over his thoughts. *Gameswood.* That was what Lennox had used to paralyse him and drag him out into the countryside of Willowdale.

Gods. The tournament, Swinton realised, struggling to free himself from the binds. *How am I going to explain this? What will Father think? What will the* king *think?*

He forced himself to slow down. *One thing at a*

time. He managed to loosen the rope and twist his wrists free. Wincing, he stretched both hands out before him. His back and shoulders ached. Lifting his shirt, he found a collage of blue-and-violet bruising across his ribs.

Bloody bastard, he cursed Lennox as he staggered to his feet.

A rush of nausea hit him. Leaning against the trunk of a tree, Swinton hurled his guts up, praying it was the last of the poison leaving his battered body. He wiped his mouth with the back of his hand and looked around. They couldn't have travelled more than an hour out of Grayside. This was still very much Willowdale county – the green paddocks in the distance, the cluster of woodland, the deer grazing happily on the nearby foliage. If he hurried, Swinton could be at the tournament by noon.

It was harder than he anticipated, finding the strength to trek across the farmlands in his injured state. But every time he wanted to collapse, he pictured Lennox's sneering face. He pictured his knighthood slipping from his grasp. He wasn't going to let that happen. He had worked too damn hard to get to where he was, had spurned his father's influence to make a name of his own. When he became Sir Dimitri Swinton, it would be because he and he alone had got himself there.

Finally, he saw the town of Willowdale in the distance. From the sound of the crowd, the tournament was in full swing. He had no idea how he would explain his absence, or his dishevelled state; all he thought of was getting there.

At last, Swinton entered the town and headed straight for the makeshift stands where the jousting was in full swing.

'Dimi!' Fi exclaimed, catching him by the elbow. 'What in Liir's name happened to you?'

'It's a long story,' Swinton muttered, spotting his father and King Arden side by side in the royal box in the stands.

'So shorten it.'

'Lennox.'

Fiore whirled around. 'What did he do?'

Swinton gestured to his swollen face. 'You need further explanation?'

Fi's gaze clouded with fury. 'Where is he. That piece of scum. I'll —'

'Not now, Fi,' Swinton said, grabbing his friend's arm. 'Not in front of the king and my father. This has to be handled differently.'

There was a loud crunch as one opponent's lance splintered against the other's armour. The loser was sent flying across the field with a loud cry, hitting the ground with a thunk.

The crowd erupted with applause as the victor removed his helmet.

Lennox.

Fiore made to charge forward again, but Swinton grabbed him.

'Not like this,' he hissed, spotting King Arden motioning for him to join them.

Leaving Fiore behind, Swinton approached the foot of the dais and bowed, flushing furiously. He knew how disrespectful he looked.

'Your Majesty. Sir Caleb.'

His father said nothing, but the shame in his umber eyes was piercing.

From the corner of his eye, Swinton could see his mother, Lady Yuliana, with Queen Vera and the little prince and princess.

The king, however, stood. 'What in Rheyah's name happened to you, Commander?'

Without so much as a glance at Lennox, Swinton bowed deeply. 'An embarrassing tale, my king. One that involves much ale and stupidity. I apologise for my tardiness.'

King Arden's eyes narrowed as he scrutinised the bruising and swelling on Swinton's face. He pursed his lips before turning to Sir Caleb.

'Every young man makes mistakes, eh, Caleb?'

'Indeed, sire,' Sir Caleb said stiffly.

King Arden turned back to Swinton. 'Get yourself cleaned up, Commander.'

'Of course, Your Majesty.' Swinton made to leave, but behind him, someone cleared their throat.

'Your Majesty,' called Lennox, stepping forward, helm in hand. 'If the commander will allow it, I'd like the honour of challenging him.'

Swinton froze.

Frowning, the king leaned forward in his throne. 'Now?'

'If the commander doesn't object.'

The king beckoned Swinton forward once more. 'Do you accept Lennox's challenge?'

Swinton met Lennox's cocky stare. Like he had a choice.

'I accept.'

'Very well, then. Prepare yourself. The next round is in fifteen minutes.'

Swinton bowed once more and ducked away to the staging area, mind racing. He'd have to borrow armour. His own was still back at the tavern. He didn't like the idea of using someone else's, but there was nothing for it.

A hand grabbed his arm. 'Are you mad, old friend?' Fi hissed, dragging him out of earshot. 'You can hardly stand straight. Let alone joust.'

'What do you expect me to do? Reject a challenge from that bastard?'

'If it means you remain in one piece for the day, yes.'

Swinton simply shook his head and walked on.

The weight of the armour pressed painfully against Swinton's battered body. He grit his teeth as Fiore strapped the breastplate in place.

'You're still sluggish from the poison,' Fi muttered. 'You don't have to —'

Swinton cut him a glare. 'You know I do, or you wouldn't be helping.'

Fi gave an exasperated sigh. 'Fine,' he said. 'But gods, Dimi, you'd better be careful. He's the best jouster we have. And you're …'

'Not experiencing my finest hour.'

On the field, the trumpets blared and Lennox was announced as the reigning victor. He rode up and down the pitch, shaking his fist triumphantly at the onlookers. A true champion. The crowd cheered and stomped their feet in the stands. To Swinton, it sounded like the thunder before a storm.

'Here,' Fi said, handing him a helm.

Swinton took it and fit it over his head with a wince. The cold steel pressed against his swollen face.

'Dimi?' Fi asked.

'What?'

'I'm sorry.'

'Sorry? What for?'

'I should have been there.'

'Not your fault, Fi.'

'All the same. I should have been there. I hope you've got a plan.'

Swinton took in the jousting pitch before him, littered with the remains of splintered lances. 'We're about to find out.'

A young squire helped Swinton up onto his horse. The heavy armour was cumbersome, but he didn't doubt for a second that he'd need it. He brought his steed to the end of the tilt barrier and halted. Stefan handed him his lance.

Swinton cursed the weight of the damn thing. Fi had been right – he was still affected by the gameswood.

Stefan offered his shield.

'Gods,' Swinton muttered as he heaved it up alongside him. At least it was his own: crafted to his specifications, with his house sigil painted proudly on the face – the crossed battleaxes of Sir Caleb. He gave Stefan a nod of thanks for retrieving it.

At the other end of the barrier, Lennox looked formidable. He held his lance and shield high at the ready. And although he wore his helm, Swinton could tell he was sneering behind it. Lennox's lackeys were trading bets nearby.

Swinton nodded to Stefan, who signalled the herald.

The trumpets sounded. And at the centre of the tilt barrier, the flag dropped.

Swinton forgot his pain. Forgot the weight of his shield and lance. He charged.

The horses' hooves thundered across the packed dirt, matching the pounding in Swinton's chest as the gap between him and Lennox grew smaller. He positioned his lance, already feeling the strain on his body.

He tensed, preparing for impact.

There was a sharp intake of breath from the

crowd. And Lennox's lance crashed into Swinton's shoulder.

He clung to his horse, remaining upright in the saddle but reeling from the blow. The roar from the spectators was deafening.

Suppressing a groan of pain, Swinton reached the other side, passing his lance to Stefan.

'Dimi?' Fi's voice sounded from nearby.

'I'm fine,' Swinton growled. He couldn't stop now. Couldn't think of his injuries, lest they get the best of him.

Across the field, Lennox had removed his helm and was egging on the boisterous crowd. Looking right at Swinton, he took a full tankard of ale from a nearby soldier and downed it. Ale ran down his chin and armour. He smacked his lips before putting his helm back on.

Fuming silently, Swinton took up his lance again.

'Good luck, Commander,' Stefan said, a note of concern quavering in his voice.

Swinton merely nodded before the trumpets sounded again.

The flag hadn't yet touched the ground as they charged for each other, lances pointed. Nothing else existed for Swinton. This next impact would define the tournament. Would define things between him and Lennox, if it went according to plan. Swinton had watched Lennox joust hundreds of times. He knew his tells, knew when his arrogance got the better of him, knew *how* to make his arrogance get the better of him …

It was over in a blur, Lennox grazing Swinton's neck this time. Swinton could feel the warm, wet trickle of blood running into his armour, and the intense gaze from his father, seated beside the king.

Have faith, he wanted to tell Sir Caleb. *I can make this right.* But he didn't meet his father's stare. Not yet.

'Gods, Dimi,' Fiore exclaimed, meeting him back in position, handing him a cloth to staunch the bleeding on his neck.

But Swinton didn't take his eyes off Lennox. The bastard was laughing with his lackeys, pouring ale through the mouthpiece in his helm. He had Swinton poised for defeat – so he thought.

Swinton hardly heard the trumpets' blast. He only saw the flutter of the flag falling.

His horse surged ahead. He braced himself with every bit of strength he had left and leaned forward, lance at the ready.

Wood shattered against steel. Plates of armour flew. And so did Lennox, his large frame tumbling to the ground, a muffled cry escaping him.

The crowd erupted. Their victor had been unseated. And what was more triumphant than a reigning champion, but for a new hero emerging from the dust?

Swinton let his men pull him from his horse and stand him before the king. He didn't notice someone removing his helm, or taking his lance and shield. He was dazed. It had worked. He had won.

'We have a new victor,' King Arden bellowed over the noise.

Nearby, Lennox swore at the men trying to help him up. He threw his helm to the ground, whirling around to face Swinton. But before the king and court, he could do nothing. He turned on his heel and stormed off, leaving his splintered lance and broken armour in pieces in the dirt. Swinton watched him go. He'd have to answer for his crimes later.

Swinton tried not to grimace as the men clapped him heartily on the back. Tried not to wince as they lifted him up in the air.

'Brothers, put the commander down,' Fi laughed. 'He's bleeding all over you.'

Swinton shot him a grateful look before turning to the king.

'May I have Your Majesty's leave to retire?'

King Arden nodded. 'Along with my congratulations, Commander.'

'Thank you,' Swinton said, bowing. His knighthood was still within reach.

He managed to keep himself upright until he was out of the crowd. Behind the stands near the stables, he staggered with a gasp.

One of his men ducked under his arm and helped support his weight.

No – not one of his men, he realised. *A woman.*

Long golden hair fell over her face as she helped

him to a nearby tent and guided him to a chair. He couldn't stifle his moan of pain as she dropped him into it. Finally, he caught a glimpse of her face. Milky skin, freckles dusting her nose, and a storm in her eyes like no other Swinton had seen before.

The woman's hands went to her hips. 'Serves you right.' Her voice was dark, and she surveyed his injuries with an air of satisfaction.

'Excuse me?'

'Serves you right,' she said, nodding to the blood on his armour.

What? He couldn't be hearing her correctly. He'd never known a young woman to be so *rude*.

'For scaring the wits out of the horses!' she exclaimed, shaking her head in disbelief. 'Jousting is a cruel, unnecessary sport —'

'The horses are fine,' Swinton started.

'Fine? You think the horses are *fine*? Tell me, do you feel *fine* after that valiant display?'

Swinton frowned.

'Didn't think so. I thought the Commander of the King's Army would have some measure of mindfulness, but —'

Someone was calling in the distance. Something Swinton couldn't quite make out. But the girl froze, listening.

Catching him watching her, she scowled in his direction, and he found himself smiling.

'What's your name?' he asked, as she made to leave.

She scoffed. 'What do you care for the name of some stable girl?'

'Wait —'

But she had scooped up her muddied skirts and hurried out, passing Fiore as he entered.

Swinton couldn't tear his eyes away from where the girl had been. 'Who in Rheyah's name was that?' he heard himself ask.

Fi placed a medical kit on the nearby table and grinned. 'Eliza Carlington,' he said. 'The stable master's daughter.'

FELDER'S BAY

Even though the sun had beamed down all day, its warmth hadn't quite reached the foamy beaches of Angove. The crisp evening air now bit into Bleak's bones, cutting through her coat. She grit her teeth against the icy wind as she made her way back up to the marina. Senior waved at her from the garden of their cottage – they were running late for dinner with the Claytons.

Senior's weathered face cracked into a grin when she reached him. 'Bit brisk, eh, Half-Pint?'

'I'll say,' Bleak replied, stuffing her numb hands into her pockets.

'Come on then, ya know Mrs Clayton's a fan of an early supper.'

He pulled a woollen hat down over her messy hair and closed the small gate behind them.

The Claytons lived closer to town, and so Senior

and Bleak took the small path up the steep coastal hills towards the village. Both man and girl turned up their collars against the wind.

'Damn gale coming down from Havennesse, eh, Half-Pint?'

'Don't care where it's come from,' she muttered into her coat.

'It'd be savage out on the water.'

'Glad we're not.'

'For once, I gotta agree with ya there,' said Senior, his eyes bright.

They shuffled up the path in companionable silence. Despite the sting of the wind on her cheeks, when they reached the top, Bleak paused to take in the great expanse of sapphire water, stretching all the way out to the horizon. The wind whipped across its surface, creating cresting waves far out to sea and rocking the pleasure yachts moored in the harbour.

'Best view in Angove, this,' she said.

Senior glanced down at her. He opened his mouth, and closed it again, before turning back to the water.

I'm glad, yer know. Glad I took ya in that day, he spoke to her mind. *Glad you've come to call this place home, with me.*

Her eyes burned with tears, but she blinked them back.

Senior had taken to doing that lately. When something was too much for him to say aloud, he would think it, knowing that sometimes, she could hear him.

'Come on,' she said. 'Before we freeze to death. Or Mrs Clayton kills us.'

Senior huffed a laugh and started after her.

'And what time do you call this?' Mrs Clayton scolded as they traipsed through the Clayton mudroom. 'Supper will be damn near cold by now.'

'I'm sure it'll be as delicious as ever, Nora,' said Senior, brushing a kiss to her cheek.

Mrs Clayton clapped a hand to her face with a gasp. 'Your face is like an ice brick. And if the pie is cold you've got no one to blame but yourself.' Mrs Clayton's tone was sharp, but her eyes smiled.

'Evening, Mrs Clayton,' Bleak said as Senior moved from her path.

'Suppose you're just as frozen?' Mrs Clayton said by way of greeting, kissing Bleak on the cheek.

A strong arm swung around her and pulled her close. 'She's alright, Ma.'

Bren gave Bleak an extra squeeze around the shoulders and Mrs Clayton glanced between them. She shook her head and led them through to the dining room.

'Look what the cat dragged in,' quipped Willem, the eldest of the Clayton brothers, who sat at the head of the table. Senior was already seated beside him, pouring himself a mug of ale. Bleak went to her usual place opposite Senior, her chair scraping back noisily as she sat. Bren plonked himself down next to her. The table was set for ten, which meant all seven Clayton boys were home.

'Behave yourself, Willem,' Mrs Clayton said. She placed a large, steaming palma pie in front of her eldest. 'Start serving, will you?'

Bleak's mouth watered at the sight of it. Mrs Clayton made the best palma pie in all of Angove. The pastry was always light and golden, while the meat and gravy inside were deliciously spiced.

Willem pulled the pie towards him and took up the carving knife.

'No Mr Clayton today, Nora?' Senior asked, eyeing the empty chair at the other end of the table.

Beside Bleak, Bren stiffened, and the rest of the Clayton brothers' eyes shot protectively to their mother.

'Just us, Senior,' Mrs Clayton said, putting another pie down in front of Tobias, the second eldest. She patted his arm fondly.

Thank the gods for that, Bleak heard her mutter internally. It wasn't the first time Bleak had heard a thought like this from Mrs Clayton. She'd heard enough snippets from the rest of the Clayton clan to have a notion of what happened behind closed doors when Mr Clayton was around. But now the Clayton boys were grown, Mr Clayton was scarcely present.

'Always two steps ahead, you are, Ma,' Tobias said,

nodding to the second pie and picking up the second carving knife.

'I don't think to kid myself when it comes to my boys and their food,' she said. She untied her apron and finally sat down beside Tobias, next to the empty chair.

Bleak caught Senior glancing between the empty chair and Mrs Clayton.

Is that a bruise on her cheek? Bleak heard his concern immediately. His eyes flicked to hers and she shook her head ever so slightly. She knew for a fact that Kearne Clayton hadn't returned from his travels for the past month. It had been at least four weeks since his giant, dirt-caked boots had sat in the mudroom and Bren had pushed her back out the door, his face panic-stricken, images of his mother bloodied and broken crowding his mind.

Senior nodded once, taking the plate Willem offered him and passing it down the table.

Bleak looked around at the Clayton boys: Willem, Tobias, Bren, Aaron, Sampson, Van and the youngest, Hutch. They all had the same sun-streaked fair hair, with the three eldest sharing Mrs Clayton's charming crooked smile and Mr Clayton's labourer's build. The younger boys hadn't yet grown into their frames, their limbs lanky and clumsy as they teased and pinched each other under the table.

Bleak bit into her pie, savouring the incredible taste, and studied Mrs Clayton in hidden wonderment. How had the woman survived? Seven boys. No partner worth mentioning, and yet here they all sat. Happy.

'Best one yet, Ma,' Bren said between mouthfuls.

Mrs Clayton frowned. 'Crust is a little overdone.'

'Nonsense,' said Tobias, pouring his mother a drink.

'Boy's right. You've outdone yourself, Nora,' Senior added. 'Best be careful or you'll never be rid of me and Half-Pint.'

Mrs Clayton smiled. 'You two know you're always welcome.'

'Bless you, Nora. Yer the only woman I know who's happier when she's got more mouths to feed.'

'Ma likes having a big family, don'tcha, Ma?' piped Hutch, reaching for the serving spoon.

'My father always said "the more the merrier". I've found that to be true often enough.'

Visions of a teenage Mrs Clayton flashed before Bleak's eyes. Mrs Clayton and a young woman who could only have been her sister, kneading dough, flour dusting their noses as they laughed. She realised that these were Nora's memories. Bleak brought her pint of ale to her lips and took a long drink. Senior raised his brows as she leaned across to refill it.

The warm chatter hummed across the table, but the thoughts were the loudest of all. Bren was talking to her, something about going out on the boat together, but the mental commentary around her was too great. Dozens of thoughts rolled into her mind, breaking upon her like waves on the shore.

Bren nudged her. When she didn't respond, he gripped her arm. At the contact, his thoughts drowned out the rest.

Is she alright – she looks pale – is she —

Bleak shook him off and took another long drink. The liquor was a blanket over the loud scramble in her mind.

Hurt flashed across Bren's face, but was gone in an instant. He drank from his own mug.

Bleak came back to herself, noticing Senior's head tilted in concern. Again, she shook her head slightly, and he returned his attention to Mrs Clayton.

'I said, I reckon we should take the boat out, just you and me,' Bren was saying.

'Where'd you wanna go?' she said.

'Well, I don't reckon Senior'd let us go north.'

'Not likely,' Senior cut in.

'Where then?' Bleak insisted, suddenly excited. She loved the idea. Senior was a good man, a good guardian, but wouldn't it be something – being out on the open water, just her and her best friend?

Senior scratched the stubble at his chin, looking from Bren to Mrs Clayton. 'Reckon you'd be fine going down to Felder's Bay. If ya stick to the coastline.'

'What's this?' Nora looked up from fussing over Hutch.

'Felder's Bay,' Senior said. 'Bren and Bleak wanna do a trip.'

'Oh? Is that a good idea?' she replied, her eyes flicking between the two.

'How do you mean?' Bren said, frowning.

But Bleak heard her thoughts loud and clear.

It's not appropriate for them to be off adventuring together anymore ... What if — Bleak shoved the internal voice away.

'Well …' Mrs Clayton struggled to find her words.

'You know what she means, lad,' Senior said. 'But Nora, we're not in the capital – nor are they, no offence, noblemen's children. I don't think it'd do any harm.'

Bleak's chest swelled with pride as she took in Senior's tanned, lined face. Despite spending more of his life out at sea than on land, he was by far the most grounded person she'd ever met.

'Felder's Bay, you said?' Mrs Clayton asked, starting to gather the empty plates.

'Aye, safest spot for a little sail.'

'Overnight?'

'Well, it'd be safest to anchor overnight, Nora. The waters are calm in the bay. Don't want them caught out in the currents on their way back in the dark, eh?'

Bren and Bleak were hardly breathing. Could Senior do it? Could he persuade her?

Mrs Clayton sighed. 'Alright then. *One night*. And you do exactly as Senior's instructed you to do.'

'I'd trust Bleak with me life out there, Nora,' Senior said kindly. 'Half-Pint knows what she's doing.'

'It's not Bleak who concerns me,' Nora replied. 'It's those damn butter fingers I'm worried about,' she added, nodding to Bren.

His brothers roared with laughter.

The next day, the savage winds had calmed, and Senior rowed them out to *The Daybreaker*. As they made to climb aboard, Senior cleared his throat.

'Now listen, you two …'

'Senior, we'll be fine. Like you said, I know what I'm doing —'

'That's not what I was gonna say …' Senior cleared his throat again and his gaze shifted between them.

Do I need to take the lad aside? Make sure his intentions —

'Oh! No … All good,' Bleak stammered. 'No need. *Really*. No need.'

Bren's brow furrowed, looking questioningly at Senior.

But Senior's shoulders sagged with relief and finally, he merely shrugged. 'Alright then. Remember, keep to the coastline.'

'Got it,' Bleak said, heaving herself up onto the larger boat.

'Thanks, Senior,' Bren said, following her up the ladder.

They reeled in the anchor as Senior rowed back to the jetty, and started to prepare the sails.

'What was that about?' Bren asked her, nodding back to Senior.

'Nothing.'

'Was not.'

'Is now.'

Bren rolled his eyes and tossed her a spare coil of rope. 'Fine.'

The breeze was just right for sailing. The sun bathed the deck with warm, golden rays. Bleak looked back at Angove with the sort of appreciation that only comes in the face of a new journey. Nestled in the coastal cliffs and hillsides, the little village was quaint but not insignificant. Bright and full of movement, the docks hummed with the rhythm of daily life. Bleak smiled. She was fortunate.

The Daybreaker picked up speed. The breeze pulled Bleak's hair from its tie, sending it whipping about her face. She scraped it back into a messy topknot and looked over to Bren. He was manning the wheel temporarily, eyes focused on the sea ahead.

'Know where we're going, Butter Fingers?'

'I know the general direction. You'll need to navigate once we're out of Angove.'

'Stick to the —'

'Coastline, I know,' Bren said with a grin.

Angove disappeared behind them, and they set sail for Felder's Bay. Bleak revelled in the easiness of it all. She and Bren worked like a well-oiled machine, both taking on their usual duties and picking up whatever Senior usually did between the two of them. From where she now stood at the wheel, Bleak could see Bren adjusting the canvas sail. His shirt billowed in the breeze, and he was squinting past the sun's glare. His thoughts hadn't bothered her yet, thankfully, and for a time, Bleak could pretend she was normal. She and Bren were just two *normal* best friends, out on their first adventure together.

The morning passed quickly, and Bleak's face hurt from smiling so much. The sea grew a little choppy but it made the ride all the more fun. She and Bren took turns at the wheel and climbing the mast.

It was early afternoon when they reached Felder's Bay – one of its untouched beaches at the foot of the Hawthorne Ranges, stretching on for miles and miles. The water was the clearest turquoise Bleak had ever seen, and it shimmered like a sea of stars.

'Gods, I wouldn't fancy a trek up there,' Bren said, nodding to the formidable peaks covered in dark, sprawling trees.

'Me either …' Bleak said, craning her neck to look up to the highest alp.

'Reckon we anchor here?' Bren turned back to her. 'Think it's close enough to the shore for Senior's liking?'

Bleak nodded. 'Can't go much closer or we might tear our bottom on the reef.'

'What reef?'

Bleak rolled her eyes and pointed. 'See that shadow beneath the water there? That'd be a coral reef. Not sure how low the tide'll get, so wouldn't want to risk getting much closer.'

Bren's face was a mixture of awe and envy. 'Ya really are Bleaker Junior, aren't ya?'

Bleak shook her head. 'Come help me with the anchor, Butter Fingers.'

He laughed and slung his arm casually around her shoulders. She tensed, waiting for the onslaught of thoughts to invade. But they didn't. Her body relaxed, even savoured the warm weight of Bren's arm around her. Together, they released the anchor. The iron weight sent water spraying over them as it plunged into the depths of the sea below.

'Senior said it'd be safe to go for a dip, if ya fancy it?' Bren said, looking out across the water again.

'Did he?'

Bren nodded. 'Said not to stray too far from the boat, but also that the water out here is the cleanest in all of Ellest.' The way Bren said it was like a dare, like they'd be stupid not to dive into its crystal-clear currents.

Bleak loved a challenge – better still, she loved *beating Bren* at a challenge. And yet she hesitated.

'Scared?' Bren teased, one brow raised in amusement.

'No,' she bit back.

Bren was already tugging his shirt over his head, revealing the tanned, muscular torso beneath. Bleak flushed.

'Come on then,' he said.

But Bleak squirmed uncomfortably. It was all very well and good for *him* to strip down and go swimming, but it was different for her. Beneath the layers of fabric, her skin was marred with scarring.

Bren clocked her discomfort and smiled kindly. 'Ya don't have to, obviously.'

'It's just …' Her hand went to the side of her thigh.

'Ya know I don't care about that —'

'It's embarrassing —'

'It's *not*. I'm *glad* ya got that scar. Without it, yer wouldn't be here.'

It was true. The large scar on her leg was a reminder of how close she'd come to leaving this realm. Young, fevered and delirious from the plague that swept across the continent, she had hung on dearly to life's fragile thread. Senior had done the only thing he thought might cure her. He'd taken her far out to sea, and carved out and burned the infected section of flesh – scarring her, but saving her life. She shuddered at the memory.

'I —' she stammered.

'Bleak, if ya don't wanna swim, that's fine. Ya make yer choices for you and you alone. But I don't want ya ever thinking that scar is somethin' to be ashamed of. 'Cause it's not.'

Bren's wintry eyes bore into hers until she nodded, a smile tugging the corner of her mouth.

'Good,' he said, pushing his boots off at the heel and swinging himself overboard without another word. A splash sounded and Bleak rushed to the side of the boat and peered over. Bren surfaced, slicking his wet hair back from his face with a grin.

'Cold?' Bleak said.

'Perfect.'

Before she could think twice, Bleak jumped.

The water *was* perfect. Refreshing, but not icy. She let herself stay fully submerged. It felt as though time had stopped, and the realm around her had a blanket pulled over all its sounds and worries. Lungs bursting, she kicked reluctantly, propelling herself up, emerging from the water.

Bren was smiling. 'Told ya.'

They swam for hours, until the sun dipped behind the mountains and Bleak's teeth began to chatter.

In the small cabin below deck, she peeled away her wet clothes and towelled herself dry, pulling on the nightshirt she kept onboard. Wrapping herself in a thick woollen blanket, she went back on deck to hang her clothes up. Bren was stoking the small cooking fire and turning the venison they'd brought with them.

'Smells good,' Bleak said, sitting down beside him, suddenly very aware that she wore very little clothing.

'Ma gave me some herbs to use. Rosemary mainly, but I added some thyme and a bit of wine.'

'Wine?'

Bren laughed. 'In the flask,' he pointed.

The sun had set and night settled around them. The round, yellow moon was mirrored on the glassy surface of the sea. They ate hunched over in comfortable silence, passing the flask back and forth.

'It was a good idea,' Bleak said thoughtfully, wiping her hands on the blanket.

'What?'

'Coming here. It was a good idea.'

'I have those occasionally.'

'Only occasionally.'

Bleak noticed the goosebumps covering Bren's arms, and the way his shoulders were caved inwards.

'You're cold,' she said.

'I'm alright.'

Bleak studied him for a moment, and then raised the blanket, motioning for him to move closer.

Bren didn't hide his surprise, but he did as she bid and closed the gap between them, pulling his side of the blanket around them tightly. Bleak could have sworn she could hear her own heart pounding. She held her breath, waiting for his thoughts to come crashing into her. But they didn't. Again. She exhaled a sigh of relief and focused on the flames before them. They didn't speak for a time. And Bleak realised that this quiet was different … She had to say something. *Anything*. She opened her mouth –

'What's that?' Bren said suddenly.

'What?'

Bren rushed to the side of the boat. 'That …'

Bleak ran to where he stood and looked out. Her stomach dropped to her feet and she gripped Bren's arm.

Mist. Thick mist rolled towards them from the open sea. Mist that had been feeding on their realm, encroaching on it inch by inch for decades. Mist that was used as a death sentence for traitors to the crown. Mist that should be nowhere near the shores of Felder's Bay … Bleak swallowed. Mist that would kill them at first touch.

'What the …' Bren muttered, staring in disbelief as the mist crept towards them.

'Bren.' Bleak shook his arm. 'Bren!'

His eyes met hers, shock etched upon his face.

'Bren, we have to go. Now.'

'*Go?* Where?'

Bleak pulled him across the deck to the other side of the boat. 'To shore. We have to swim to shore.'

Something sounded in Bleak's ear. A whisper. A word she couldn't make out. She glanced back and saw the mist creeping closer. The silken voice sounded again, melodic and mesmerising.

'*Now*,' she yelled.

They dove into the water.

When Bleak broke the surface, the silence was eerie. The only noise was the gentle slap of the current against the side of the boat. She couldn't see Bren.

'Bren?' she called.

Nothing.

She swallowed. 'Bren?'

'Here,' he said, paddling towards her.

Momentary relief flooded through her. 'Come on, let's get out of here,' she managed.

They swam for what felt like an age, as the current tried to suck them back towards the mist.

'How is that possible?' Bren spluttered.

'I don't know …'

Exhausted, they finally felt sand beneath their feet. They staggered from the water and onto the hard, wet shore. Something crunched under the sole of Bleak's foot. She bent down to retrieve it. A piece of dead coral, she realised, holding it up to the moonlight. It had been bleached bone-white by the sun. She pocketed it.

When they made it onto dry sand, Bleak turned to Bren. 'What are we going to do?'

Bren sat down, resting his elbows on his knees. 'Wait.'

They sat shoulder to shoulder, gazing out onto the sea, Bleak turning the piece of coral in her hands. The mist roiled across the water's surface and crept up the sides of the boat. Bleak only noticed she was trembling when Bren put his arm around her.

'You okay?' he said quietly.

Bleak watched as the deck disappeared entirely, until only the canvas sails stood tall and strong above the mist.

'I don't know,' she whispered. 'You?'

'I don't know either,' he said.

. . .

Sometime in the early hours of the morning, as the dark sky melted into hues of soft pinks and golds, the mist started to recede.

Bren was asleep on Bleak's shoulder.

'Bren.' She nudged him. 'Bren, look ...'

Bleary-eyed and tousle-haired, Bren followed her gaze.

'It's ... it's leaving ...' he muttered.

'Yeah ... It is.'

The boat reappeared, as though nothing had happened. As the sun rose high into the sky, the mist grew fainter and fainter, until it had completely vanished.

'Gods ... What happened?' Bren rubbed his eyes, as though now he didn't quite believe what had occurred.

Bleak shook her head. 'I don't know ... Do you think it's safe?'

Bren stood and stretched, and took a tentative step toward the water. 'Only one way to know ...'

'I'm coming too.'

'Expected nothing less.'

'Good,' Bleak said, moving past him and into the low tide.

They swam quickly and quietly towards *The Daybreaker,* anxiety tight in Bleak's chest.

It's gone, she told herself. *It has to be okay ...*

They hauled themselves up onto the deck and waited, waited for something to happen. Nothing did. Everything was the same. Everything was exactly where they'd left it. Tentatively, they walked the length of the boat. Once, twice.

'I think everything's fine ...?' Bren said finally.

Bleak nodded. 'I think so ...'

Bren came to stand beside her, leaning on the railing and looking back to shore.

'What do we tell Senior?'

They locked eyes, and understood one another.

'Nothing,' said Bleak. 'We tell him nothing.'

Bren nodded and offered his hand. 'Agreed.'

'Agreed,' she replied, taking it.

And then Bren's thoughts slammed into her, stronger and louder than ever before.

WILLOWDALE

Commander Dimitri Swinton and Captain Fiore Murphadias stood tall on either side of their king and queen's thrones, overlooking the festivities. The capital's amphitheatre had been transformed for Princess Olena's name day, though the little girl was far more interested in the wooden horse someone had gifted her than the decadence below. Unbeknownst to her, the circular, open-air structure was awash with colour; the best blooms from the royal gardens framed the stone archways, and the surging crowds wore their finest silks. Revellers clutched mugs of cold mead and cheered the troupe of dancers on, eager to enjoy another of Heathton's annual holidays.

Swinton had briefed his guards on the heightened security threat only this morning, stressing the importance of teamwork and being alert. Now, his gaze wandered to the furthest end of the amphitheatre, where Siv Lennox was stationed. The former unit leader bore the same scowl he'd adopted after the King's Tournament a few months earlier. He'd been unseated as jousting champion, and demoted after a vicious attempt to ruin Swinton's reputation. Lennox hadn't taken his punishment gracefully by any stretch of the imagination.

Swinton felt Fi's gaze follow his to Lennox, his Battalonian friend's nose scrunched up in distaste. Were it up to Fi, Lennox would have been thrown out of the King's Army, but Swinton knew it was better to keep his enemy where he could see him.

Nearby, a trumpet sounded, signifying the end of the performance and the start of the gift-giving ceremony. Down below, noblemen and women queued to present their offerings to Heathton's young princess. Queen Vera helped her reluctant daughter to her feet and sat her in the small throne beside her brother's. The princess kicked her slippered feet and turned her clouded gaze in her mother's direction, a deep frown appearing on her face. Prince Jaxon was also squirming restlessly in his seat, but after a wink from Fi, Swinton caught the prince whispering something to Olena that wiped the crease of frustration from her brow.

Adjusting his stance, Swinton surveyed the crowd as prominent families presented Olena with rare fabrics for gowns, jewels from the finest artisans in Ellest, and baskets of fresh fruit, which

Swinton knew the little girl would turn away in private in favour of sweets from the local confectioner. Queen Vera sat beside Olena, describing each gift to the princess so she could give her thanks to the person before her. The ceremony went on without incident, though Swinton kept his eyes on Lennox. There was unfinished business between them – that much he knew.

At last, the final nobleman stepped forward. The crowd burst into applause at the sight of the famous sigil emblazoned on the chest of the man's tunic. Swinton took a steadying breath. Sir Caleb Swinton, his father, had entered the arena. The knight tugged gently on a lead rope he held, coaxing a young filly out from behind one of the piers.

'Your Majesties, Your Highnesses.' Sir Caleb's voice projected up to where the royal family sat and the arena fell silent under his spell. His eyes settled upon Princess Olena. 'Princess. On behalf of my family, I wish you a happy name day. We offer this prize filly from the best horse-rearing establishment in all of Ellest.'

Olena's attention locked onto the knight before her. 'A horse?'

Sir Caleb smiled. 'A young horse, Your Highness. She will grow to be one of the most valuable mares in the realm …'

'For me?' The princess turned to her mother in disbelief.

Queen Vera exchanged smiles with the knight. 'Yes, my love. For you. Now, what do you say?'

As dusk fell, the amphitheatre emptied, with the royal family having retired to the castle for the evening. Swinton watched the drunken revellers and entertainers clear the arena, but his attention snagged on something. Lennox. He lingered in the shadows, head ducked close to two other guards. Swinton's fists clenched at his sides. The bastard was stirring unease within his army.

'Hope you've got that under control,' said Fi from beside him, arms crossed over his chest.

'It's under control,' Swinton replied, not tearing his gaze away from Lennox. He had ordered Stefan to monitor the situation from the lower ranks in the guard, and he and Fi were tracking Lennox's movements. There wasn't much more they could do without feeding the already existing tensions between the men.

He elbowed Fi. 'Come on.'

'Where?'

Swinton shook his head. 'Dinner? At my father's estate. You don't remember?'

Fi stared at him blankly.

'I'll take that as a no.'

'Sorry, old friend. Of course.'

Swinton frowned at his Battalonian brother. Fiore had been distracted of late; anxious, even, which was unusual for the ordinarily jovial captain. He had been disappearing, writing hurried letters and sealing them with his own emblem, the one that matched the flame tattoo on his forearm rather than the royal sigil. Whenever Swinton questioned him, he merely shrugged and said: 'Not to worry, old friend, not to worry.' Swinton didn't like to press him, but he got the distinct impression something simmered below the surface there.

The Swinton family estate was located just outside of Heathton, surrounded by woodlands and acres of prosperous fields: King Arden's gift to Sir Caleb along with his knighthood. Swinton and Fi rode up the gravel road leading through the trees to the towering manor beyond. Swinton slowed his horse as they approached the gates and nodded to the guard stationed at the entrance. He rarely returned to the family estate nowadays and the staff were all different from those he'd grown up with. Torches lined the path to the courtyard, and they dismounted at the doors, an attendant waiting to take their horses to the stables.

'Dimitri,' his mother said warmly as the doors opened. Lady Yuliana was a tall woman who stood poised like a dancer. But while her posture was always formal, her broad smile remained inviting. She kissed both his cheeks and did the same to Fiore. 'Welcome. You must be famished after today's duties.'

She led them inside through the parlour, where Sir Caleb stood by a drinks tray, goblet of wine already in hand.

'Father.' Swinton bowed his head.

Fi followed suit. 'Sir Caleb,' he said in greeting.

The knight came forward and shook both their hands. 'Glad you could join us this evening. I've had one of the servants fetch a good vintage from the cellars. We should toast to the princess.'

'It's being poured in the dining hall,' Lady Yuliana interjected. 'Come now, Caleb. The young men are hungry.'

They followed Lady and Sir Swinton through to the dining hall, where numerous animal hides were draped from the walls, and a great hearth burned steadily. The mouth-watering aromas of roast vegetables and boar wafted in from the kitchen as they took their places at the table, which was much too large for the four of them. Sir Caleb sat at the head, his wife to his right.

A servant placed a goblet in front of Swinton. He murmured his thanks as Fi accepted one as well.

Sir Caleb raised his glass. 'To Princess Olena.'

'To Princess Olena,' they chorused.

The wine was delicious. His father had indeed selected one of their finer bottles, and Swinton savoured the bold flavours, so different from the watered-down tavern liquor he and Fi were used to.

As the food was served, Lady Yuliana smiled at him encouragingly. 'So, Dimitri, do tell us. What's been happening in the castle lately? Any news to share with your ageing parents?'

Swinton glanced at his father. 'Well …'

His mother nodded, her eyes bright.

'I … I am due for a knighthood any day now.'

'A knighthood?' Lady Yuliana beamed. 'That's wonderful, Dimitri.'

Sir Caleb cleared his throat. 'The king has spoken of this with you?'

Quiet settled over the table, and Swinton didn't dare look to Fi. He forced himself to meet his father's stare. 'Not in so many words, as yet.'

Sir Caleb nodded slowly, his gaze suddenly far away.

Swinton nearly hissed as Fiore's boot connected with his shin under the table.

'That was quite a gift today, sir,' the Battalonian said, with a pointed glance at Swinton.

The knight looked relieved at the change of topic. 'Yes, thank you. I hand-picked the filly from the Willowdale stables myself.'

'Willowdale?' Swinton heard himself say.

'Yes, son. You know those stables are the most revered in all of Ellest, perhaps even the whole realm. They breed King Arden's stallions there.'

Swinton nodded. Yes, he had known that. Fi delivered another swift kick below the table, clearly knowing full well that it was not the quality of the horses that had snagged Swinton's attention.

'She will need to be fitted for tack, and given

proper training in the round pen with the stable master,' his father was saying. 'Perhaps an errand for your disgraced underling?'

'Lennox?'

Sir Caleb nodded. 'Yes. His punishments were not nearly severe enough for his atrocious actions at the King's Tournament.'

'He was demoted, Father.'

'For what he did to you, for the disrespect he showed this family, he did not pay enough. What would he have done to you, were the boot on the other foot?'

Swinton suppressed a sigh. His father was not alone in that opinion. Humiliation. That was what Caleb and Fiore had advised. Humiliate Lennox into submission. It was the only way degenerates like Lennox complied, they had argued. But Swinton hated that aspect of being commander, hated playing the petty political games. They detracted from his actual duties: ensuring the safety of the royal family, and the readiness of the King's Army.

'That's not the sort of commander, or knight, for that matter, that I wish to be, Father.'

'Being a commander or a knight is not about what you wish,' Sir Caleb said, studying him. 'And that, my son, will come back to bite you in the backside, I promise you.'

Swinton shook his head and took another sip from his goblet, the wine suddenly tasting sour. 'Fi and I will take the filly to Willowdale.'

'What? Dimitri, that's no task for a commander. Certainly no task for a *knight*,' Sir Caleb scoffed.

Swinton saw Fi open his mouth to make an objection, but this time, Swinton delivered his own kick to the Battalonian, and his friend fell silent. In truth, Swinton hadn't stopped thinking of the sharp-tongued, golden-haired woman who'd spoken to him after the tournament. Spoken *at* him. Fearlessly. Which he'd liked. That she had the audacity to lecture the Commander of the King's Army … He didn't know many people of whom he could say the same. Her bright eyes and unexpected roughness had ensnared him, and he'd told himself he'd seize any chance he had to see her again.

Sir Caleb looked between his son and Fiore. 'Your time would be better spent elsewhere.'

Swinton ground his teeth, but his mother rested a hand on his arm.

'Hush now, Caleb,' she interjected, calling a servant over for more wine. 'Dimitri can make his own decisions, and waste his time as he sees fit. Leave him be.'

Swinton didn't refrain from rolling his eyes. His mother was skilled at delivering backhanded support like this when he and his father opposed each other, which was often.

His father's umber eyes didn't leave his. 'You're right, Yulie,' he said, before draining his goblet.

Later, as they stood around the sitting room, Swinton studied his parents, seemingly unchanged in the home in which he'd grown up. The son of a famous knight, now soon to be a knight himself. He wondered if it would be enough then. If it would ever be enough.

'It's late,' he heard himself say. 'I have to get back to check on the guards before I retire.'

'Surely your men are capable of guarding a few doors?' his father said.

Swinton scowled. 'I take my position at the castle seriously, Father.'

Behind him, Fiore gave him a push and laughed lightly, trying to diffuse the tension as always. 'Yes, Sir Caleb. We know Dimi is *always* serious.'

Swinton placed his goblet on the table deliberately. 'Shall we?' he said to Fi.

'As you wish, old friend.'

In the formal throne room the next day, Swinton requested leave from the king to go to Willowdale. If King Arden was surprised by this, he hid it well. But just as Swinton bowed and made to leave, the king called him back.

'Commander?'

'Yes, Your Majesty?'

'Upon your return, there is a matter I wish to discuss with you.'

Swinton bowed his head. 'Is there anything I can assist you with now, my king?'

King Arden studied him for a long moment,

before shaking his head. 'No, Commander. Upon your return.'

Swinton and Fiore started the ride to Willowdale that day, with the princess' filly in tow. His father had been right: she was a beautiful horse. Even at such a young age, it was clear that at maturity, she was going to be one of the most revered mares in the realm. Though riding with her now was making their journey twice as long.

As they trekked across the rich green lands, Swinton stole glances at his captain. Fi was restless in the saddle, his hand absentmindedly straying to the lick of fire tattooed on his forearm.

Fi finally clicked his tongue in frustration. 'What is it, Dimi?'

'What?'

'You keep watching me.'

'I'm checking the surrounds.'

Fi snorted. 'You've never been a good liar, old friend.'

Swinton sighed. 'Not to you.'

'No, not to me.'

'So will you tell me, then?'

'Tell you what?'

'What has been bothering you.'

'Nothi—'

'Now who's lying?'

Fi gave a grim smile. 'There is some family business back in Belbarrow that needs attending,' he allowed. 'And so far, it's been difficult to find a solution here in Ellest.'

Swinton frowned. Fi rarely spoke of his family, so it was surprising to hear that he was dealing with Murphadias matters from abroad. 'What sort of business?'

'The usual sort of family squabbling, old friend.'

'Is there more to it than that, Fi? It's unlike you to let family politics affect you …'

Fi raised a brow. 'There's also the matter of my brother-in-arms being smitten with some golden-haired girl —'

'What —?'

Fi merely grinned and urged his horse into a canter.

They stayed at the same tavern as always in Grayside. The oily barman, Jasper, kicked patrons out of their favourite booth to accommodate them. Swinton and Fi sipped their ale in companionable silence, watching the card games and debates unfold as the night wore on. The last time they'd been here had been on the eve of the King's Tournament, where Lennox and his lackeys had drugged and kidnapped Swinton. Sometimes he could still feel the burn of the chemicals in his nostrils, and the rising grip of panicked helplessness.

Fi nudged him with his elbow. 'Before my days

are done, that bastard will pay for what he did to you here, old friend.'

Goosebumps shot across Swinton's arms, but he forced himself to shrug. He wouldn't let Lennox get the better of him, wouldn't let Fi see how much that night had affected him.

'I'm going to retire for the evening,' he said, draining his mug.

A dark look crossed Fi's face, but the Battalonian let the matter be.

Swinton gave him a reassuring smile. 'I assume you'll find other entertainment for the remainder of the night?'

'Nothing is more preferable than my brother's company.'

'Rubbish,' Swinton scoffed.

'You're right,' Fi laughed. 'Get a move on, your brooding is deterring my admirers.'

Not failing to notice the women lingering near their booth, Swinton laughed and bid Fi goodnight.

Their packs had been taken up to their double room upon their arrival and basins of hot water had been prepared. Mind churning, Swinton readied himself for bed. He mulled over the potential stupidity of his decision to come here. He knew nothing about Eliza Carlington, other than the fact that she wasn't afraid to speak her mind. And that she was beautiful. Breathtakingly so. Perhaps she already had a suitor. Why wouldn't she?

Swinton had been with women. One didn't grow

up beside Fi without being exposed to such matters. Though Swinton always suspected any success he had was due to who his friend was, rather than who *he* was. But as his thoughts moved between the brief dalliances of his past, he realised he'd never met anyone like Eliza Carlington.

Feeling suddenly restless, Swinton decided to rejoin Fi at the bar. There would be no sleep for him this evening.

Downstairs, the rowdiness of the tavern had increased tenfold. Swinton stood at the bottom step, trying to spy Fi in the crowd, no doubt surrounded by eager ladies as he shared one of his many captivating tales. But Fi was not where Swinton anticipated. He spotted the brawny Battalonian tucked away in a corner booth, his head bowed close beside another's. Swinton couldn't see the stranger's face, only Fi's, his mouth a tight line of concern. Swinton suppressed the urge to storm over and demand to be let in on their secret. Instead, he pressed himself against the wall as the stranger stood, a tattered tailcoat falling about his legs. The two men shook hands, and the stranger left, his coat vanishing beyond the door as though he'd never been here.

Swinton debated confronting Fi, but his friend looked rattled as he called Jasper over to refill his mug. Without a word, Swinton slipped back upstairs. It was a conversation for another day.

. . .

The next morning, Fi was conveniently occupied when Swinton woke and readied the horses for the ride to Willowdale stables. The captain had made some thinly veiled excuse about an errand, and Swinton didn't know whether to be grateful or annoyed.

As he started the ride to Willowdale with the young filly trotting alongside his own horse, Swinton's stomach churned. What if she wasn't there? What was he going to say if he saw her? Or what if, at worst, she didn't want anything to do with him? He took a deep breath. There was only one way to know.

The ride seemed to take forever and yet no time at all. Swinton stared at the gates of the Willowdale stables and swallowed, hard. This was a battle of a different kind. Clicking his tongue, he urged his horse and the filly forward. Inside the gates, the cobblestone courtyard was bustling with stable hands and carriage drivers. Swinton dismounted and approached a young man carrying a bale of hay.

'Excuse me,' he said.

The man's eyes grew wide as he took in the crest on Swinton's chest. 'Commander Swinton ... We weren't expecting you.'

Swinton didn't recognise the man, but he dealt with many people in his line of work. 'I'm here on the king's business,' he said. 'Might I enquire after Eliza Carlington?'

'Of course, Commander. I believe she's at the southern end of the stables,' he replied, pointing.

'Thank you.' Swinton made to leave.

'Commander?'

'Yes?'

'I just have to say. That final joust at the King's Tournament … That was really something. Even my pa said so. Said he'd never seen a manoeuvre like it before. That you'll make a fine knight.'

Swinton blinked. It was not the first time someone had said as much. It was often followed by questions of when he next intended to compete. He wouldn't speak of that now. 'Thank you,' he replied with a nod.

Leaving the horses tied outside, Swinton ventured into the grand stables, the scent of sweet hay and horse manure instantly filling his nostrils. Slowly, he walked past the rows of stalls, heading towards the southern end. In truth, he'd never been inside the stables. During his visits to Willowdale, his horse had always been ready and waiting for him in the courtyard. Now, as his boots tapped against the stone floor, he was surprised to find how peaceful it was within. The comforting scent, the warmth and the sound of the horses shuffling about and whinnying in their stalls, soothed him. And it was just as he relaxed that he spotted her, his breath catching in his throat.

She was shovelling fresh hay into a stall at the end of the row. Swinton paused at the gate, watching her golden hair fall like a curtain over her face. She wore a white apron over a simple dress, both smeared with dirt, and patches of perspiration darkened the fabric beneath her arms.

At last, she looked up. 'Oh,' she said. Then, with a critical survey of his bruise-free face, she added: 'You're looking better than the last time I saw you.'

The first and only time Eliza Carlington had seen him, he'd been in a bloodied state after the jousting match.

'Thanks,' he found himself saying. 'You look …' In truth, she looked a mess. With her facing him now, he could see the streaks of dirt on her cheeks and the straw caught in her hair. She seemed flustered. 'Like you need a bath,' he finished.

For a second, Eliza's eyes bulged, incredulous. Swinton's stomach dropped. What was he thinking? Coming all this way to insult her?

But Eliza did something he didn't expect. She laughed. Not just a polite chuckle. She tipped her head back and laughed from deep within. The sound made Swinton giddy. 'You're right about that,' she said finally, wiping her hands on her apron and turning to him fully. 'What can I help you with, Commander?'

He cleared his throat. 'I'm here on the king's business. The princess' new filly needs to be fitted with tack and is to receive additional training.'

Eliza raised a brow and joined him outside the stall. 'An errand fit for a commander, was it?'

'I do as the king orders.'

Swinton didn't fail to notice the slight tug at the corner of Eliza's mouth at his words, but she said no more. Instead, she motioned for him to follow her to the tack room. Inside, it smelled like oiled leather, and Swinton marvelled at the dozens of saddles mounted on the walls.

'Do you have the king's specifications?'

Swinton dug a hand into his pocket and fished out the folded piece of parchment. Eliza took it from him, her fingers brushing his. With a glance at him, she studied the parchment, chewing her bottom lip.

'This can be done,' she said. 'Though it will take a few weeks.'

'A few weeks?'

She nodded. 'For any royally commissioned work, we have a specialist from Havennesse do the detailing. It takes longer. It's the best work in the realm.'

Something struck Swinton. 'In that case … might we add some additional detailing? I think the princess would appreciate it being more tactile.'

Eliza looked at him then – *really* looked at him. 'I think you're right,' she said slowly. 'I'll see what we can do.'

'I'd be grateful.'

She pocketed the parchment and nodded again. 'Fine. You'll leave the filly to board here for training?'

'Yes. I believe your father trained the princess' last pony?'

'He did.'

'It's the king's wish that he oversees this filly's training personally.'

Eliza fiddled with her apron. 'Is that all?'

'I believe so.'

'Very well then,' she said, turning towards the door, her golden hair swishing down her back.

'I gave it up,' Swinton blurted out.

Eliza turned back. 'What?'

'The jousting. I gave it up.'

'But …' She frowned. 'But that tournament … You won. It's all people have been talking about.'

'I know.'

Silence lingered between them as Swinton's eyes met hers. He wouldn't say it aloud – the reason he'd retired from competing. He didn't need to. He felt himself flush, but he wouldn't break eye contact. It was Eliza who looked away first, tucking her hair behind her ear.

'Would you like to see something?' she asked.

'Like what?'

'Something beautiful?'

Swinton had to refrain from saying that he was, in fact, already looking at something beautiful. Instead he merely nodded, and followed her from the tack room.

Eliza led him from the southern exit of the stables towards a round grassy pen on the far end of the grounds. A pregnant light-grey mare stood grazing inside, her white mane dancing in the breeze.

'That's my horse,' Eliza told him, resting her

elbows against the fence and peering into the pen. 'Her name is Silver.'

Silver ... Swinton had heard that name before. 'Isn't she ...?'

Eliza nodded. 'Yes, she's one of three rare Ellestian thoroughbreds. We managed to breed her with one of the last wild stallions before he died.'

'So her foal ...'

'Father says it's a colt. And yes, he'll be one of the most valuable in the realm when he's born.'

Swinton let out a low whistle. 'He'll go to the highest bidder, then?'

Eliza shook her head. 'Xander won't be for sale.'

'Xander?'

She flushed. 'I've already named him.'

Swinton felt himself smile. 'It's a good name.'

'Eliza!' someone shouted. 'Eliza, come quick!' An attendant ran towards them, the young woman's face tight with panic.

Eliza went to her. 'What is it, Frieda?'

'Something spooked one of the king's stallions. He smashed through the fence —'

Eliza was already running, skirts hiked up around her knees, and without thinking, Swinton broke into a sprint too.

'Is he injured?' Swinton asked Frieda.

'We don't know. He's bolted into the woods —'

'Show me,' Eliza said.

They followed Frieda past the corrals and grazing steeds to the edge of the woods. There, a dozen or so stable hands and attendants lingered, pacing in dismay. Relief flooded their faces at the sight of Eliza.

'We didn't know what to do. He's in there, rearing and kicking anyone who comes near —'

Eliza tucked her loose hair behind her ears and placed her hands on her hips. 'There are too many of you. You're only spooking him more.'

'We didn't want to lose him, Liza – he's the king's favourite.'

Swinton's stomach lurched at that thought. For the stable hands to lose a prized stallion at all was bad news for everyone, but to lose the king's favourite ... People would be punished *severely*.

Eliza took a deep breath. 'Get back to work,' she said. 'I'll fetch him.'

'But Liza —'

She merely raised a brow at the challenge. Her father might have been the official stable master, but there was no doubt who really commanded the place. The crowd left.

'I can't let you go in alone,' Swinton heard himself say.

Frustration flashed across Eliza's face. 'Are you a trained horseman?'

'No, but —'

'Then don't presume to think I need your assistance.'

'You might need my assistance if you get kicked in the head and need someone to carry you back.'

Eliza rolled her eyes. 'That's not going to happen.'

'You never know.'

She clicked her tongue. 'Just be quiet, then. And no sudden movements.'

Swinton shrugged. 'Fine.'

Shaking her head, Eliza entered the woods, Swinton close behind her. Her footsteps were light atop the leaf litter, and she called out to the stallion in a soft, gentle tone. With the horse nowhere in sight, they crept further into the woods, where the trees became denser and darker. Swinton copied Eliza's tentative pace, noticing the hem of her dress was nearly black with dirt.

'Eliza,' he whispered.

She turned, scowling at him. 'What?'

He pointed. A nearby tree trunk glistened. Slowly, he approached and touched his fingers to it. They came away wet with blood.

Eliza's face fell. 'He's hurt.'

Swinton nodded and peered into the woods beyond. 'Over there …' he breathed, spotting a white coat amidst the trees.

'Stay here,' Eliza said, not taking her eyes off the horse.

Swinton did as she bid, remaining rooted to the spot as Eliza hiked her skirts up once more and called softly to the horse as she approached. The stallion's ears flicked back and he bared his teeth, shifting anxiously.

'It's alright,' Eliza said. 'It's alright.' She held her

palms out and took another step forward. The horse reared violently.

Swinton flinched, but didn't move. Eliza knew what she was doing; his interference might only put her in more danger. She spoke in soothing tones to the spooked steed, all the while holding her hands out, so he could see she meant him no harm. She inched closer and closer, calm and confident, though the horse was huge next to her lithe frame. Swinton had never seen such patience in a person. Especially in someone who had seemingly so little patience for people. He watched on in awe as Eliza reached up and stroked the stallion's neck – the horse let her. She ran her hands along his flank, to where a patch of blood shone.

'Just a scratch,' she muttered.

Swinton suddenly realised they had no rope, nothing to pull the horse back to the stables. But Eliza showed no such concern. She continued to stroke the horse, running her hand down from the black star on his forehead to his white velvet nose. Still talking, she turned to Swinton and stepped towards him.

What is she doing? We need to tie him —

But to Swinton's surprise, the horse took a step after her. And as Eliza made her way back through the undergrowth towards him, the horse followed.

How ...? He stared as Eliza passed him, the great stallion calm and obedient at her side.

. . .

After returning the king's prized steed to his pen, Swinton and Eliza walked through the stables in silence, and Swinton chewed the inside of his cheek, trying to come up with things to say. Everything seemed inadequate.

'There you are,' said a familiar, melodic voice. Fiore met them midway through the stables. 'Miss Carlington,' he said with a polite nod to Eliza. 'I've had the filly set up in one of the larger stalls.'

Confused, Swinton and Eliza followed Fi to the stall in question. Fi had done as he said, though Swinton had no idea why he felt the need to inform them …

'She's stunning,' Eliza breathed, stepping into the stall and approaching the filly.

Swinton stood at the gate, staring as she ran a gentle palm down the horse's nose.

Fi nudged Swinton in the ribs.

What?

But Fi was already stepping away. 'I forgot my riding gloves. Meet you out front, Dimi.'

Fi's riding gloves were peeking out of his pocket as he turned heel and left.

Swallowing his nerves, Swinton entered the stall and, beside Eliza, ran his fingers through the filly's mane. He could have sworn Eliza was holding her breath.

'You were … impressive,' he stammered. 'With the stallion earlier, I mean.'

She glanced across at him. 'Thank you,' she said. 'I

trained him when he was little more than a foal, so it wasn't so hard.'

Swinton nodded, and then once more, was lost for words. His mind stumbled over possible sentences but ultimately left him speechless. Instead, he looked at her hands. They were not the soft, delicate palms of a lady. They were worker's hands. Rough and calloused, red and raw in some places, the nails cut short and lined with dirt.

'I'm glad you quit,' she said finally, her voice low.

'Quit?' Swinton's own voice came out hoarse.

'Jousting.'

'Oh,' he managed. 'Why?'

Her rough hand met his, tangled in the filly's mane. 'I just am.'

The ride back to Heathton was different. When Fi teased Swinton, he couldn't help but return the captain's grin. The two of them cantered across the territories with a newfound ease, or so it seemed to Swinton. He felt a lightness he hadn't felt in a long time. And there was such promise on the horizon.

'Upon your return, there is a matter I wish to discuss with you ...' King Arden had finally decided to knight him – he knew it in his bones. He would be *Sir* Dimitri Swinton.

His mind drifted back to Eliza. His father would never approve of the stable master's daughter. Especially if he saw the state of her hands. But as a knight … Perhaps it wouldn't matter. Perhaps he'd be able to offer Eliza the world, and the need for his father's approval would fade into the past.

Swinton urged his horse into a gallop. The sooner they returned to the castle, the sooner his life could well and truly begin.

NORTHERN WATERS

Every year, as Belbarrow celebrated the Festival of Lamaka, the Battalonian trout favoured by much of Ellest disappeared from the East Sea. The shoals swam northwest to breed in the warmer shallows of Battalon's capital, leaving the cooler waters to the swarms of common cod.

With the deck rocking steadily beneath her bare feet, Bleak breathed in the briny sea air and examined the day's catch, noting that amidst the flapping on deck, the silver scales were few and far between.

'They've already started to migrate,' she called out to Senior.

Her guardian's tanned, leathered face appeared from behind a barrel of salt. 'What's that?'

'She said the trout's on the move to Belbarrow already,' Bren yelled from the hull, where he sat cross-legged, mending one of the spare sails.

Senior dusted his hands off and approached Bleak's catch with a frown. 'Bit early yet …?'

'That's what I thought,' Bleak replied, palming through the thrashing fish. 'I don't understand, we come out this time every year. Always catch plenty.'

Senior's eyes scanned the catch and then met hers. 'It'll be that damn mist,' he said. 'Keeps forcing the shoals north —'

Bren joined them on the main deck. 'Senior, the king says it hasn't moved an inch since —'

'Believe everything yer told, do ya, Butter Fingers? That stuff out there is shifting. You'd be a fool to deny it …'

Bren flushed.

'Plenty of fools out there,' Bleak muttered.

Senior grunted his agreement, but his brow knitted in concern as he surveyed the catch again.

'Not enough, is it?' Bren said.

Senior shook his head. 'Not enough for the queen's birthday celebrations. The king won't be best pleased if we bring a third of the order.'

'Then we follow them,' said Bleak.

Senior laughed, giving her shoulder a gentle squeeze. 'Think it's that simple, do ya, Half-Pint? The northern waters in high season are rough enough to turn any sailor's gut.'

As if in answer, the northern wind picked up, the sails flapping madly. But Bren merely snorted. 'Come on, Senior,' he said with a wink at Bleak. 'We can handle it. We're seasoned sailors.'

'Seasoned sailors, eh?' Senior barked a laugh. 'You're greener than Half-Pint over there.'

Bleak smirked at her friend's outrage.

'Horseshi—'

'If ya wouldn't say it in front of yer mother, don't be sayin' it in front of me. Won't be blamed for yer bad habits, lad.'

Bleak clutched her stomach, laughing.

'Shut up,' Bren muttered.

'Well, don't be letting this lot die on deck.' Senior waved his hand at the catch.

Bleak and Bren dove, scooping up the fish and dumping them into the waiting barrels of seawater. Senior left them to it, returning to his usual post at the helm.

'What d'ya reckon?' Bren asked Bleak under his breath. 'Ya think we could do it?'

'What? Follow the trout north?'

Bren nodded eagerly.

Bleak shrugged. 'Don't know. Senior isn't joking about the northern waters.'

'How bad could it be? We've managed some rough seas just fine, the three of us.'

'True, but we knew those waters.'

'So? Water's water.'

Bleak deposited the last of the cod into the barrel and picked up the wet netting. 'Don't let Senior catch you saying that,' she said, raising a brow. Bren should know better than that. Each part of the sea had its own rhythm, its own currents and depths. Senior had been preaching that song for as long as she could remember. There was no knowing what sorts of winds whipped up over foreign waters, what storms brewed beyond their usual routes. They'd always stayed south of Battalon and Havennesse. They didn't have the right to be fishing there. But … they didn't have to go *too far* northwest. Just enough to catch the rear end of the shoal of trout.

'Well?' Bren said.

'We might be able to do it. With the right wind.'

'So ask him.' Bren elbowed her.

'*You* ask him,' Bleak countered.

However, as they worked up the courage over the course of the afternoon to broach the topic, it turned out that Senior had come to the decision of his own accord.

'There's nothin' for it,' he told them over dinner. 'We can't return with common cod for the queen's birthday. We gotta chase the wind north.'

Bren beamed and Bleak shook her head at her fair-haired friend. Uneasiness squirmed in her gut. She knew Senior was right. One bad catch would see his regular, lucrative trade with the royals, nobles and market folk plummet. He'd conquered the fishing trade decades ago, and despite constant new players to the game, had managed to stay afloat ever since. But although he'd been clever and reliable with his routes thus far, the high society of Heathton was unforgiving. A single bad spell could be a man's undoing in the Upper Realm.

Senior downed the rest of his ale. 'At first light, then ...'

Bleak and Bren took to the hammocks up on the main deck while Senior retired to the cabin below. They were quiet for a time, listening to the waves slapping against the side of the ship and the splash of the fish they'd caught in the barrels. The inky night sky was studded with millions of stars glinting down on them, and the briny breeze toyed with the loose fabric of the sails they'd taken in.

'Do ya reckon Senior's right?' Bren said suddenly.

Bleak craned her neck to look at him. He was gazing up at the sky, hands clasped across his abdomen. 'About what?' she said.

'That the trout are moving earlier 'cause of the mist. That the mist is encroaching more than the king's letting on.'

'We saw it ourselves, Bren ...'

They hadn't talked about it. That day in Felder's Bay, when the mist had come for them. Bleak remembered the panic vividly. Remembered swimming to shore with Bren, wondering if they'd survive the night.

'I know ...' he said quietly. This time his eyes met hers. 'I still dream about it.'

'Me too.'

'Do ya think we should have told Senior?'

Bleak drew her blanket up to her chin, suddenly chilly. 'I don't think it would have made a difference.'

Silence pulsed, and Bleak flinched as Bren's thoughts pummelled into her.

Why won't she look at me? Doesn't she realise —

It was happening more and more often now. Since that day in Felder's Bay. Since the mist. Regret churned in Bleak's gut. If she'd told Senior about the mist, she might have been able to ask him about it. She wanted to know if her encounter with the mist had amplified her Ashai ability somehow, with Bren in particular. It was his thoughts she heard the loudest.

'Bleak?'

'Hmm?'

'Do ya ever think what might have happened, if the mist hadn't appeared?' The words were laced with vulnerability, words he'd wanted to ask her for weeks, months even, and hadn't found the courage. She'd done all she could to avoid it so far, but now the question had been asked aloud, it hung heavy between them.

Had she thought about what might have happened? Every *damn* day. She couldn't help but lean into Bren's touch, couldn't help but watch him work the rigging, sweat gleaming across his tanned skin. Most of all, she couldn't help how her heart soared every time they laughed together. Had she thought about it? Gods, yes.

'Bleak? Do ya ever think about it?'

Bleak swallowed the lump in her throat. 'No,' she said. 'I don't.'

She heard him exhale shakily from his hammock.

'Good,' he told her. 'Me either.'

Bleak was awake long after Bren drifted off. Her usual love for the gentle sway of the sea and the reassuring sound of Bren's light snoring nearby was stifled by the guilt that swelled in her chest. She nestled deeper into her hammock and blankets, and watched as dawn bled into the dark sky.

Bleak got through the morning in an uneasy daze. Bleary-eyed, she tended to the sails and washed the lower deck. Glancing up at Bren scrubbing the main deck, her stomach squirmed. They hadn't talked over breakfast, and Bleak could feel the awkwardness pulsing between them. Senior had noticed too.

Everything alright with you two? he'd asked into her mind, jutting his chin towards Bren over porridge.

Bleak had just shaken her head and taken their empty bowls to the galley, eager to throw herself into more physical work. It was times like these she relished pushing her muscles, her endurance, to breaking point. It meant sleep would find her more easily come nightfall.

As the morning progressed, the winds picked up, and *The Daybreaker* gained speed. Bleak's hair escaped its tie and whipped about her face wildly. The breeze was a welcome respite against the hot day as they headed northwest towards the waters of the fire continent. The sun's rays soaked into Bleak's skin, and a glance at Senior's leathery face made her wonder if she'd one day have the same tanned, weathered appearance after years out at sea.

She peered into the turquoise depths below. No sign of the Battalonian trout yet, not from where she was standing. No, she needed to see further out. Passing Senior at the wheel, she plucked his spyglass from his breast pocket and headed to the mast.

With her usual surefootedness, she scaled the structure easily and settled in the crow's nest. Holding the spyglass to her eye, she gazed out at the expanse of sea, watching the choppy current churn across the glassy surface. She adjusted the lens and focused, looking for shadows beneath the clear waters. They couldn't be far behind the shoal of trout now.

'How are we tracking?' Bren called up to her.

Bleak nearly dropped the spyglass and swore under her breath. But with a glance down at her friend she answered, 'Nothing yet.'

'We can't be far off,' he said.

She chanced another look in his direction, surprised to find a green tint to his skin, his face lined with discomfort.

Before she could say anything, Senior cut in. 'Give us another quarter hour, Half-Pint,' he called. 'Gotta cover a bit more distance first, should be on 'em soon enough. Butter Fingers, drop the nets, will ya?'

She watched Bren tuck his fair hair behind his ear and roll his shirtsleeves up before he threw the last of the nets overboard. Tentative relief flared in Bleak as she watched Bren go about releasing the nets. He looked a little queasy from the stronger currents, but he'd spoken to her. That had to mean he was okay, that *they* were okay. For the moment at least.

Yes, she thought. *We'll be fine.*

Movement up ahead caught her eye, and Bleak cursed herself for not paying closer attention to her duty. She brought the spyglass back up to her face and peered through, her pulse quickening.

'Senior,' she shouted as soon as her eyes fell upon the foreign vessel. 'Senior!'

'Eh?'

'There's a ship ahead. I don't recognise the crest.'

Senior remained calm. 'How far?'

'A half-dozen leagues or so …'

Senior frowned. *And you're just seeing this now?*

Bleak ignored his mental quip.

'What's going on?' Bren asked, joining Senior at the wheel.

Senior merely pointed.

'That's not a Battalonian flag …' Bren murmured, squinting at the red rectangle of fabric waving in the wind.

'No,' agreed Senior. 'It's not.'

Following their gazes, Bleak focused the spyglass on the flag. They were right. It wasn't any flag of Battalon she recognised. It didn't have the required stitching anywhere she could see. Instead, the flag showed the hand-painted face of a woman. It was none of the goddesses Bleak knew. And the ship was now heading straight for them.

Bleak climbed down the mast swiftly. There was nothing more she could do from the crow's nest. 'They're coming,' she said.

'We're not doing anything wrong.' Bren turned to Senior. 'Haven't caught any Battalonian trout yet, so they can't claim we're breaching trade agreements, right?'

'Nets are down, lad. No hiding our intentions now … But I don't think it's that type of ship …' Senior narrowed his eyes at the approaching vessel, glancing back up at the strange flag.

'What do we do now?' asked Bleak. This was all her fault.

Senior shrugged. 'We wait.'

They didn't have to wait long. The foreign ship rivalled *The Daybreaker* for speed easily. Before Bleak knew it, the vessel was pulling up alongside them, its crew staring the trio down.

'Greetings, sailors,' said a woman's voice.

Bleak scanned the crew until she found the source leaning against the mast, hands outstretched before her.

Definitely not Battalonian, Bleak thought as she took in the woman's elaborately embroidered shawl and pale skin.

'Greetings to you as well,' Senior said from beside

Bleak, hiding his surprise. It wasn't often a woman was found at the heart of a ship.

'Bit far north to be fishing for Ellest, aren't you?' the woman said, approaching the side of her ship and taking in the Ellestian colours marking their flag.

'Got caught in a rip,' Senior said casually. 'Yourself?'

'Returning to Qatrola after a leisure visit to Belbarrow.'

Bleak noticed Bren's utter stillness beside her, his thoughts milling freely into her mind. She followed them across the way to the weapons each of the crew clutched.

Weapons? Bleak had to stop herself from gaping as her eyes swept across the shortswords and daggers. Why would the entire crew have weapons?

'Begging your pardon.' Senior bowed his head. 'We'd best be turning home then.'

Bleak's stomach squirmed as the woman blatantly assessed her. Her gaze lingered on Bleak's odd-coloured eyes.

'I would ask that you wait a moment,' she said. It wasn't a request. A threat laced between each of her words. 'My lady may wish to speak with you ...' she added, flicking her hand in the direction of their captain's cabin.

'Yer lady?' Bren cut in. 'Who is yer lady?'

Bleak winced at the demand in his voice, and heard Senior's thoughts mirror her own. A tone like that wouldn't do them any favours.

The woman smiled, a smile that didn't quite meet her eyes. 'You don't strike me as the sort of fellow who would be familiar with nobility.'

From the corner of her eye, Bleak saw Bren's face flush scarlet.

Serves you right, she thought, glancing nervously at the opposing crew.

Half-Pint. Senior's voice filled her head. *If something should happen, don't fight them. Don't reveal what you are. If there's a chance to escape with Butter Fingers, take it. With or without me.*

She swallowed hard, but gave Senior a subtle nod.

One of the crew members addressed the woman. 'Madame Farlah,' he said. 'Our lady does not wish to delay. She asks that we leave the travellers and depart now. She is eager to return to Qatrola.'

Bleak didn't dare exhale the breath she'd been holding. Not yet.

Madame Farlah's eyes slid back to hers, once more pausing on Bleak's hazel and blue irises.

A humming sound buzzed in Bleak's ears, gradually infiltrating her mind. It grew louder and louder. She strained to keep her facial features neutral as the noise became a painful intrusion, demanding her acknowledgement.

What. Is. This? She gritted her teeth and tried to breathe steadily through her nose. She couldn't hide it for much longer. Couldn't –

A hand slipped into hers. A calloused thumb ran over her middle knuckle. Bren.

He squeezed her hand and the sound retreated, fading into the background. Another squeeze of his hand and she could feel her feet beneath her, feel the cool breeze on her face once more.

Madame Farlah was staring at her. A dark, piercing stare that sent a shiver down Bleak's spine. The woman tilted her head slightly, and then adjusted her shawl across her shoulders.

'Very well,' she said. 'As our lady commands, then ... May the seas be kind to you, travellers.'

She heard a soft sigh of relief from Senior. Bleak dropped Bren's hand, her pulse still racing.

As the foreign ship departed, the strange red flag billowed in the wind, giving them one last glimpse of the illustrated woman's face. A wave of goosebumps broke out across Bleak's arms, and she crossed them over her chest, turning to the men.

'Well, that was different,' she said, her voice not nearly as steady as she'd intended.

'Different's one word for it,' Senior muttered.

Bren suddenly made a mad dash for the side of the ship, and was violently sick. Beads of sweat broke out across his brow and he vomited again.

Bleak glanced at Senior, who was trying and failing to hide his smirk.

'Not feeling so good, eh, Butter Fingers?' he said. 'Told you these waters are rough enough to turn any sailor's gut ...'

Bleak gave Senior a shove and went to Bren. She

rubbed his back as his body heaved again. Gods knew he'd done the same for her countless times.

Senior was chuckling to himself as he set about getting *The Daybreaker* back on course.

Bren went down below with a bucket for company, and Bleak escaped once more to the mast. Her mind wandered back to the painful hum that had broken through her thoughts. And then Bren's touch, and how it had grounded her, brought her back from the pain. She had so many questions, and no one to voice them to. While she loved Senior with all her heart, he didn't have the answers she needed. With a sigh, she pressed the spyglass to her eye and gazed out across the churning waters again.

A dark shadow flickered below the surface. A seamless movement. A shoal of Battalonian trout.

'Senior,' she called out, jumping to her feet. 'They're straight on! We've got them!'

She and Senior scrambled to the nets, watching as they began to fill. Beside her, Senior's body sank with relief. The tension of the day lifted from his shoulders.

'I wouldn't have left you, you know …' Bleak told him, not taking her eyes from their catch.

Senior put his arm around her neck. 'You never were one for doing as you were told.'

Before long, the nets were sagging with fresh Battalonian trout. Bleak and Senior reeled them in from the sea, water cascading onto the deck.

Bren reappeared, letting out a low, appreciative

whistle as the flapping silver bodies spilled out across the deck. He looked pale, but no longer carried the bucket with him.

'Reckon we've earned ourselves a decent supper, Butter Fingers?' Senior said, nodding to one of the fatter fish.

Bren laughed weakly. 'Maybe once we're back on Ellestian waters …'

The waters calmed as they sailed south, back into the familiar currents of the East Sea. Colour came back to Bren's cheeks, and he smiled at Bleak from across the cooking fire, his hands busy descaling a fat silver trout.

She smiled back. *We'll be fine,* she thought again.

Night fell once more and they anchored not far from the coast of Angove. Bleak bit into the smoky Battalonian trout and took a swig of dark ale. She watched the lights flicker from the cliffs. Mrs Clayton and the boys would have supped long ago now, and Van and Hutch, the youngest, would be tucked up in bed. The others would be drinking and talking around the kitchen table, likely with Mrs Clayton simultaneously chastising and laughing at their bawdy jokes. That was, unless Mr Clayton was home.

Senior left to get more ale, and Bleak looked to Bren again, his fair hair falling over his eyes as he gathered the empty plates.

'I do think about it, you know,' she heard herself say. 'What might have happened.'

Bren glanced up, surprised.

'I do think about it,' she said again.

Her friend smiled warmly and nodded. 'I know,' he told her. 'Our story's only just beginning, Half-Pint ... No need to rush it, eh?'

She felt a smile break across her own face. 'No need to rush it,' she agreed.

Senior rejoined them, pouring fresh ale into their mugs. 'Next time you two suggest sailing up north, remind me to knock yer heads together,' he said.

Bren laughed. 'Won't be suggesting that again in a hurry ...'

Bleak clapped him on the back. 'Never seen someone turn so green before.'

'I was not green.'

Senior scoffed. 'Were so, lad. After all that malarkey about being a seasoned sailor too, eh?'

'Imagine what your brothers will say ...' Bleak teased.

'Ya wouldn't ...'

'Wouldn't I?'

'Cut it out,' Senior barked. 'Can't an old man enjoy some peace and quiet on his own damn ship?'

Bleak and Bren stifled their laughter and went to the bow of *The Daybreaker*, gazing out onto the black waters ahead. Finally, the day was behind them. Now they would only look forward.

THE VALIAN WAY

The bitter cold of Havennesse had plunged its teeth into fourteen-year-old Henri's bones and latched around her heart. As she sank into the deep snow and buried her ice pick into the side of the mountain, everything hurt. Around their unit of eleven, the winds screamed, whipping snow into their eyes and stinging exposed skin. Despite her layers of palma furs and winter leathers, Henri couldn't stop her teeth from chattering. She hauled herself up and swung her ice pick again.

Upon their arrival in Wildenhaven, they had been received by an ageing King Stellen, who had apologised for the absence of Princess Eydis and Prince Jarel. Both were off in the hinterlands, training a new litter of wolfdogs. Henri hadn't been able to hide her disappointment, but the king assured her and Sahara that his unruly royal children would be here upon the Valians' return from the mountains.

They had trained hard in Wildenhaven before they set out, completing brutal drills and hikes in varying degrees of snowstorm. Somewhere along the way, Henri and Sahara had celebrated their fourteenth name day. Allehra's gift was an additional five drills of hand-to-hand combat in the frozen arena. Henri had pushed through it with gritted teeth. The thought of seeing one of her oldest friends was what kept her strong.

After four weeks of training, they had finally begun their trek up the Kildaholm Alps: the coldest and harshest mountain range in the realm. A sheet of white stretched as far as Henri's eyes could see, punctuated only by jagged mountain ridges and peaks; steep, savage and desolate.

'It will test the limits of even your *endurance ...'* Allehra had said.

Well, Henri thought, *she got that right.*

They had been climbing for almost three weeks now. Three weeks of utter exhaustion and no reprieve from the freezing conditions, all the while racing other Valian teams dotted around the ranges. The first unit to retrieve the Valian flag at the summit would be the team from which Allehra selected the heir's elite kindred. Henri had never wanted something so much in her life ... but she'd also never been in this much pain. She looked to her companions. Sahara, Athene, Petra, Marvel, Tilly,

Addi, Greer and Keegan were all suffering as well. Addi had developed a hacking cough, though she was doing her utmost to conceal it from their mentors, Makena and Quinn. Henri had noticed, though. She'd also noticed how Addi's steps had become shorter, the swing of her pick weaker. Beside Henri on the slope, Sahara followed her gaze and lowered the scarf wrapped around her face.

Henri shook her head frantically. She knew what Sahara was thinking, but she couldn't –

'When do we make camp?' Sahara called out over the howling winds.

If she'd had the energy, Henri would have slapped her sister. Sahara knew better than to question the leadership of a Valian mentor. The whole point of this training exercise was to showcase their endurance, their hardiness. Requesting a break was suicide.

'When I say so,' Makena's stern voice shouted from above. 'Do you want to win this thing or not?'

'Of course we want to win. We don't need to stop,' Athene yelled. She climbed just below the sisters, bringing up the rear of the unit.

Henri didn't miss Sahara's glare, or the spray of snow she sent down over Athene.

'Watch yourself,' Athene snapped in her direction. Henri should have rounded on Athene for speaking to their heir like that, but truth be told … Sahara was making life more difficult for all of them.

Addi, however, after another muffled coughing

fit, gave Sahara a sad yet grateful smile. But her gratitude didn't matter. Not here. They would not be stopping for some time yet.

Darkness fell like a heavy blanket over the craggy ridges and gullies. It wasn't until hours later that the Valians sought shelter, tucked into the side of a ravine. Numb, starving and exhausted to the core, they set up their tent in silence. Inside, they huddled around a small fire, its feeble flames doing little to bring warmth to their frozen fingers. Henri forced herself to chew the grain bar that had been pressed into her hand. She didn't want to eat, but she knew her body needed the sustenance now more than ever. Across the fire, she watched Sahara give her own steaming cup of broth to Addi.

'She's slowing us down,' Athene whispered in Henri's ear. 'Her *and* Sahara's sympathies.'

'Athene,' Henri warned.

'You know I'm right.'

As though sensing she was the subject of their murmurings, Sahara's head snapped up. 'Something to say, Athene?'

Athene lifted her chin. 'Nothing you'd care to hear.'

Henri scowled, resisting the urge to shove her friend. 'Stop it,' she hissed. 'Sahara is our heir.'

'I'm aware of that.' Athene turned away from Henri, leaving her food untouched.

Henri pushed the canteen of broth towards her. 'You need to eat something.'

But Athene shook her head. 'Can't stand the smell of that.'

Makena cleared her throat as Quinn unfurled their map. 'We're less than a day's climb from the summit,' Quinn told them, scanning their faces. 'If my estimates are accurate, we're an hour or so ahead of Allehra's unit. We'll rest here for three hours, then start the final ascent before dawn.'

Three hours? That's all the rest we get? The others' faces mirrored Henri's thoughts. But no one protested, no one complained. That was the Valian Way.

Henri dozed fitfully, her mind littered with strange dreams of dogs barking. Addi's cough worsened during the night and her hacking noises kept them all from sleep. Almost as soon as Henri had managed to warm her frostbitten toes, she was roused by a rough shake from Makena.

'Up,' was all the mentor said, before moving along to wake the others.

They had to chip the icicles from the tent before they packed it away in the blistering gale. Henri's body was aching before they even started moving.

Less than a day till the summit, she reminded herself. As she shouldered her pack and sank into the knee-deep snow, she imagined the feeling of victory they'd experience as they clutched the Valian flag in their hands on top of the world. *It will all be worth it,* she thought. *It has to be.*

The conditions were worse than the day before. A blizzard raged around them as they climbed their way to the base of the final peak. It was harder to breathe up here, and Henri found herself gasping for air. Endurance. She, *they,* had to endure. To endure was to be the best warriors of the Valia kindred. And so she put one boot in front of the other.

There was a soft cry from behind her. Henri whirled around as quickly as her bulky layers would let her.

Addi had slipped and fallen. She wasn't getting up.

Sahara was suddenly at her side, hauling her upright. But Addi's breathing was shallow and her eyes were closed.

'She can't go any further,' Sahara called out to Makena and Quinn.

The two mentors exchanged looks. 'Then she stays here,' Quinn said, gesturing to the savage surroundings.

'*What?*'

'There is no place in the kindred for the weak.'

The rest of their unit was silent. Only the wind howled around them.

But Henri had never seen such fire in her sister's eyes as Sahara took Addi's full weight and said, 'I will not leave her behind.'

'It is the Valian Way,' Makena said sternly. 'The way by which you will one day rule.'

Henri watched on in shock as her sister steeled herself against their superiors. 'I'll not leave her.'

Athene cursed. 'For Rheyah's sake. What does that mean for our mission, then? You and Addi would sabotage us like that?'

'You don't think a Valian's life is worth the loss of some flag?' Sahara snapped.

'That's enough,' Henri heard herself say.

The others did nothing to hide their surprise.

'Sahara stays with Addi, the rest of us go on to the summit and retrieve the flag. There is no rule against splitting up that I'm aware of. Is that correct, Makena?'

Makena considered this, clutching her furs tightly around herself. 'That's correct.'

Henri locked eyes with Sahara. 'So be it?'

Sahara nodded, taking the pack with the tent from Quinn. 'So be it.'

They left Sahara and Addi halfway up the final slope. Addi's lips were blue, her face grey, and she was rambling incoherently. Sahara said no more, but clenched her teeth and began to set up the tent herself. Soon, she and Addi were mere specks in the sheet of white stretching down the alps. Henri knew she wouldn't feel at ease again until her twin was back in her sight.

'It's not looking good for her,' Tilly murmured as they paused to sip from their half-frozen canteens.

'She's a dead woman,' Athene said. 'She should have been left. Our heir should be with us.'

'Athene —' Henri started to reprimand, but Athene bolted from their line to throw up in the snow. She retched violently, ending up on all fours to heave.

'Athene …' Henri's voice softened. She hadn't realised her friend was unwell. She went to her and held back her braid as Athene emptied the contents of her stomach. But Athene wiped her mouth with the back of her hand and straightened, looking determined.

'Let's just get this done.'

By the time they reached the summit of the highest peak of the Kildaholm Alps, the Valia kindred-in-training were not the same girls they had been. Henri was only just able to stay upright. Tilly and Marvel had been reduced to a staggering crawl. But it didn't matter. They were all here. Well, *almost* all of them.

It was Henri who clutched the Valian flag in her aching fist. A forest-green backdrop with a silver Valian oak tree emblazoned at its centre. Beside her, Athene embedded a pole deep in the snow, and with numb fingers, Henri raised their wavering emblem into the blistering winds.

'We've done it,' she told their unit. 'We made it.'

Her voice echoed between the gullies, but she didn't feel the relief she thought she would. And scanning the blank, exhausted faces staring back at her, she knew the others didn't either. Their group, including their mentors, lay sprawled in the icy white powder, crippled by fatigue.

At last, Henri allowed herself to sink to her knees. Athene did the same, huddling close.

'You know what this means?' the redhead murmured.

Henri was too tired to talk. She gave a slight shake of her head.

'When Sahara becomes matriarch, we'll be her elite kindred. We did it, Henri. We're the next *elite kindred* of Valia.'

Athene was right. Reaching the summit here meant they'd achieved the goal they'd shared their whole lives. Henri gave her friend a weak squeeze. They were exactly where they needed to be.

They took a short break at the top, but the air was thin and they were utterly exposed to the piercing winds. Henri shouldered her pack once more, eager to begin their descent. Climbing down was even more taxing. Henri slipped on more than one occasion, Athene grabbing her elbow or her pack before she went skidding down the slopes.

Keegan and Tilly had developed the same cough as Addi, and the sound of their rattled breathing travelled down the mountain. Henri wondered if the other Valian units were faring as badly as they were.

It began to snow in earnest. Thick flakes rained down on them, managing to find their way between the heavy layers, so cold against bare skin that they burned. No one had the energy to talk. All they could do was push forward, ever so slowly, through the now thigh-deep powder, following the coordinates they'd marked for Sahara and Addi.

Henri glanced at Athene. She hadn't been sick since the ascent – that was something, at least. She knew many people did grow ill as they climbed the alps. Henri would have to watch her closely.

When they reached the coordinates for Sahara and Addi, they couldn't see the tent. The ravine that unfolded before them was a sea of brilliant white. Henri's heart caught in her throat.

'Where are they?' she croaked. Sahara was *her* responsibility. She never should have left her. She should have stayed in her place if Sahara was going to be that immovable. Makena and Quinn's faces betrayed nothing, but Henri could feel their energy with her magic; they were rife with paralysed panic.

'They're here somewhere,' Athene murmured, scanning the mountainside.

'We can't just start digging away at the snow,' Petra chimed in. 'That could start a snowslide.'

'Well, what do you suggest? I'm not sitting here waiting for my sister to freeze to death,' Henri snapped.

'No one's going to die,' Quinn intervened, her face a mask of calm. She pointed to a subtle mound in the snow, a hundred or so yards away. 'There,' she said. 'That's where we left them.'

There was no movement. No sign of life.

Henri could scarcely breathe as they approached. Her footsteps were like lead and her mind raced. *If Sahara* – She wouldn't finish that thought. She wouldn't let herself go there. The tension among their group was stifling, and they moved slowly, as though they weren't ready to face whatever waited for them at those coordinates.

'There!' Athene exclaimed.

There was a flutter of movement from the ridge. Henri squinted. It could be a stray caribou or a lone wolf ... but ... Her eyes strained –

Relief flooded her to the core. Sahara's charcoal furs emerged from the snow, her midnight braid unmistakeable as she made her way down to them. *Thank the gods. She's alright. She's alive.*

But as Sahara drew closer, Henri's relief froze in her chest. From the look on her sister's face, she knew something was wrong. Terribly wrong.

'Where's Addi?' Makena demanded when Sahara reached them.

Sahara scanned the group, her gaze lingering on the grey tinge to Tilly and Keegan's faces. Her graphite eyes were cold.

'Gone.'

'What?' The word was like a punch to Henri's gut. There was no way Addi had been in any shape to leave. She couldn't have started back down the mountain on her own. What had happened while the rest of them had been at the summit?

Sahara's gaze met hers, steeled with anger. 'Addi's dead.'

Quinn stepped forward. 'That's not …'

Sahara closed the gap between them, her chin raised. 'Not *what*? *Possible*? I tried to tell you. I told you —'

No one had ever spoken to a mentor like that before. No one. As though in answer to her quickening heart, Henri's magic thrummed wildly through her veins. She couldn't believe what she was hearing here, what she was seeing.

'Where is she?' Makena interjected.

Sahara tore her glare away from Quinn and pointed to the mound of snow. 'In the tent.'

Without another word, Makena left them shivering in the snow. Without thinking, Henri went after her. She needed to see this. To acknowledge the fall of a comrade. She trudged behind their mentor silently, reaching the half-buried tent. Makena started to dig into the pile of snow with her gloved hands. Henri joined her. It was a mindless task that numbed her spiralling thoughts. But with each push of the snow, the questions grew louder in her head … *Is it true? Is she dead?*

Finally, they found the entrance to the tent, and Henri followed Makena inside.

'Gods …' Henri covered her mouth.

There was Addi. She lay there, lifeless, her lips a dark shade of blue and her eyes closed. Ice had formed on her eyelashes.

Beside Henri, Makena took a deep breath. 'May she rest well with Enovius.'

Henri's hands shook as she reached out to touch the fallen Valian. 'May Rheyah keep her.'

Henri and Makena worked in silence to disassemble the tent while the rest of their unit remained further up the slope, taking what little shelter they could. Henri kept stealing glances at her mentor, but Makena's face was a mask of steel. Addi's body was already blanketed with fresh snow. When the tent was packed away and hoisted onto Makena's back, the mentor made for the group.

'What are you doing?' The words burst from Henri's mouth.

Makena gave Henri a hard stare. 'We have to move.'

'But … what about Addi?' Henri stammered.

'She belongs to the mountain now.'

'What? We can't leave her up here. With no proper burial, with no —'

'She stays. We are in *no* condition to lug a body down these slopes.'

A lump formed in Henri's throat as the truth of it latched around her heart. Makena was right; their unit was fading. Two of their kindred shared the same cough as Addi. Athene was suffering from mountain sickness. Henri herself was bone-weary. None of them had the strength to spare.

Makena was already moving towards the others, but Henri hesitated. Hands trembling, she approached Addi's lifeless body and removed one of her woollen gloves. Her friend wore a ring passed down from her grandmother, who had been an elite kindred. Henri pulled the silver band from Addi's cold finger. Her mother would want something to remember her by.

When the company arrived back in Wildenhaven, there were no celebrations. Another unit had lost a member as well. Tilly and Keegan were ushered into the medical wing, their faces grey and their coughs violent. Athene's mountain illness had returned and she, too, was rushed away for treatment.

In the great hall, Henri handed the Valian flag to Allehra without a word and followed Sahara to their rooms. Only once the door had clicked closed behind them did her twin turn to her, tears in her graphite eyes.

'She didn't have to die,' Sahara said quietly.

'It was the —'

'For Rheyah's sake, Henri. Don't say *the Valian Way*.'

'But —'

Sahara shook her head. 'Was it worth it? For some stupid flag? Some outdated notion of what it means to be a Valian? Her death is on *our* hands. And who knows who else's …'

'Sahara …'

But there was nothing Henri could do to comfort her sister, or herself.

Later that evening, there was a knock on their door.

'Come in,' Henri called wearily from her place before the roaring hearth.

The door opened a fraction, enough so that a head of snow-dusted caramel hair appeared. 'It's me,' said a soft voice.

'Eydis!' Henri darted forward, pulling their friend into the room. She grabbed Eydis in a warm embrace. The princess' long arms wrapped around her and squeezed her back.

'I've just heard,' Eydis said, crossing the room to greet Sahara. 'I'm sorry for your loss.'

Sahara said nothing, but accepted the princess' embrace.

'Thank you,' Henri heard herself say. 'I'm sorry we're meeting again under such circumstances.'

Eydis nodded and peeled off her cloak, revealing bulky men's clothing beneath. The winter princess had been this way ever since Henri could remember, always hiding her lanky frame beneath baggy knits and trousers. She sank into the free armchair before the fire with a sigh.

'How was your trip?' Henri asked.

'Never mind that.' Eydis waved her away. 'How are you both?'

'Fine,' Henri said automatically.

The glare Sahara shot her from across the room nearly burned through her.

'We're not *fine*,' Sahara snapped. 'We've —'

'Sahara,' Henri warned.

Sahara folded her arms across her chest and looked out the window.

'Henri,' Eydis said. 'I actually came to tell you that one of your friends in the medical wing is asking after you.'

Henri's pulse quickened. 'Athene?'

Eydis nodded.

'Is she alright?'

'All I know is that she was asking to speak to you. Go. I'll stay and talk with Sahara.'

Henri looked from the princess to her sister, hesitating.

'Go,' Eydis told her with another wave.

Henri's heart raced as she followed an attendant's directions to the medical wing of the third Wildenhaven tower. Athene needed to speak with her? How bad was her illness? In what state was she about to find her friend?

She burst through the doors to find Athene sitting on the edge of a cot, tying her boots with trembling hands.

'What is it?' Henri asked. 'What happened?'

With a glance from Athene, the attendant left them. Athene patted the space on the cot beside her, cheeks tipped pink. Bewildered, Henri sat.

'What's wrong?' she demanded. 'How bad is it? I thought the mountain sickness had passed.'

'It …' Athene turned to her. 'It wasn't mountain sickness.'

'What then? Do you have what Tilly and —'

Athene shook her head. 'I'm not ill,' she said. 'I'm pregnant.'

Henri stared. 'What?'

'I'm pregnant.'

'You can't be.' Henri knew how stupid the words sounded as soon as they left her mouth. How would she know? Athene was her friend, but they … they never talked about —

'Well, I am,' Athene was saying.

Henri swallowed. 'Who …?'

'It doesn't matter.'

'Doesn't it?'

'Do you know who *your* father was?'

Henri baulked. No one had ever asked her that. No one in Valia *ever* asked about people's fathers. She shook her head.

'It's the Valian Way.'

Henri was numb. 'What … what are you going to do?'

'I want to keep her.'

'Her? How do you know it's a girl? You can't be that far along.'

'I'm just over six weeks. It's early, but I can just tell.'

'Just over six weeks … So it happened here?'

Athene raised a brow and waited.

'You're going to have to tell Allehra,' Henri said.

'I know.'

They left the medical wing and wandered the frozen grounds together. Henri's head was spinning. Athene had been with someone … someone Henri had no idea about. And now – now Athene was going to be a *mother*.

A feeling Henri didn't recognise stirred within her, creeping into her chest like the cold had crept into her bones.

The Valians stayed in Wildenhaven another week, until those who'd fallen ill had recovered. Athene vowed to tell Allehra of her condition upon their return to the forest. Only Henri knew. But Athene seemed at ease with her fate, and so, despite Henri's inner turmoil about the situation, she remained quiet.

It was Sahara for whom Henri feared. Her sister had barely said two words since leaving Addi atop the mountain. Their fallen comrade's ring was tucked safely in Henri's pocket. She had told Makena that she would be the one to break the news to Addi's mother. She didn't know why, but it felt important that she should be the one to do it, as though it were her responsibility. Perhaps it was guilt, for not listening to Sahara when she'd demanded that they stop. Guilt for not having the guts to challenge what she knew.

Now, Henri stood beside her twin on the deck of their ship, watching the white horizon of Havennesse disappear.

'Was it what you thought it would be?' Sahara asked her quietly.

'I don't know what I thought it would be.'

Sahara raised her brows. 'You thought it would be a big adventure. Bookended by a glorious victory.'

Henri grit her teeth. Her sister knew her well, perhaps better than she knew herself.

'So was it?' Sahara pressed, resting against the ship's rail.

'You know it wasn't.'

'Something has to change.'

'There is no changing the Valian Way.'

Sahara unsheathed her dagger and twirled it in her hands as she gazed at the sheets of ice floating atop the dark water. 'Maybe not.'

Feeling queasy, Henri left Sahara scratching something into the wooden railing. Sea travel had never agreed with her and she needed a distraction from the churning in her gut. She found Athene repairing a net by the bow.

'How are you feeling?' she asked her friend, watching her work.

'Better than you, by the looks of things. I didn't realise someone could actually turn green.'

'Thanks,' Henri muttered.

'What's going on with Sahara?' Athene nodded to their heir, standing alone at the stern.

'What d'you mean?'

'She's not the most subtle person … Something's wrong.'

Henri sighed. 'She's upset about Addi. We all are.'

'Addi was weak, Henri. She wasn't meant to be a Valian.'

Henri frowned. 'Does that mean she was meant to die, though?'

Athene met her gaze. 'Yes.' She said it with such certainty, such conviction, that Henri herself nearly agreed.

'Athene …'

'You need to accept what it means to be a Valian,' Athene said. 'The sooner you do that, the sooner you will find your place here.'

'I know my place,' Henri snapped. 'It's by Sahara's side.'

But over the next five days, Henri barely saw her sister. The heir had made herself scarce with everyone, it seemed.

It wasn't until the Valians moored at Felder's Bay that Henri saw Sahara's carving on the rail.

OREMERE.

Henri had never heard the word before. What did it mean?

She would ask Sahara later. If there was one thing she knew about herself and her sister, it was that they didn't keep secrets from one another.

. . .

Back atop the Valian canopies, Henri was glad for the summer wind that kissed her face and toyed with her braid. Even all these months after her return from Havennesse, she still shuddered at the memory of the bone-snapping cold. She thanked the gods she was back home. Here amidst the living bridges, her ancestors' magic hummed around her, ancient enchantments rustling in the leaves and dancing in the warm breeze.

She sighed, remembering why she was up here. 'Sahara?' she called. 'Sahara, where are you?'

Unlike Henri and the rest of the kindred, the Valian heir had a tendency to lose herself among the treetops – when she risked climbing that high, that was. Sahara had a loathsome fear of heights, an affliction that should have been trained out of her by now, but had gone largely undetected by their mentors. Henri shook her head at the thought.

'Sahara!' she called again, turning onto a new bridge. Frankly, half the time she didn't think Sahara *wanted* to be found, much to Henri's frustration. She was meant to be her twin's right-hand woman, her constant guard and companion. Sahara didn't exactly make it easy for her. The heir of Valia was a difficult —

'What do you want?' Sahara's sharp voice interrupted Henri's thoughts.

Henri turned. 'I —'

But her words caught in her throat as she clapped eyes on her sister.

'What have you done?' she breathed.

Sahara's waist-length side braid was gone.

Her midnight hair now swung loose at her jaw. She folded her arms over her chest, staring back at Henri, her mirror eyes inviting a challenge.

'Sahara ... how could you?' Henri managed.

'With a pair of scissors and help from a groundling.'

'Allehra's going to —' Henri stopped. 'A *groundling*? Tell me you didn't go out to the Sticks?'

'So what if I did? I'm the heir of this place, so you all keep reminding me. Surely I can go where I please. And do what I want with my own hair.'

Henri didn't know what to say. Her sister had been different, lately: darker, angrier. Athene had put it down to mood swings and the impending pressure of ruling Valia, but Henri wasn't convinced. She had a feeling – or, more accurately, her magic had a feeling; she could sense that something about Sahara's energy had changed since they'd returned from Havennesse.

A lump was suddenly caught in her throat. 'Sahara,' she pleaded. 'Let's switch. Just until your hair grows back. We can't have the kindred see you punished. Let me —'

Sahara was staring at her.

'What?'

'You would truly do that for me, wouldn't you?'

Henri frowned. 'I'd do anything for you.'

Something akin to sadness filled Sahara's eyes. 'Yes, I'm starting to realise that.'

Later that evening, Henri sparred with Athene. Sweat glistened on both their brows as they parried and feinted their way around the treetop circuit.

'Should you *really* be doing this?' Henri asked for the millionth time, keeping her blows light.

'Stop asking me that. I'm just as capable —'

'It's not about your capability. It's about your *child*.'

The word still felt foreign to Henri; wrong, somehow. Athene was too young to be pregnant. She was a Valian in her prime – a member of the heir's elite kindred …

'I know,' Athene murmured, lowering her practice sword.

Henri huffed a sigh. 'You said you'd tell Allehra when we were back. We're back now.'

'I will, alright?'

'Well, you won't have to if you wait much longer.' Henri looked pointedly at her friend's stomach. She was just beginning to show, and Henri had noticed her hand often rested there protectively. That tic would only increase as the child grew inside her.

'Come on,' Athene said. 'We'll be late for supper.'

The dining area of the keep was bustling by the time they arrived. Several fires roared, game roasting atop the flames, while Valian wine flowed generously from great barrels. Their group was in the usual spot: in the far corner, by the largest Valian oak tree. Sahara, Petra, Marvel and Tilly sat at a round table, laughing loudly.

After loading their plates with roast boar and root vegetables, Henri and Athene slid into the spare seats beside their kindred.

'What's all this about, then?' Henri asked, biting into a piece of well-seasoned pumpkin.

Tilly snorted and wiped the tears streaming from her eyes. 'Petra quite —'

Petra elbowed her, hard. 'Shut it.'

But it was no use. The group burst into another fit of hysterics.

'Petra fancies Jarel,' Marvel managed between hiccups.

'Jarel?' Athene frowned. 'Princess Eydis' younger brother?'

'The very one,' Tilly crowed, her eyes bright with mischief.

Petra flushed profusely. 'What's wrong with liking a crown prince of one of the realm's most powerful continents?' she snapped defensively.

'Well … nothing …' Henri found herself grinning. 'He's quite pretty, isn't he?'

Her comment earned her a glowering glare from Petra and another bout of knee-slapping laughter from the others.

All except Sahara.

The smile faded from Henri's lips as she studied

her sister across the table. Her expression was faraway, and Henri suddenly knew exactly what she was thinking. Shame rushed through her.

Of course. They were making light of a time that had been the scene of monumental loss for the Valian people. Addi had died, along with another young Valian from Allehra's unit. The image of Addi's blue lips and frozen hair was etched into Henri's memory – as was the look on Addi's mother's face when Henri had returned her daughter's ring to her with no body to burn. Sahara, even as heir, had been voiceless against the Valian Way.

Guilt seized Henri's gut. She should have had more respect for their fallen comrades.

The others had noticed the change in their moods and lowered their voices to soft chatter, glancing at the twins, concern knitted into their furrowed brows.

Beside Henri, Athene scrutinised Sahara's freshly chopped locks.

'What does our queen think of your new look?' she asked, her words icy.

Henri started, unable to believe Athene's nerve. It was one thing for the heir's twin to question her choices, but *Athene* ...

Sahara raised her brows and took a deliberately long drink from her goblet. 'What does she think of yours?' she said, with a pointed glance at the hand resting across Athene's stomach.

The chatter around them died.

Blood pounded between Henri's ears. How did Sahara know? Henri hadn't told a soul, and now —

Suddenly, she realised it wasn't just *their* table that had quietened. It was the whole keep. For Allehra, Matriarch and Queen of Valia, had entered, dressed in spotless leathers, two of her elites by her sides.

Her eyes sought her daughters, finding them sat where they always were. Her gaze lingered briefly on Sahara's cropped hair, but her expression gave nothing away as she approached. The rest of the keep resumed their meals, albeit a little more quietly.

Athene shifted in her seat and, with another look of distaste at Sahara, said, 'Let's see what she thinks of us, then.'

Henri panicked. No – Athene couldn't tell Allehra like this, not in front of everyone – what was she thinking?

Allehra reached their table.

'Athene,' Henri pleaded. 'Don't —'

'Don't what?'

Allehra's voice was smooth and her gaze was cool as she surveyed Athene batting away Henri's hand. She stood between Marvel and Petra, resting her palms on their table.

Athene sat up straight and met Allehra's look. 'Henri's asking me not to tell you that I'm pregnant, Your Majesty.'

Henri saw Tilly's jaw drop, and Marvel and Petra exchange glances of disbelief.

'All I meant,' Henri blurted, 'was not to tell you like *this,* Matriarch.'

Allehra's gaze hadn't left Athene's face. 'You wish to keep the child?'

'Yes, Majesty.'

'You have considered *all* your options?'

'I have.'

Allehra let the words settle over their group and across the rest of the keep. At the sound of their queen's slightly projected voice, all the kindred in the dining area had stopped to listen.

Henri recognised her mother's actions for what they were: not a form of reprimand, but a lesson, to all kindred, that there were, in fact, options. At least here in Valia.

'If you are sure ...'

Athene nodded. 'I'm sure.'

'Then Valia will welcome another warrior into its fold soon enough,' Allehra said. 'Be sure to see Maman, the groundling healer. She will monitor your health and adjust your training regime.'

'Thank you, Majesty.'

Allehra merely bowed her head once, and with a final glance at Sahara, left their table to rejoin her elites.

Henri, along with the rest of her friends, let out a breath of relief. Then she rounded on Athene.

'What in the name of all the gods —'

'You're *pregnant?*' Tilly blurted.

'How? *When?*' Marvel added.

But as the shock rippled across their table, Athene was grinning. She turned to Henri. 'Told you it'd be fine,' she said, resting her hand confidently on the small bump at her stomach.

Henri glanced towards Sahara, wondering what she was making of all of this, and how in the realm she'd known in the first place.

But her sister was gone.

A COMMANDER'S PLACE

In the deep woodlands by the Swinton family estate, the sharp sound of shortswords clashing echoed through the trees. Even in the shade, Swinton was sweating as he defended against Fiore's oncoming attack. His boots scraped across the damp earth, but he held his ground. They sparred Battalonian-style: a closer form of combat with precise jabs and tight spins.

Fi grinned. 'You're getting good, old friend.'

In the little downtime the commander and captain had, Fi had been teaching Swinton a range of Battalonian swordplay techniques. These manoeuvres weren't part of the Ellestian guards' training – they were frowned upon, in fact – but Swinton was committed to being the best warrior he could be. And that meant mastering a range of combat styles.

'Not as good as you,' Swinton huffed, noting that his friend wasn't out of breath or perspiring in the slightest.

'Well, nobody's *that* good.' Fi delivered a strong strike that knocked Swinton's sword to the ground.

Swinton laughed. 'You're probably right. At least, no one in Ellest.'

'We Battalonians are used to these duels with the desert heat blazing down on us … It makes fighting in the cooler climates much easier. You know this.'

Swinton felt fatigued just thinking of the fire continent. 'I hope to never return to that godsforsaken home of yours,' he said.

'Hmm … You can hope as much as you like, Dimi. But we don't always get what we want, eh?' Fi uncorked a flask and passed it to him.

Swinton took a grateful gulp of water. 'I'll be hoping all the same. Shall we go again?'

'If you think you can handle it …' Fi teased, nodding to Swinton's sword lying discarded in the dirt.

But as Swinton leaned down to retrieve it, they heard footsteps. One of his father's servants, James, appeared at the edge of the clearing.

'Commander Swinton, Captain Murphadias …'

'What is it?' Swinton asked, sheathing his sword with a sigh. There never seemed to be enough hours in the day. If it were up to him, he and Fi would spar all afternoon until he could best his friend.

'Your father requires your assistance. The delivery of the Willowdale thoroughbreds has arrived —'

Swinton was already moving.

King Arden was travelling abroad and had taken his best horsemen with him, which meant Swinton, Fi *and* Sir Caleb had added duties, like overseeing the board and final training of His Majesty's horses before their transfer to the royal stables. Swinton had suggested the additional work himself, with the hopes of seeing a particular golden-haired woman from the revered East Farmlands stables.

He hadn't stopped thinking about Eliza Carlington since their last encounter. He'd written numerous letters, but all had seemed inadequate and remained unsent. He wasn't even sure what he wanted to say, only that he wanted to talk with her, wanted to listen to what she had to say.

'Is the Willowdale stable master in attendance?' Swinton asked James.

'Yes, Commander,' the servant said.

'Anyone else join him, old friend?' Fi asked, with a sly smile in Swinton's direction. Though the Battalonian had been distracted of late, Swinton's 'pining', as Fi called it, hadn't gone unnoticed. He'd found one of Swinton's half-written letters in his chambers a number of weeks ago and had been relentless ever since.

The teasing no longer bothered Swinton, though. He had a good feeling about the future. Upon his return from Willowdale, the king had called a meeting with him ... *There is a matter I wish to discuss with you.* Knighthood. An impending knighthood. There was just one task Swinton would have to complete when King Arden was back from his travels. He couldn't wait to find out what it was.

'— young stable hand,' James was saying. 'And his daughter. She has a natural gift with horses, I'm told.'

'Eliza's *here*?' Swinton heard himself say.

Fi's sideway glance was one of sheer glee. He elbowed Swinton in the ribs. 'We'd best not keep them waiting, eh?'

A thrill went through Swinton as they headed to the gates. He was going to see Eliza ...

They spotted Emmett Carlington first. The man brought up the front of the company, riding atop a speckle-backed gelding, his sandy hair tied back in a messy knot. He greeted them with a smile and dismounted with ease, then shook their hands.

'Commander, Captain.'

'Mister Carlington,' Swinton said. 'I trust your journey wasn't too arduous?'

'Not at all, Commander. And please, call me Emmett.'

Swinton gave a stiff nod, wondering if the man would be so casual if he knew Swinton's intentions regarding his daughter. 'Very well, Emmett.'

'In that case,' Fi said, 'call us Dimitri and Fiore —'

But Swinton had stopped paying attention, for just past the stable hand, in the middle of the thoroughbreds, was Eliza, bringing up the rear.

Wearing well-worn riding pants and a dirt-smudged shirt, she sat astride her mare, Silver.

Fi nudged him. 'Go, brother,' he murmured. 'She came here for you, no?' The Battalonian mounted one of the saddleless thoroughbreds and urged the steed beside Emmett's gelding. 'This way to the stables and paddocks, Emmett.'

Swinton dropped back. Approaching Eliza, he smiled at her and Silver. 'So, she had her colt? Xander, was it?'

'Morning, Commander.' Eliza's eyes were bright. 'She did indeed. Xander is already flitting about the corrals back home. He's strong.'

'I'm glad to hear it.'

She dipped her head. 'These are stunning grounds you have here,' she said, eyeing the acres of verdant paddocks, the nearby woodlands and the grand manor looming beyond.

'Thank you,' he said, not quite knowing what to do now he'd reached her.

Fortunately, Eliza gracefully dismounted and led them on, following Fi and Emmett. 'How are you?' she asked as they walked.

The question momentarily stumped Swinton. He couldn't remember the last time someone other than Fi had asked him that and truly wanted an answer.

'Well enough,' he told her. 'Glad for your company.'

Her smile floored him. 'You shall have it a little longer, then.'

He found himself beaming back. 'How long are you here?'

'We stay tonight and ride for Willowdale tomorrow at first light. Your father offered us rooms in the southern wing of the estate.'

Swinton swallowed. *The servants' wing*. 'I see.'

All too soon, they reached the stables, where Fi and Emmett were waiting. Between Fi, the Carlingtons and their stable hand, they managed to house the thoroughbreds quickly and efficiently in the nearby paddocks. Swinton had always liked being around horses, but seeing Eliza working was a completely different matter. She seemed in tune with their body language, their fears and hesitations. She could calm one with a feather-light touch and a soothing whisper.

'She has a gift,' Emmett said, following his gaze.

Flushing, Swinton cleared his throat. 'She's very talented, yes.'

'Better than any of the lads I've got working for me, that's for sure. Truth be told, Commander ... I'd love for her to take over the stables when it's time, but it's unheard of in these parts. A woman as a stable master.'

'In these parts, maybe,' Fi interjected. 'In Battalon, women take many a role like it.'

'I doubt Eliza would much fancy the heat, Captain.'

'Can't blame her there,' Swinton quipped, not

taking his eyes off Eliza as she brought three horses into an empty corral.

'Don't let us delay you, Commander, Captain,' Emmett said, wiping his hands on the sides of his trousers. 'We know you are busy men.'

Fi shrugged. 'Sir Caleb has provided refreshments for you in the gardens. We'd like to join you before returning to our duties.'

Swinton stopped himself from shooting Fi a look of incredulity. His friend couldn't have been more blatant if he'd tried.

The small group strolled towards the gardens, Swinton once more finding himself beside Eliza. He kept stealing glances at her, unable to quite believe she was here at his family's home.

'How do you like Heathton?' he asked, shoving his fidgeting hands in his pockets.

'I've never been one for the city. It's too compact,' she said. 'But it's beautiful out here. I've never been to this estate before ...' Then, boldly, she added: 'Perhaps you could show me around?'

'I'd love —' Swinton cut himself off. 'Won't your father mind?'

'My father knows I'm my own person.' She walked ahead and squeezed Emmett's shoulder. 'Da, Dimitri's going to show me the grounds.'

Swinton didn't know what sort of response he'd been expecting from the stable master, but Emmett's content nod was not it. Having grown up around strict noblemen and their daughters, this ease between Emmett and Eliza was dumbfounding.

Eliza caught his look of surprise as they peeled away from Fi and the others.

'What?' she asked.

Swinton frowned. 'It's just … I've not known a man to let his daughter —'

'*Let?*'

'Well —'

'Da doesn't *let* me do anything. I'm a grown woman, Dimitri. Not a child. My choices are my own.'

'But —'

'But nothing. That's something I can't stand about the capital. For all its promise and development, it's backwards in so many ways.'

Swinton chewed the inside of his cheek as they crossed the wet grass of another field. He knew Heathton wasn't perfect – what city was? But backwards? He'd never thought of it like that.

Studying him, Eliza raised a brow. 'Ask your friend, the captain. I'm sure he'd tell you much the same …'

A flush crept up Swinton's neck as he realised she was right. Fi had been treated differently by Ellestian squires from the moment he'd arrived in the capital. While he'd won over the majority with his wicked charm and outstanding battle skills, there were still those who muttered about his origins behind his back, no matter what Swinton did to quell such behaviour.

'I ... I didn't think,' Swinton said slowly.

'Men of your upbringing usually don't.' Her tone wasn't unkind, but her words hit Swinton square in the chest.

'Is it that different in Willowdale?'

Eliza considered this, waiting for him to open the gate they'd reached. She tucked a loose strand of hair behind her ear. 'It's that different in my family. In our community. I cannot speak for a whole village, nor can I know what goes on behind closed doors. All I know is that I was lucky. I *am* lucky.'

She gazed at their surroundings as she spoke. Swinton had turned them back around to face the manor. Despite her father's lack of concern at her absence, Swinton was still wary of keeping her too long. As they slowly made their way back, he churned over what Eliza had shared, risking sidelong glances at her. She took in the lush paddocks stretching across acres, the towering hedges framing the outer grounds of the estate, and the rose gardens, where Fi had led her father and their stable hand.

'This property is probably as big as the Willowdale stable grounds,' Swinton offered, gesturing to the greenery and grazing horses nearby.

Eliza chewed her lip. 'Perhaps ...'

'You don't think so.'

'I think it's hard to compare a working farmstead to a knight's manicured lawns ... no matter the acreage.' Her mouth tugged up in the corner, her eyes dancing.

She was teasing him. Swinton met her gaze, laughter bubbling out of him. He felt lighter than he had in a long while. How was it this simple with her? This comfortable? He couldn't remember the last time someone other than Fi had made him laugh. Feeling bold, he reached for her hand. It was a skill of hers, he realised, as her rough fingers laced through his. Making people feel at ease.

Suddenly, his skin prickled. Movement from the manor caught his eye. Sir Caleb was standing on one of the private balconies, staring out at them. Swinton dropped Eliza's hand quickly. But it was too late. He was close enough to see the subtle shake of his father's head before he turned and went back inside.

Eliza looked from their now unlinked hands to the curtains fluttering on the balcony. Swinton could have sworn he saw a flicker of disappointment cross her face, but she said nothing.

Swinton had the sinking feeling he'd done something wrong as they re-joined the others in the gardens. Eliza was now quiet and tight-lipped, standing beside her father by the refreshment table. Swinton's stomach churned. He wanted more of her opinions, more of her ideas on the world. He opened his mouth to say something – what, he wasn't sure – but there was a light tap on his shoulder.

James was holding out a folded piece of

parchment. 'It seems you are needed at the castle, Commander.'

Frowning, Swinton opened the note and cursed under his breath. There had been an altercation between two of his guards. He nodded to Fi, who was instantly at his side.

'Emmett, Eliza, my apologies. The captain and I have unforeseen duties at the castle. Please, enjoy the grounds. Should you need anything, James would be happy to oblige.' His gaze settled upon Eliza as he added: 'We shall see you at dinner.'

Swinton's stomach was in knots as he and Fi rode into the city. *An altercation ...* The missive hadn't said who was involved, but he had his suspicions. There was only one person in his guard on whom he'd put money for causing trouble.

Perhaps his father and Fi had been right. He should have removed Siv Lennox from the King's Army, should have humiliated him and beaten him down into submission.

Swinton hadn't planned on coming into Heathton today. He wanted to be back at the estate for dinner with the Carlingtons. If they hurried, they might be able to make it in time. The flicker of disappointment on Eliza's face flashed before him. He needed more time with her.

Swinton urged his horse into a gallop. Beside him, Fi followed suit.

When they reached the castle courtyard, Swinton took a deep breath. It was in absolute disarray, crowded with squires, soldiers and castle guards. Heat rushed to Swinton's face. Were the king here, this would be disastrous. Sitting straight-backed in the saddle, he pressed his horse through the throng of people.

'What is the meaning of this?' he boomed.

Quiet settled as Swinton dismounted. He and Fi made their way to the heart of the fray, where, sure enough, Siv Lennox was being restrained.

Eyes narrowed, Swinton met Lennox's glare. One of the man's eyes was swollen shut. 'What happened here?'

'Your boy thought he'd take a swing at me,' Lennox spat, eyeing someone on the ground behind Swinton.

Swinton turned and nearly groaned in dismay. It was Stefan. His own squire. Stefan gave him a regretful look through the damp hair hanging about his face.

'Stefan?'

Fi was helping the lad to his feet. Stefan's face was bloodied, but the way his body was sagging made it clear Lennox had fought dirty. The bastard was known for slipping knives into hand-to-hand combat.

'I'm sorry, Commander.'

'That's all you have to say? I want to get to the bottom of this.'

Stefan cleared his throat. 'It's as Lennox says. I took a swing at him.'

'Why?' Swinton demanded.

Silence fell.

Gods, Swinton hated this. Hated Lennox. Nothing was ever as that bastard said. He'd done something, something awful to provoke Stefan.

'You're both suspended —'

Lennox jerked away from the guards restraining him. 'What —?'

'Effective immediately.'

Lennox stormed up to him, his breath hot on Swinton's face. 'You can't do that —'

'I can do whatever I like, Lennox.' Swinton's voice was steely, fury radiating from him as he stared his rival down. 'I'm the Commander of the King's Army. You, however – *you* were already on probation. You're suspended. Now, get out of my face, before I give that black eye some much-needed company.'

Lennox swore.

'Walk it off, Lennox,' Fi said, stepping in beside Swinton. 'Or suspension will be the least of your concerns.'

'Is that right, you Battalonian bastard?' Lennox sneered.

Fi's fist was a blur as it smacked into Lennox's face with a crack, sending him sprawling across the cobblestones.

Cursing, Lennox scrambled to his feet, nose bleeding. He made to lunge at Fi, but thought better of it, clearly sizing up the captain. He rounded on Swinton. 'What's *his* punishment, then?'

With a sideways glance at Fi, Swinton frowned. 'What do you mean?'

'For hitting a guard of the King's Army!'

'I don't know what you're talking about,' Swinton mused. 'Fi?'

'No idea.'

Swinton nodded. 'That clears that up, then. Now get out of my sight, Lennox.'

When the crowd had dispersed, Swinton and Fi took Stefan aside.

'What did he do, old friend?' Fi asked, offering the squire a cold compress.

Stefan winced as he moved, but simply shook his head.

'Stefan, I know you,' Swinton said. 'You were provoked. We need to know how, and why.'

Stefan met his gaze with apologetic eyes. 'I understand that, Commander. But ... I can't help you.'

Fi's muscular arms crossed over his chest. 'He threatened you?'

'I —'

'Stefan,' Swinton warned. 'It's your sworn duty to —'

'It wasn't me he was threatening. It was you.'

'Me?'

Stefan nodded. 'He had a group of his lackeys. I caught them rallying against you, plotting how they would sully your reputation and have you expelled from the King's Army.'

'Oh.'

'I wouldn't let that happen on my watch, Commander. Nor would most of the guards. We are loyal to you, not that brute.'

It was worse than Swinton thought. He offered Stefan a grim smile. 'Thank you for telling us. Fi and I will deal with this.'

'I was hoping you'd say that.'

Fi patted the young squire on the shoulder. 'Head on home, old friend. Rest up. We'll see what we can do about this suspension. You understand why Dimi had to make the call then and there?'

Stefan nodded, getting to his feet. 'I'm sorry, Commander.'

Swinton shook his hand. 'Don't be. We'll see you tomorrow.'

It was dusk when Swinton and Fiore started their ride back to Sir Caleb's estate. Swinton had known the situation with Lennox was less than ideal, but this ... this was outright unacceptable.

'What are you going to do about him?' Fi asked, glancing Swinton's way in the fading light.

'He needs to go.'

'That he does, old friend.'

'When the king returns from abroad, I'll have Lennox dismissed.'

'Is that all?'

'What do you mean?'

'I mean, there are more permanent ways of getting rid of someone, Dimi.'

Swinton barked a laugh. 'You can't be serious.'

'You'll never know now, eh?' Fi grinned.

But Swinton's smile faltered when he recalled the venom in Lennox's voice as he'd spat that slur at Fi.

'It was a good swing,' he allowed.

Fi quirked a brow. 'It was.'

'You wanted to hit him.'

'Didn't you?'

''Course I did. And I would have done, for what he called you —'

'Don't need you to fight my fights for me, Dimi. Besides,' Fi added with a wink, 'we both know my right hook's better than yours.'

Swinton laughed again.

'Now,' Fi said, suddenly businesslike. 'Let's get you back for dinner, eh?'

Swinton and Fi burst into the formal dining room at the family estate.

'Sorry we're late,' Swinton blurted, taking in the crystalware glimmering in the firelight, the unfamiliar faces seated at the dining table.

'Nonsense,' Sir Caleb said, his wine glass paused before his lips. 'Your duties come first, always. Lord Moore and his family understand that.'

The nobleman seated to Sir Caleb's right gave an agreeable nod in Swinton's direction. Swinton noticed they'd seated a young woman, whom Swinton could only imagine was Lord Moore's daughter, opposite his own empty seat.

A servant entered with the first course.

Swinton looked to his father. 'Where are the Carlingtons?'

Sir Caleb met his gaze with cold eyes. 'We thought they'd be more comfortable dining in the southern wing.'

The servants' wing.

Rage blinded Swinton. He'd had enough —

'Sir Caleb,' Fi's melodic voice interjected. 'Might Dimitri and I clean up before joining you? We still have the road on our clothes.'

'Of course, of course.' Swinton's mother, Lady Yuliana, waved them away. 'Fancy making them stand there in their dusty riding gear, Caleb.'

Swinton barely felt Fi tug his sleeve. Numb with anger, he followed his friend from the dining room and out into the hall. Fi started towards the east wing, where their chambers were. But Swinton had stopped short.

'Dimi?'

'I won't be joining you for dinner, Fi.'

'What?' Even Fi didn't like to upset Sir Caleb.

'I'll be dining in the southern wing tonight.'

'Dimi, your father —'

But for the first time in his life, Swinton didn't

care what his father thought. 'Tell him what you like, Fi. I'll be dining with the Carlingtons regardless.'

Swinton waited for the onslaught of protests. *Sir Caleb will be furious. Lord Moore will be offended. You're the* Commander, *customs must be honoured –*

But none of those words left Fi's mouth. Instead, Swinton found his friend smiling. Fi turned towards the east wing and walked off alone, loudly whistling a Battalonian tune.

Swinton didn't clean up or change before making for the southern wing. He was already late enough. As he half-ran through the manor, he realised with a flush of shame that the hallways in this section of the house were foreign to him. He didn't know his way around these parts. When he reached the southern wing, he had to ask a shocked-looking attendant for directions to the servants' dining room.

'There is no servants' dining room, Commander ...'

'What? What do you mean? Where does everyone eat, then?'

'Uh ... In the kitchens, Commander.'

'Take me there, then, please.'

Still bewildered, the attendant led him through the dimly lit corridors to a set of double doors. 'Through there,' he said, pointing.

'Thank you ...' Swinton trailed off, realising he didn't know the man's name.

'Oliver, Commander.'

'Thank you, Oliver,' Swinton said, before pushing through the doors.

The chatter that had filled the kitchen merely seconds ago died upon Swinton's entry. Knives and forks froze, suspended above plates.

'Commander Swinton,' James said, standing abruptly. 'Can I get you something? Do you need assistance?'

'No, everything's fine,' he said, spotting Eliza and Emmett at the end of the table. 'I thought … I thought I'd dine with you this evening, if it's alright.'

The silence was agonising, but finally, there was the scrape of a chair. Emmett waved him over. 'Glad you made it,' the stable master said. 'Come, sit! Tell us about this drama at the castle today.'

Flooded with gratitude, face flushed, Swinton went to him, taking a seat opposite Eliza.

'You made it,' she said, smiling.

'Wouldn't have missed it,' he told her.

They ate bread, dried meat and cheeses, a far cry from the roasted lamb and goose his father's guests were enjoying in the northern wing. But the stress of the day seemed to fall away as Swinton listened to Emmett and Eliza talk of Willowdale. He watched them keenly as they spoke of everything and nothing, the words between them completely effortless. Swinton found himself laughing, his eyes streaming as Eliza told the table story after story of stable life. He sipped his wine and took it all in.

It was one of the best meals he'd ever had.

. . .

It was late when he and Eliza realised they were the only ones left in the kitchen. 'I'm sorry,' he stammered. 'I've kept you far too long.'

'It's alright, Dimitri,' she said, smiling kindly as she stood. She stretched her arms above her head. He, too, was sore from sitting for so long.

He walked her to the door, debating whether or not to take her hand, wondering where they now stood. She turned to him, suddenly close – much closer than she'd ever been before. The faint scent of lavender soap filled his nose.

Panicked, he took a step back. 'Goodnight, Eliza,' he said.

Disappointment flickered across her face once more. 'Goodnight, Dimitri.'

The soft hues of dawn were tinged with regret as Swinton readied himself for the day. He'd missed his chance. He'd lost his nerve at the worst possible moment. He was still cursing himself over his bootlaces when his bedroom door flew open with a bang.

'Just what in the name of all the gods were you playing at?' Sir Caleb's face was a mask of rage.

'Father, I —'

'First, you had the nerve to insult our esteemed guests. *Then* – dining with the *servants*, Dimitri?

Don't think I don't know what, or *who*, this is about. Courting a commoner – have you lost your mind?'

'Father —'

'No.' The word cleaved through Swinton's chest. 'I forbid it, Dimitri. I do not want to discuss this again.'

Swinton was still standing there, open-mouthed, when his father left, closing the door behind him with a deafening click.

Swinton skipped breakfast and instead, wandered the grounds. He couldn't believe his father. Couldn't believe how he'd treated the Carlingtons, couldn't believe how he'd spoken to his own son. But what could Swinton do? He was trapped, hands tied. It wasn't fair, any of it. As anger churned in his gut, a voice stirred at the back of his mind. Eliza's voice. Her words from the day before …

My choices are my own.

Swinton lifted his chin and started across the paddock he'd ended up in. His choices would be his own as well.

He found her in the stables, readying the horses for her and Emmett's departure. 'I'm sorry,' he said from the stall gate.

Eliza looked up in surprise. 'Sorry? For what?'

He swallowed the lump in his throat. 'I'm sorry you were made to eat in the kitchens. It's not fair.'

She busied herself adjusting a stirrup. 'No, it's not. But I've made my peace with who I am and my place in the world.'

'Your place in the world?'

She nodded. 'Someday, you'll make peace with your place, too.'

Swinton closed the gap between them. 'The only thing I know about my place in the world,' he said, taking a deep breath, 'is that it's near you.'

His hands were at her waist, her warm eyes gazing up at him. This time, he didn't hesitate.

This time, he kissed her.

A CURRENT SO STRONG

The seaside village of Angove was bustling with excited townsfolk. People chattered in the streets and flitted from shop to shop in a manner that was rarely seen. It was all due to the Eery Brothers. The famous fiddler duo was touring the taverns of Ellest, and the brothers were due to play at the annual Angove dance later that evening.

Bleak couldn't have cared less.

The hot coastal sun blazed down on the back of her neck as she hammered another nail into the scaffolding. Up on the cliffs in the centre of town, there was no shade, no shelter, no relief from the rays. She longed to be where she belonged out on the water, where the briny breeze eased the grip of the sun. Wiping the sweat from her brow with a sigh, she hammered another nail in.

She, Senior and Bren had taken on the extra work

of setting up the marquee for the evening's festivities with a handful of the townsmen. Though it should be high trout season, the schools of fish had been few and far between, so much so that Bleak could have sworn she saw fresh wrinkles line Senior's face each morning.

'Alright there, Half-Pint?' he called out to her now.

'Fine, fine,' she muttered, waving him away. The less attention she drew, the better. While she was generally accepted amongst Senior's crews out on the water, working amidst the townsmen was another matter entirely. Their thoughts battered into her mind every time they glanced in her direction.

What's he got a scrawny girl working here for? She should be in the scullery or the damned kitchen –

That little bitch is doing half the work and taking the same cut as the rest of us –

The old man's gone mad, bringing his feral stray here –

Each insight was more unpleasant than the last, and knowing it was not yet noon didn't help Bleak's growing rage. Bren and Senior, however, were naturally oblivious. There they stood, holding beams of timber in place and erecting the framework needed for the giant marquee. Supposedly the whole town, and even people from neighbouring farmlands, were coming to see the Eery Brothers.

Bleak went to fetch more nails. All she knew was

that she'd steer well clear of the village square come nightfall. What did she know about dances, anyway?

With her supply of nails replenished, she headed back to her workstation – and went sprawling. Her bag of nails scattered across the ground and her palms stung against the dirt. She looked around quickly enough to see one of the tradesmen tuck his foot away.

'Oi, Senior,' he called out. 'This is what happens when you bring a girl to a work site.' He gestured to the nails.

Bleak rounded on him. She was just as damned skilled as any boy here. Better than most, thanks to working with Senior so long. She rounded on the bastard. 'You bloody well —'

But Senior was already by her side, tanned arms folded over his chest and a stern look on his weathered face.

The pounding of hammers and the scrape of saws ceased.

'Ya take me for some kind of lug, Braxley?' Senior scoffed. 'I don't miss a damn beat, not on the seas. Not here with you lot.' He turned to the group. 'If anyone else has a problem with Bleak earning her keep here, ya come and ya take it up with me.'

No one spoke. Senior simply shook his head and returned to Bren, who was waiting, axe in hand.

Bleak flushed but didn't turn her glare away from Braxley. Her fury sparked the magic in her veins and set her teeth on edge, but she ignored it. Instead, she forced herself to crouch, starting the tedious task of picking up dozens of nails in the dust.

Knees creaked beside her. 'Just be grateful for Senior and be done with it,' said Bren, combing through the dirt.

Bleak's brows shot up. 'What?'

'I'm just saying —'

'Just be *grateful* and be done with it?' Bleak's fury was bubbling close to the surface. 'Spoken like a man who's never had to justify his presence anywhere.' The words had more venom than she intended, and were directed at the wrong person —

'Yer right,' Bren said with a shrug.

Bleak hid her surprise. 'I know.'

'Ya need help with the frame?' Bren waved towards the structure lying horizontal on the ground.

'Yeah. You hold it upright. I'll hammer.'

Bren nodded, picking up the now-full bag of nails.

But Bleak paused, seeing someone familiar talking to Senior: Willem, Bren's older brother.

'What's he doing here?' Bleak pointed.

'Dunno,' Bren replied, already heading over to the scaffolding she'd been working on.

'Don't you care?'

'Not really?'

Bleak frowned. 'I'll be back.' Willem gave her a wave and made towards the path down the cliffs as she approached. 'What was that about?' she asked Senior.

'Can't help yerself, can ya, Half-Pint?'

'No.'

Senior sighed. 'Willem reckons he and Tobias saw a school of rainbow trout just off the coast of Felder's Bay. Reckons if we're quick and follow the tides, we can net 'em and make some coin at the markets tomorrow.'

'Since when does Willem know so much about fishing?'

Senior laughed. 'Since we spoke about market prices at the tavern last night. He's found a girl he wants to impress, so having some extra coin would do well for him.'

Bleak scoffed. She was fairly certain none of the Clayton brothers needed extra coin to impress the ladies of Angove. The broad-shouldered, fair-haired lot barely went anywhere without someone batting lashes in their direction.

'Well?'

'Well ... if you and Butter Fingers are alright here, I'll take the boys out in an hour or so.'

'Why can't I come? I'd rather —'

'Yer've been paid to work here. Here's where you'll work.'

'But —'

'No buts. I've stuck me neck out for ya, now you need to stick the work out, eh?'

Bleak rolled her eyes. 'Fine.'

'And Bleak?'

'What?' She followed Senior's gaze to Bren. '*What?*'

'Just ... be careful there, eh?'

'What's *that* supposed to mean?'

'I mean, ya know Butter Fingers over there fancies ya. And I'd hate to see him hurt, hmm? Just don't go leading him where ya don't want him –'

Bleak's face was burning, and her magic crackled. 'What in the realm gives you the right –'

'Now, calm down, Half-Pint. I only –'

'You only *what*? You don't get to tell me what to do. How to act –'

'*Bleak* ... It's my responsibility to help ya through –'

Bleak saw red. 'You're *not* my father.'

The words had left her mouth in a vicious rage, but now, as they hung between her and Senior, she felt their poison linger. She couldn't take them back.

Senior's eyes were glassy. 'Have I ever pretended to be?' he said quietly.

Bleak's fists were clenched at her sides, and despite the shame that rushed through her, she didn't avert her hard gaze.

Senior stared at her a moment longer, before he shook his head and left.

'What was that about?' Bren's voice sounded at her side.

'Nothing,' she said. 'Let's get back to work.'

They worked well into the afternoon. Bleak refused to take a break for lunch, knowing the men would only use it as ammunition against her. Instead, she lifted frame after frame, hammered nail after nail, and ignored the splinters in her calloused fingers.

As the afternoon wore on, the stage and the marquee structure began to take shape. Bleak found herself stepping back to look at what they'd achieved. It was a nice feeling: being able to create something from the ground up with a few pairs of bare hands. She glanced at Bren. His hair had fallen across his furrowed brow as he helped one of the others carry the steps they'd made to their place.

Just don't go leading him where ya don't want him ... A wave of anger washed over her again. She didn't know how she felt about Bren yet. They'd been friends since forever, but hadn't had a chance to be anything more. How could she possibly know what she wanted? Especially if people didn't give her the space to find out? She gave a frustrated sigh as she packed away Senior's tools. She felt as though everyone wanted a say in her life, but none of them understood what it was like. Her growing magic, the past she could barely remember ...

She spotted a group of young women across the square, their heads bent close together, an air of secrecy about them. Hit with a sudden pang of envy, she watched them. The women were at complete ease with each other; it was clear they'd known one another for years – since childhood, probably. Even from a distance, Bleak could feel the relief in their minds as they conversed, a bond in place that Bleak had never experienced: sisterhood.

With a start, she realised she had no female friends. None whatsoever. Her main companions were Senior and Bren and Bren's brothers.

Her thoughts were interrupted by a decorated carriage pulling up abruptly by the nearby tavern. A small crowd stood behind it, eagerly trying to peer inside. The driver hopped down from his perch and opened the door, where two men emerged. The Eery Brothers. They greeted the gathering crowd with bright smiles and easy conversation before heading into the tavern with their fiddle cases.

'So that was them, eh?' Bren said, dusting his hands on his thighs.

'That was them.'

'Lot of fuss about nothin', in my opinion.'

'How would you know? You've never heard them play.'

Bren frowned. 'Suppose yer right —'

'Oi. You two!' It was the head builder, stomping towards them.

What now? Bleak steeled herself.

'We're done for the day,' the man said gruffly. 'Here's ya pay. And Senior's. Tell him apologies for the trouble. We'd have you help us again. Tell him that, alright?'

Bleak's hand closed around the pouch of coin. 'Alright.'

. . .

Bleak and Bren ate an early supper sitting atop the white cliffs, overlooking the sapphire water. The freshly baked bread was still steaming as Bleak pulled it apart in her hands and dipped it into the jar of strawberry jam.

Bren eyed her jam-covered fingers. 'Ya didn't think to use a knife?'

Bleak shrugged. 'No.'

Bren huffed a laugh and followed her example. 'Senior went with Willem and Tobias?'

'Uh-huh. Said they'd spotted some trout off the coast of Felder's.'

'Hmm …' Bren was fidgeting. 'So,' he said, turning to her.

'So, what?'

'I meant to ask … Have *you* ever seen the Eery Brothers play?'

Bleak laughed. 'No. When would I have done that? In between scrubbing the decks on *The Daybreaker* and gutting fish at the docks?'

'Well, do you want to?'

'Want to what?'

'See them play?'

Bleak frowned. She had no idea what Bren was getting at here. She ripped off another piece of bread.

Bren stilled her hand with his. 'Come to the dance with me.'

Bleak nearly choked. 'What?'

'Come to the dance with me. It'll be fun. We can see if these fiddlers are any good.'

'I …'

'You what?'

'I … I don't have anything to wear,' Bleak managed. 'I don't even own a dress.'

Bren shrugged. 'Doesn't matter. Just wear what yer wearing now.'

Bleak might never have been to a dance before, but she was savvy enough to know that young girls didn't wear sawdust-covered breeches. 'I don't think so.'

Bren clicked his tongue in frustration. 'Well, I'm going.'

'Fine. Go, then.'

'Fine.'

Bren got to his feet and left her sitting on the grass alone.

Back at the cottage, Bleak didn't know what to do with herself. She paced the tiny kitchen, back and forth, back and forth, until she felt dizzy. She didn't know why she was the way she was. Why she was always so difficult. Senior and Bren had only ever shown her kindness, and yet she felt the need to push back. She knew it made no sense, but more often than not, she just couldn't help herself.

She pictured Bren at the dance and longing squeezed her insides. *Of course* she wanted to go. He was her best friend. But … to show up to that marquee in the Clayton boys' dusty old hand-me-downs ... She couldn't do that. Not this time.

Throwing on Senior's waxed coat, she found herself closing the cottage door behind her, and heading up the hill.

'And what can I do for you, Bleaker Junior?' Mrs Clayton asked, pulling her inside out of the wind and planting a kiss on her cheek.

Bleak shifted from foot to foot. 'Uh ... I came ... I came because ...'

'Well, spit it out, lass, I've got stew on the fire.'

Bleak wrung her hands. 'Bren's going to the dance.'

'Aye, I know. He's already up there. Said you didn't want to go.'

'Well ...'

'You changed your mind?' Mrs Clayton asked, leading her to the hearth and fetching a large wooden spoon.

'No!' Bleak blurted.

Mrs Clayton raised a brow.

'It's not that. I always wanted to go.'

Mrs Clayton began stirring the stew. 'Then why'd you say no?'

'I ...' Bleak gestured to her dusty trousers.

'Ah.'

Bleak sighed. 'I'm not good at this.'

'No one became any good at anything by not

trying, eh?' Mrs Clayton looked her up and down. 'I might have something for you.'

'What?'

'Wait here. Stir the stew, will you?'

Bleak took the spoon and did as she was told. It smelled delicious – it always did in the Clayton household.

Mrs Clayton reemerged from her bedroom with a handful of blue fabric. 'This was my sister's,' she said, holding out a dress. 'Now, you're quite a bit smaller than her, but I reckon we can bring it in with a sash of some sort.'

Bleak didn't know what to say.

'Well, don't just stand there. I'm heating some water for you, you'll need to bathe before you head out. You're a mess. But don't worry, there's plenty of time. The Eery Brothers won't be playing until later.'

As Mrs Clayton ushered her into the bathing chamber, Bleak stopped her and looked her in the eye. 'Thank you,' she said.

Mrs Clayton merely waved her towards the bath.

The melodic notes of the Eery Brothers' fiddles travelled to the very outskirts of town, as did the rhythmic stomping of the crowd on the floorboards Bleak had hammered into place earlier that day. Clutching Mrs Clayton's cloak around her against the night's chilled air, Bleak made her way to the illuminated marquee at the village centre. She had never heard such merriment.

Standing at the entrance, she peered inside. The townsfolk were laughing and clapping along to the tune. The handsome duo was centre stage, their fiddles tucked neatly under their chins and their boots tapping to keep time. Spotting the makeshift bar, Bleak found her purpose. She managed to slip a full glass from the table easily and retreated to the shadows to drink the sweet wine and watch the revelry unfold. She looked for Bren, but instead found the gaze of Maz, the blacksmith's son, on her. He strode over.

'You scrub up alright, little Bleak.'

She flushed, feeling the eyes of the other girls on her as the popular apprentice ran his gaze over her dress.

'Thanks,' she said. 'You too,' she added awkwardly. That was the polite thing to say, wasn't it?

'Do I?' he asked with a wink.

Bleak frowned. 'Sure ...'

She could have sworn she saw a flicker of frustration cross Maz's face, but on the other side of the marquee, a bobbing head of fair hair caught her attention.

Bren. He was guiding one of the baker's daughters through a clumsy waltz. A sour taste filled Bleak's mouth as she watched them, Maz forgotten. She backed further into the shadows with her drink.

What should I do? Go home? She felt stupid. Stupid

for dressing up. Stupid for wanting to come to this damn event in the first place. But her feet wouldn't move. And she realised with a start that the fury roiling around inside her wasn't for Bren, or Senior, or even those cursed builders today. She was furious with herself. For always sabotaging her own happiness.

Shaking her head, she saw Bren step off the floor and leave his companion with her friends. With a deep breath, Bleak put her empty glass down and approached him.

Bren's eyes widened at the sight of her. 'What are you doing here?'

'Wanted to see what all the fuss was about —'

Her usual smart-mouthed reply was second nature. She stopped herself and said more seriously: 'You invited me.'

'You didn't want to come.'

'I didn't have – I …' She sighed. 'I'm here now.'

Bren took in the blue dress she wore, cinched in at the waist with a black sash. 'You look different …'

'Good different?'

Bren nodded. 'But ya coulda worn a sack and I wouldn't have cared.'

'I cared.'

He shrugged his shoulders. 'That's fair enough. Ya wanna dance, then?'

Bleak was suddenly panicked. 'I don't know how.'

'No one does. Come on. We'll make it up, eh?'

But it certainly didn't feel like Bren was making it

up as he swept her across the floor. She was practically weightless in his arms, and for the first few moments, she focused so hard on her feet that she barely heard the music. Then, something within her told her to look up.

Bren's face was close to hers. So close she could feel his warm breath tickle her cheek. She breathed in his familiar smell: rose soap, and tonight, a hint of ale. She followed his lead as he spun her around the floor, the building notes of the Eery Brothers' melody filling her chest with a lightness she hadn't felt in a while. Happiness. And Bren … Bren was smiling at her, his large hand enveloping her waist. She could feel the heat from his palm through the fabric of her dress. The fingers of his other hand threaded through hers.

'So, what d'ya think?' His words vibrated against her chest.

She knew he wasn't talking about the music. 'Better than I imagined,' she murmured, smiling back at him.

His wintry gaze dropped to her mouth and her heart sped up.

He was going to kiss her. Here, in front of the whole town. She didn't give a damn. She wouldn't miss her chance this time.

She reached up so her arms wrapped around his neck, and she drew him in close. His nose brushed hers. She forgot the Eery Brothers and everyone else. There was only them –

'Bren.'

Bren jolted and Bleak pulled away sharply at the sound of Senior's rough voice. But her guardian didn't look angry, she realised. He looked … She didn't know how he looked. She'd never seen this expression on his face before. All too suddenly, his thoughts – no, his *memories*, recent memories, crashed into her mind. Images from that very afternoon.

A choppy sea and a black, swirling current, breaking into a giant, wild whirlpool. The Daybreaker *rocking from side to side, nearly tipping over, as powerless as a child's toy up against the will of the gods. Willem going over first, not even having time to scream as he plunged into the dark depths, disappearing into the churning white foam.*

'Willem!' A massive wave breaking across the deck and Tobias being swept away, his brother's name still on his lips.

Senior's own shouts being swallowed by the roar of the sea as he, too, was flung overboard.

'What is it?' Bren was saying as he closed the gap between himself and Senior.

Senior's chin quivered, but his gaze met Bren's. 'You're needed at home, lad.'

Concern flickered across Bren's face and he took another step towards Senior. 'Is it Ma?' His voice cracked.

'It's not your ma,' Bleak said quietly, forgetting herself.

But Bren gave no sign of hearing her. Instead he stared at Senior. 'I should go?'

Senior nodded slowly. 'You should go.'

Bren didn't turn back to her, didn't feel the ghost of her hand reaching for his arm. He ran from the marquee with the speed of someone trying to outrun a change to their entire world. And so it would be.

Bleak couldn't hear the music as Senior's eyes met hers.

'You know?' he asked.

She nodded numbly. Willem and Tobias Clayton were gone. Senior hadn't been able to find them amidst the lashing waves and dark, churning waters. They hadn't made it. The seas had claimed them both. The seas had nearly claimed Senior too …

'You're not my father,' she'd spat at him. Despair hit her in the gut. Those could have been the last words she ever said to him. Her only family. The only father she'd ever known.

She hardly noticed as Senior led her from the marquee. She hardly noticed as they began to follow the path down the cliffs toward home. They passed the Claytons' cottage and paused at the gate, swinging ajar on its creaking hinges. Candlelight danced in the windows and Senior started down the pebbled track to their front door. Bleak tugged gently on his sleeve, stopping him. He looked at her in a daze. His eyes were bloodshot, and in the bright moonlight, she could see that his lips were tinged blue. Beneath her hand, his jacket was still damp.

He pulled her towards the house. 'Come on, we should see how —'

But Bleak shook her head and brought her guardian into a warm embrace. It felt strange, being the one to offer comfort. Usually, it was Senior supporting her. But after a moment of surprise, his long arms wrapped around her back.

'Bren needs to be with his family,' she told him. 'And you need to be with yours.'

THREE BRONZE COINS

The ride to Willowdale in autumn was nothing short of glorious.

At least, that was how Dimitri Swinton felt as he guided his horse through yet another tunnel of gold and crimson leaves beside the Angove River. He and Eliza Carlington had been meeting in secret for months now, snatching stolen snippets of time together away from the rest of the world. Each visit, each moment they shared made the young commander's life richer, his chest fuller.

As usual, he bypassed the high street of the village and made his way to their little woodland clearing. From beneath a great willow, he could see the corral where Eliza trained the horses most days. Xander, the colt birthed by Eliza's mare, Silver, was grazing in the nearby paddock. Though the foal was still young, his fine breeding was already evident.

Swinton dismounted his own horse and sat beneath the tree, excitement fluttering in his chest. He'd had to call in a number of favours back in Heathton in order to be here, but it was worth it. It always was, to see her.

'Glad you've made yourself comfortable.' Laughter laced Eliza's voice as she approached. The streams of sunlight escaping the willow's canopy caught in her gold hair. It had come loose from its usual messy knot and now fell about her face in waves.

Swinton was already on his feet, his long strides closing the gap between them. He brought her bright smile to his face and slipped his arms around her waist, drawing her in tightly. Her body fit against his as though the gods had made it so.

'I missed you,' he said into her hair. She smelled of hay and honey.

Her laugh vibrated on his chest. 'And I you. Though it hasn't been so long, has it?'

'It's been a lifetime,' Swinton murmured against her lips. With her, no amount of time would ever be enough. Which was precisely why he'd come to Willowdale this time.

'I need to speak with your father today,' he told her, suddenly serious.

'Oh?'

'Castle stable logistics, I'm afraid.'

'You're mixing business with pleasure now, are you, Commander?' she quipped, squeezing his side.

Swinton kept his arm around her shoulder as he took up his horse's reins and started towards the stable grounds. 'Xander's getting big,' he remarked, nodding towards the colt, who was still grazing happily.

Eliza smiled. 'He's responding well to early training. He's a smart horse. He'll be a much sought-after stallion in a few years.'

'The king will buy him, no doubt.'

Eliza shrugged. 'He won't be for sale.'

They continued across the paddocks, their steps in time with one another's. Swinton marvelled at the ease of it all: the conversation, the comfortable quiet, the little touches between them – feather-light, but brimming with meaning. He had to stop himself from staring at her.

As they reached the gates of the stables, Swinton reluctantly withdrew his arm from around Eliza. He wanted nothing more than to tell the realm they belonged to each other, but ... not yet. They had agreed on that together. Their worlds weren't ready.

'Da will be in the tack room.' Eliza waved vaguely towards the stables. 'One of the boys made a mess of a delivery, so he's been in there since dawn sorting through a hundred different sets of reins.'

Swinton laughed nervously. 'Right ...'

'I'll saddle up Silver,' Eliza continued. 'Perhaps we can meet up for a ride when you're done?'

Swinton nodded. Grateful for her unsuspecting nature, he watched her walk towards the southern stalls before he made for the tack room, to ask Emmett Carlington for his daughter's hand.

Dusk settled around the woodland where Swinton once more waited for Eliza. Across the paddocks, the horizon glowed with pink-and-orange clouds. Swinton stared skywards as he paced, recalling Emmett's words.

'If she wants you, she wants you, Dimitri. She hasn't needed my permission to do anything for a long while, and it's certainly got nothing to do with things now.'

But at the end of the conversation, the stable master had pulled him into a firm embrace and wished him luck. It meant more to Swinton than he could say.

Now, beneath Eliza's favourite willow, Swinton was wearing the ground thin. He couldn't tell if he was nervous or excited, or both. This was, he hoped, the beginning of a new life. As he walked back and forth, he thought briefly of Fi. His friend would be happy for him – ecstatic, even. It had been Fi who had encouraged him to pursue Eliza in the first place —

A twig snapped. Swinton's gaze shot up.

Eliza was still in her worn work clothes, her boots caked with mud, brushing her hands on her trousers as she approached.

'What's this about?' she asked by way of greeting. 'I thought we were going for a ride?'

'I ...' Suddenly, Swinton realised he hadn't prepared what he was going to say. He'd been so focused on imagining their life together that the details of the proposal itself had been overlooked. He'd heard tales of grand gestures and gifts, stories of poetry and fine jewellery. But that wasn't him, and it wasn't Eliza, either. They were –

'I want to marry you,' he blurted, finding his feet rooted to the spot.

Eliza laughed. 'I want to marry you, too. I thought we already knew that.'

'No ... I want to marry you now. Soon. Within the month.'

Now it was Eliza's turn to freeze. 'What?'

Swinton took her hands in his. 'I don't want to live in a world where you're not my wife. We're meant to be together, you and I.'

She took a half step back, her eyes full of surprise. 'Oh.'

'Oh?' Swinton faltered. 'I ... I don't have much to offer you, yet. But when I'm a knight –'

Her expression softened, and a warm smile spread across her face as her gaze met his. 'I meant, yes.'

Something within Swinton flared to life. 'Yes?'

'Yes.'

She was already in his arms. He lifted her off the ground and kissed her deeply. Then, Eliza was laughing.

'What is it?' Swinton asked, smiling into her neck, unable to let her go.

'It seems I owe Ma three bronze coins,' she told him, still grinning.

'What?'

Eliza kissed him again. 'She bet me that you would propose before autumn was over.'

'She *bet* on me?' Swinton asked, amused. '*You* bet on me?'

Eliza elbowed him gently. 'Welcome to the family, Dimitri. There's no backing out now.'

Swinton rode into Heathton a new man.

Within the month, he and Eliza would be married. They would start their new life together. Though they hadn't quite worked out the logistics of *where* yet, Swinton couldn't help but feel stupidly happy. He had to find Fi. Next to Eliza, there was no one with whom he'd rather share his joy.

The journey to the castle flew by, and before Swinton knew it, he was passing through the gatehouse and dismounting before the entrance steps. He handed his reins to the waiting attendant, planning to head straight to his chambers to wash up and then send for his friend. But as he entered the castle, he saw a small group of his guards peering into the throne room.

'What is the meaning of this?' he demanded, startling a good few.

'Commander! We … uh …' stammered one of the newer guards.

Swinton waited.

Stefan appeared at his comrade's side, facing Swinton with a stony expression. 'Perhaps it's best if you see for yourself, Commander …'

Swinton looked past the guards. His gaze fell on King Arden, who had recently returned from his travels across the seas, and a broad figure standing before him.

'What in Rheyah's name …?' Swinton pushed his way past the rest of the guards and strode into the room.

Siv Lennox turned at the sound of Swinton's boots on the marble floor, a satisfied smirk on his face.

Fuming, Swinton ignored him and made for the foot of the dais. 'Your Majesty.' He bowed low.

'Commander Swinton,' King Arden greeted him warmly.

'My apologies for the intrusion, my king. But this man has no right to be in your throne room.' He paused, waiting for Lennox to object and bombard the king with his lies, but the man was silent – smugly so. Swinton's stomach was sinking fast. 'Your Majesty, I dismissed Siv Lennox in your absence. He was stirring dissent amongst the guards, and attacking his comrades.'

King Arden's expression remained unchanged. 'I heard that it was *Lennox* here who was attacked.'

'With all due respect —'

'No guard is ever dismissed in my absence, Commander.'

Swinton's throat constricted, his mouth instantly dry. *What is happening here?* Stunned, he glanced between king and former guard. He could still feel the eyes of the rest of the guards from the doorway. They were hearing every word. Seeing the authority stripped from their commander.

He had to try again. This wasn't right. 'My king —'

The lift of a single ringed finger silenced him. 'This is not up for debate, Commander. Lennox here has served in my army for the past seven years, and his father before him. I will not have him turned out onto the streets based on the gossip of some doltish squire. Lennox will be a part of your unit until I order it otherwise. Is that understood?'

Swinton's face was on fire. Shame seared his cheeks and only sheer willpower stopped him recoiling from the very public reprimand.

'*Is that understood?*' the king repeated coldly.

'Yes, Your Majesty,' Swinton said, struggling to keep his voice even.

'Good. Now you have my leave. I'm sure you wish to freshen up after your travels. As I understand it, you've just this moment returned from Willowdale.'

There was no mistaking the dismissal, or the less-than-subtle nod to the fact that King Arden knew his movements …

But Swinton forced himself to bow low once

more. 'Thank you, Your Majesty,' he said, and left the room. He didn't pause at the gobsmacked guards waiting by the door. Not even for Stefan. He didn't know what he'd say to them. They'd heard every word, anyway.

He walked briskly through the castle hallways, not sure where he was going until he arrived. As he raised his fist to knock on Fi's door, he realised he was trembling.

His friend answered, barefoot and smiling brightly. His grin faltered at the sight of Swinton's shaken expression.

'What is it, old friend?' he said, pulling Swinton into his chambers.

Dazed, Swinton looked around. He'd been in these quarters countless times, for official meetings and quiet games of cards over mead and bread. Fi was generally neat, keeping clothes to the wardrobe in the corner and paperwork in a tidy stack on the desk. Now, the rooms were hardly recognisable. Scrolls of parchment littered the desk and the unmade bed. Dirty clothes were piled by the door of the bathing room, and a blanket and pillow were ruffled on the settee, as though Fi had been sleeping there rather than in his bed.

'Fi —' Swinton frowned, forgetting his own affairs for the moment. 'What's going on here?'

Fi waved him away. 'Nothing, Dimi. It's been a busy week and I've just let the mess pile up. Need to get one of the housemaids to help, eh?'

Swinton began to shake his head. This was very unlike Fi. As was his mention of the housekeeping staff. Fi always tended to his own rooms —

'Don't trouble yourself, Dimi,' Fi told him, scooping the blanket and pillow from the settee and dumping them on the floor. He gestured for Swinton to sit. 'What bothers you, old friend?'

With a heavy sigh, Swinton decided he needed to pick his battles. He sank into the settee and rubbed his temples. 'Lennox,' he said.

'Ah.'

'You know?

Fi nodded. 'Stefan came to me this morning. The king is reinstating that bastard, eh?'

'Apparently.'

Fi swore. 'It's not right. He's causing trouble amongst the guards. He's undermining you. He's —'

'I know all of this, Fi. But what exactly can I do about it now? He stays on Arden's orders.'

'You should have explained —'

'*I did!* It was no use. Lennox has the king wrapped around his finger —'

Fi scoffed. 'Or Arden is using Lennox for something.'

'What?'

'Dirty work, Dimi. Every king has some. And every king needs a lackey to do it.'

'The king would come to me. I'm the commander of his army. I would do anything on his orders.'

Fi raised his brows. 'Anything? Surely not. You

have a moral compass, old friend. The king knows that.'

Swinton threw his hands up. 'What are you talking about? I'm His Majesty's right-hand man. I'm going to be a knight, for Rheyah's sake.'

Fi gave a grim shrug. 'Are you?' He rested a compassionate hand on Swinton's shoulder. 'You've been saying that for months – *years*, even. And yet, brother, nothing has changed.' The Battalonian's warm eyes were filled with something like pity.

Swinton's stomach dropped. That couldn't be right. Arden had hinted at his knighthood for a while now, but he had his reasons for the delay, surely. Swinton had no cause to doubt the king …

Did he?

Fi was watching him closely. 'I just don't want you to be disappointed. This was a bad move by Arden —'

'Careful, Fi …'

'Just stating facts, old friend. Keeping a lech like Lennox on the guard isn't a good sign, eh?'

Swinton didn't reply. Eliza flashed before his eyes. She had agreed to marry a soon-to-be knight. What now? What if his knighthood never came to pass? What if he couldn't offer her all that she deserved?

'Is there something else, Dimi?' Fi asked gently, his hands clasped together in his lap.

Swinton stared at his Battalonian brother for a moment, before slowly shaking his head. 'No,' he said, his earlier joy rapidly evaporating. 'There's nothing.'

. . .

The tavern in Grayside was as raucous as ever. Even hidden away in his room upstairs, Swinton could hear the commotion of gambling and drinking bellowing from below. Too nervous to eat, his lunch sat scarcely touched on a tray by the fire.

Eliza was late, and he felt immense guilt for asking her to travel here from Willowdale. Even during daylight, he didn't like the idea of her riding alone across the rural counties. But there had been no other option. His frequent visits to Willowdale were apparently drawing attention —

A sharp knock on the door sounded.

'Come in,' he called.

'Hello,' Eliza said, stepping inside and lowering her hood. Beneath her cloak she wore a plain blue dress and muddied riding boots. 'Have you been waiting long?'

Swinton shook his head and went to her, folding his arms around her and breathing in her scent.

'Are you alright?' Eliza asked, frowning as she drew back and studied his face.

Swinton led her to the settee in front of the fireplace and sat down beside her, holding her rough hands in his.

She squeezed his fingers. 'You're having second thoughts?' she guessed.

'Gods, no,' Swinton replied, still unable to meet her eyes.

'Then what is it?'

Swinton took a deep breath. 'I ... I just thought it was only fair to offer you the chance to retract your answer to my proposal.'

She dropped his hand. 'And why in the realm would I do that?'

'Well ... things at the castle aren't quite going according to plan ...'

'How do you mean?'

'I'm ... Well, I'm beginning to suspect that the king's intentions regarding my knighthood have changed.'

Eliza blinked.

'I'm sorry,' Swinton stammered. 'I honestly thought this was going to happen, I —'

'What does that have to do with anything?' she cut in.

Swinton finally met her gaze. Her eyes were filled with fire. 'Eliza, I —'

She held up a hand, shaking her head in disbelief. 'Do you *honestly* think your title means something to me?'

'Well ...'

'Dimitri.' She cupped his face, her eyes locking with his. 'I realise it's something you've worked hard for your whole life. I realise it's something you *deserve,* something that you were promised. So, in that sense, *of course* it's important.' She paused, kissed him gently. 'But when it comes to me, when it comes to *us*, I couldn't give a damn whether you're a knight or a street cleaner.'

Tears lined her eyes now. She swallowed. 'Do you still want to marry me?'

'*Of course* – I was just trying to —'

She gave a decisive nod. 'Then let's get married.'

Still in shock, Swinton nodded back. 'Alright. Well, in two weeks —'

'Not in two weeks. Today. *Now*.'

'Eliza.' Swinton squeezed her shoulder. 'Don't be rash. We can't get married today.'

'We can do whatever we like, Dimitri. Let's find a priestess. Let's be together.'

She was mad. There was no way they could get married here and now. It wasn't proper. It wasn't how things were meant to be. But …

She was studying him, a subtle smile playing across her lips. 'What do you say?'

Swinton pulled her to him, his lips finding hers. Eliza's hands went to the back of his neck and her fingers threaded through his hair. He could kiss her forever.

Finally, he leaned back and gazed into her eyes. 'I say yes. Yes,' he laughed. 'Let's get married today.'

They asked Eliza's parents to be their witnesses. Back in Willowdale, down by their favourite tree, they swore their vows to the local priestess, to the gods and to one another.

Taking his oath to Eliza was the highest honour of Swinton's life. He told her so as he held her hands beneath the flowing leaves of the great willow.

'I give you everything I have and will have,' he said, entwining his fingers with hers. 'I vow to love you and protect you for as long as I draw breath.'

There was a sniff from nearby. Swinton glanced over to Eliza's parents and was surprised to see Emmett, not Dorothy, shedding a tear. Swinton felt a swell of gratitude towards them. They were decent folk, and unlike so many others, they just wanted happiness for their daughter, no matter how or where she found it.

'Eliza,' the priestess said. 'Do you take this man, Dimitri Caleb Swinton, to be your husband, here and now, here and forever, before all the gods?'

Eliza grinned. 'I take him.'

The priestess nodded. 'And Dimitri, do you take this woman, Eliza Elora Carlington, to be your wife, here and now, here and forever, before all the gods?'

Swinton let out a breath. 'I take her.' He couldn't believe this was truly happening.

'Then it is with great pleasure that I pronounce you husband and wife.'

Husband and wife. Husband and wife ... Swinton had a wife. The beautiful, spirited woman standing before him was his *wife*.

Eliza leaned in and kissed him full on the mouth.

Swinton flushed. In front of her parents? In front of the priestess? But as the Carlingtons approached, they wore only expressions of pride. Emmett grasped Swinton's hand and shook it firmly.

'Congratulations, Dimitri. I know you'll do right by her.'

'Of course.'

Dorothy brushed a kiss against his stubbled cheek and echoed her daughter's earlier words: 'Welcome to the family, love.' Then she winked at him, the gesture strongly reminiscent of Eliza, and added, 'I knew I'd be three bronze coins richer, before long.'

Eliza's parents and the priestess made their excuses and started back towards the village. For the first time, Swinton suddenly felt self-conscious.

The wedding night.

Gods. Where would they stay? Were they going to …?

Eliza's voice interrupted his panic. 'Come with me.'

'Where?'

She tugged his hand. 'Just follow me.'

Swinton did as she bid, trailing after her towards the stable grounds. She led them all the way to the field where Xander was grazing, his coat gleaming in the afternoon sun.

Eliza rested her elbows on the fence. 'He's beautiful, isn't he?'

Swinton nodded. 'He is. He'll be a fine stallion one day.'

Eliza turned to him. 'He's yours.'

'What?' Swinton couldn't have heard her right.

But Eliza nodded keenly. 'He's yours. Xander. He's a wedding gift from me.'

'Eliza … you can't. He's … The king will want him. Your father —'

She waved him away. 'Says Xander is mine and mine to give to whom I please. I want you to have him.'

'I can't accept him.'

'You can, and you will.' She stepped back and crossed her arms over her chest.

'But …' Swinton looked again at the magnificent foal, then back to Eliza. 'I don't have a wedding gift for you.'

His wife smiled, unfolding her arms and taking his hands once more. 'This day is gift enough, Dimitri.'

Swinton wished there was somewhere else, somewhere finer he could take his new bride, but she insisted that there was nothing wrong with the tavern in Grayside. Swinton could think of many things wrong with it, but he had learned even before today that once Eliza set her mind to something, that mind was rarely changed.

They rode side by side back to the tavern as dusk fell, nerves fluttering in Swinton's stomach the entire time. He kept sneaking glances at Eliza, wondering if she was just as anxious. But his wife looked at ease, as she always did, smiling at him whenever she caught his eye.

The journey felt like it took an age and then, suddenly, no time at all. The grubby tavern came into view before Swinton had fully prepared himself for it. *Do we share a room?* he thought frantically. *Do I assume that? I can't assume – I don't want to put her on the spot. I want her to be —*

'Good to have you back, Commander,' the stable boy said, dipping his head as they dismounted and handed him their reins.

'Thank you,' Swinton managed, not at all sure how to proceed as the boy led their horses away.

He'd been with women before. Fi had made sure of it. But this … this was different. This was his *wife*. This was a *wedding night*. He had no idea what Eliza would expect, and he didn't want her to feel uncomfortable – or worse, disappointed.

'Your room is big enough for two, isn't it?' Eliza asked brazenly, looking to the entrance of the tavern.

Swinton flushed. 'Yes – would you … Would you like to stay with me tonight?'

'Of course.' Eliza laughed. 'But first things first: let's eat. I'm absolutely famished.'

Relief flooded through Swinton. He realised that he was starving as well, that neither of them had eaten all day. That settled things, then. He took her hand and marched inside.

In a corner booth, the newlyweds ate and drank their fill by the fire. A simple meal of beef stew, bread and wine, but hearty nonetheless. They spoke of the day, and how they wouldn't change it for the world. They spoke of their first meeting, Swinton teasing Eliza for her initial rudeness. His eyes lined with tears of laughter as she vehemently denied his impression of her scowl.

At last, they sat back against the cushions, bellies full and hearts content.

'Shall we go upstairs?' Eliza asked quietly, her warm hand on his.

Swinton laced his fingers through hers and nodded.

The door creaked as Swinton unlocked it and led Eliza inside. Had it really only been this morning that they'd been here, deciding to marry? It felt so long ago now.

Someone had stoked the fire. The shadows of its flames flickered across the settee before the hearth. Eliza, already pushing her boots off at the heel, sank into the plush seat with a contented sigh.

Suddenly nervous again, Swinton removed his boots and went to sit beside her, wringing his hands.

'Something on your mind?' Eliza said, turning to him, her legs curled up beneath her.

Swinton cleared his throat. 'I … I want to be honest with you,' he said, the words grating in his throat.

Eliza raised her brows. 'Oh?'

He took a deep breath. The last thing he wanted to do was upset her, but … the truth was important.

They couldn't start their marriage based on lies. 'You're not … You're not the first woman I've —'

'Married?' she teased, tucking loose hair behind her ear with a grin.

'No.' Swinton was sweating. 'You're not my … my *first*.'

She shrugged. 'Nor are you mine.'

Swinton's next words faltered, and clearly, he hadn't hidden his surprise well.

Eliza frowned. 'I didn't think that would bother you.'

'I …' Swinton considered this, before reaching across and taking her hand in his once more. She was right. It didn't bother him at all. 'I don't care about your first love, or loves,' he told her. 'The only love I care about is your last.'

Eliza gazed at him intently, pulling herself on top of him, a leg either side of his. She drew his face to hers, her fingers tangled in his hair.

'Good,' she said softly. 'Now will you take me to bed, Dimitri?'

Swinton awoke to beams of gold filtering through the gaps in the curtains. Eliza's hair, splayed across the pillow next to his, glinted in the sunlight. She was sleeping soundly, her bare legs entwined with his, while her dress and shift lay crumpled in a pile by the unlit fire.

Swinton watched as her torso rose and fell

steadily with each breath. He had never allowed himself to imagine that one day they would be this close. That he would be able to hold her in bed, to call her his wife. But yet … here she was.

She stirred beside him, but settled as he began to stroke her hair. Soon the magic of this morning would fade and reality would sweep in, but not yet. They had a few more hours still.

It was mid-morning when Swinton finally opened the curtains. He was due back in Heathton that same afternoon to oversee the training of the new squires, and he was already running late.

'Don't go,' Eliza said, wrapping her arms around his neck.

'I don't want to,' Swinton told her, leaning into her touch. 'I want nothing more than to stay here with you. But …'

'But you can't.'

Swinton nodded.

'I'll come with you …'

'I'd never ask that of you,' he said. 'You hate the capital.'

She leaned back and pressed her hands to his chest. 'But I love you.'

He grasped her hands in his. 'And I love you too much to force you to live in a place you deem so backwards. We will make this work. We will find a way. I just need time to sort out my duties in Heathton first.'

'I know,' Eliza allowed. 'How long will you be gone?'

'A few weeks.'

'Weeks?'

'I'm sorry. But once I've attended to my obligations, I'll come back to you, and we can finally start our life together.'

Eliza tucked her hair behind her ear and sighed. 'Do you promise?'

Swinton pressed his forehead to hers. 'With all my heart,' he vowed.

Back in Heathton, Swinton felt hollow. He missed Eliza more than he could have ever imagined. He missed her confidence and her teasing. He missed their conversations and the ease with which he could speak his mind to her. He missed her mouth on his and the sweep of her hair across his chest as they lay together.

The daily duties of his post made life no simpler. Lennox was permanently in the periphery of his guard now, smug and cocky, knowing that Swinton had no true authority over him. The other guards knew it, too.

In Swinton's absence, Fi had been granted leave to return home to Battalon for a brief visit. So Swinton spent his numbered hours of leisure time writing to Eliza. He had told no one of their marriage. Not yet. He would tell Fi once he was back in Heathton, but to tell anyone else seemed unimportant.

As the days passed, he oversaw the enrolment and training of new squires. He drilled each of his units hard, making sure the king's defences were up to scratch, and he visited his father's estate. For a moment, he considered telling his parents about Eliza, but the previous encounter they'd had with the Carlingtons stopped him.

After three long weeks had gone by, a porter arrived with a letter for Swinton. A letter from Eliza. He waited until the servant had closed the door behind him before tearing open the seal, eager to hear any news from his wife. She had a way with words, and her letters always managed to make him feel less alone.

This one was different.

His heart began to thud wildly as he read and re-read the unusually short missive:

Dimitri.

Come to Willowdale. I need you.

Eliza

Swinton rode out of Heathton in the middle of the night, panic latching onto his heart. Eliza needed him, and whatever was wrong, whatever the cost, he needed to be there for her.

When he arrived in Willowdale, it was mid-morning. He had ridden all night and stopped only once to water his horse. He was exhausted, but terror urged him on. He asked after her like a madman, stopping every porter and stable hand in the area.

He found her in a corral with Xander. She was walking beside the colt, her arms wrapped tightly around her middle, gaze on the ground.

He ducked under the fence and approached her.

'Dimitri.' His name caught in her throat, her eyes suddenly lined with tears. 'What … I … I wasn't sure you would come.'

He stopped her and gripped her shoulders, peering into her face. 'Of course I came. What happened? Are you alright? What's wrong?' The questions tumbled out of him in a panic.

'Dimitri,' she started, her eyes dropping to her hands resting across her abdomen.

'You can tell me. Has something happened? I'm here now.'

Her lower lip trembled. 'I'm not sure you'll …'

'Whatever it is, Eliza. I need to know.'

She nodded, as if to steady herself. 'Dimitri.' His name sounded like a question, but then she looked him straight in the eyes. 'I'm pregnant.'

Time stopped.

Eliza's words hung suspended between them as Swinton tried to understand them, tried to comprehend what they meant.

'We're going to have a family?' he asked, a tremor in his voice.

Eliza nodded again, biting her lip and searching his face.

Tears stung his eyes, but he didn't wipe them away. *A family. I'm going to have a family of my own ...* He let his wife see his utter joy as he scooped her up in his arms.

'You're happy?' she asked cautiously.

'Happy? I'm ... I'm more than that, Eliza,' he said, his heart full to bursting. 'There are no words for what I am.'

THE HEART OF THE FOREST

The most beautiful part of Valia was at its heart. A garden of sorts, only much larger, abundant with beds of rich green herbs that emitted a light, exotic fragrance whenever the breeze blew. It was Henri's favourite spot in her homeland, a place that seemed to nourish the rest of the forest and the people within it.

She walked between the trees in the morning light, brushing her palms against the contrasting rough and smooth bark of the towering trunks. There was nowhere else in the realm like Valia. And she'd seen her fair share of the realm.

Breathing in the fresh air and taking in the blue hue of the early hours, she waited. And sure enough, she soon heard a whoosh of leaves and a delighted shriek as a tiny redheaded girl skidded into the clearing.

'Luka!' Athene warned her daughter. 'What have I told you about making noise around here?'

But the little girl paid her no heed as she scooped up an armful of leaf litter and thrust it into the air, giggling uncontrollably.

Athene shook her head in defeat as she spotted Henri.

'Off with you, then,' she told Luka. 'Not too far.'

Henri found herself smiling. It wasn't often she saw her friend frazzled, but the five-year-old miniature Valian had a way of getting under Athene's skin.

'What's so funny?' Athene said, folding her arms over her chest as she came to stand beside Henri. That gesture alone made Henri want to laugh. She'd seen Luka do the very same thing when she didn't get her way.

'Nothing.' Henri knew better than to antagonise her – Luka had already been there, done that this morning.

Athene huffed. 'I tried to squeeze in some training before she was up,' she said, nodding to Luka, who was now drawing in the dirt with her fingers. 'But the little terror was awake and waiting.'

'Sounds like you need a break …'

'I *do*, so I can actually get things *done*. I don't remember the last time I had a full training session without being interrupted. I'm not nearly as strong and fit as I need to be —'

'That's nonsense,' Henri said. 'You're the best in Sahara's kindred.'

'We both know that's not true.'

'Except for me, perhaps,' Henri allowed.

A shout sounded. Luka was now swinging a stick before her, brandishing it like a sword, jabbing the air aggressively.

'She's been watching you spar?' Henri asked, noting the little girl's stance.

'Of course. I told Allehra she's ready to start her training.'

'She's not old enough yet.'

'But she's *good* enough.'

'That's not the Valian —'

Athene's brows shot up. 'It is the *epitome* of the Valian Way. In any case, Allehra delegated the decision to Sahara.'

Henri nodded. 'She's giving her more responsibility in the lead-up to the coronation.'

'So I've heard.'

'What did Sahara say, then?'

Athene's voice was steely. 'She said no.'

'Well …'

'Well, nothing. I know what's best for my own daughter —'

A yelp cut Athene off and she bolted towards Luka. The little girl's bottom lip trembled as she surveyed her grazed palms.

'You're fine. Up you get,' Athene told her, helping

Luka to her feet. The tears lining the girl's bright blue eyes vanished.

'I have to meet Sahara for watch,' Henri called.

Athene sighed and lifted Luka up onto her hip in one effortless motion. 'Say bye to Henri,' she told her daughter.

But Luka buried her face in the crook of her mother's neck. Athene rolled her eyes and waved Henri away, heading for the stream.

Henri watched them go, her chest swelling with pride. Despite her (and the rest of the kindred's) initial reservations about Athene's situation, she knew her friend was a brilliant mother. Firm, but not unkind, Athene had garnered a new level of respect from the kindred of the keep. And as for little Luka ... The girl was a handful, no doubt, but she was not only a daughter of one of the elites, but a daughter to them all.

Henri was still smiling as she arrived at her and Sahara's meeting point. She leaned against a tree and tipped her head to the canopies, taking in the light that filtered through the branches above.

The last few years had been a whirlwind. Relentless travels and training across all four continents; Allehra desperately seeking out any hidden magic in Sahara. Henri knew her sister was frustrated by it all. How could she not be?

Light footsteps sounded and Sahara came into view by the stream, her short hair dancing in the breeze. She'd kept it cropped over the years, despite their mother's protests. No one confused the twins anymore.

'You're late,' Henri said by way of greeting.

'Am not. You're early. As always. Can't help yourself, can you?'

'Watch duty starts in twenty minutes. If you're not early, you're late,' Henri quipped, following Sahara along the brook.

Sahara huffed a laugh. 'You're just like Allehra.'

'Nothing wrong with that.' Henri grinned. 'She's only one of the most revered matriarchs in our history.'

'Uh-huh.'

'What'd she want you for yesterday, anyway?'

'What?'

'Yesterday. You met her for something important?'

'Nothing life-changing. Tell me again why you volunteered us for sentry?'

'Because it's our duty,' Henri said, before giving her sister a wink. 'But also because I found a fresh crop of wildberries out here the other day. The rest have been harvested, but no one's seen these … Thought we could gorge ourselves.'

Just like when we were younger, and things were simpler, she thought.

Sahara laughed. 'Now there's a plan I can throw my support behind.'

Smiling, Henri led her sister to the secret patch she'd discovered. There, they picked fruit until their fingers turned violet.

'So Athene asked you about Luka's training?' Henri ventured tentatively, aware that her best friend was not always a safe topic of conversation with Sahara. But her sister only nodded.

'I think you were right to deny her,' Henri added.

Sahara looked at her, surprised. 'You do?'

Emboldened, Henri nodded keenly. 'She's not old enough yet. It's not the Valian Way.'

It was as though she'd said the wrong thing. Sahara's gaze went back to the berries, and she was quiet as they plucked the fruit from the bush.

'Think we've got enough?' Henri said finally, gesturing to the pile of berries they'd collected atop the cloth she'd brought.

'More than. We'll make ourselves sick.'

'Then we best get to the sentry post.'

Sahara clicked her tongue in frustration, but got to her feet and followed Henri.

They made their way up to the canopy, relieving the older kindred from their posts. Their gazes filled with distaste at the sight of Sahara's cropped hair before they descended to the forest floor. Henri knew the kindred saw her sister's small, ongoing act of rebellion as a disrespectful slap to their way of life. A horrific thing for an heir to do, in their eyes. As always, Henri wanted to run after the older kindred, to explain that Sahara wasn't like that, that disrespect was never her intention. She merely wanted to express a sense of individuality amongst the unit. But every time, something stopped Henri from doing so. She didn't know what.

Sighing, she looked outwards. She had chosen this post not just for the wildberries at the foot of the trees, but for the view at the top. As they climbed their way up to the living bridges and the viewing platform, Henri's breath caught in her throat.

From this part of Valia, and this high up, they could see the roiling mist that bordered the southeast of their territory. It had been that way for centuries. An impenetrable wall that rose up into the sky as far as she could see.

Even at a safe distance, her magic thrummed in its presence. The people of the realm knew little of the mist's origins, only that it was deadly. That it hungered for Ashai magic like an insatiable beast.

But that only made it more fascinating, Henri realised as she watched the cloud-like tufts drift skyward.

Beside her, Sahara was staring too. 'Do you think it's true?'

'What?'

Sahara didn't take her eyes off the mist. 'That the air is different in there? That those who go beyond it fall off the face of the realm?'

Henri considered this and shrugged. 'All I know is that those who go in don't come back out.'

'Hmm.'

Henri waited for her sister to say something more, but she didn't. Instead, they stood at their post in silence, watching the mist roil beyond their borders. But Henri didn't fail to notice that Sahara's fists were clenched at her sides, her knuckles white.

Sahara seemed to nod to herself before passing Henri the cloth of berries and heading towards the ladder.

Henri frowned. 'What are you doing?'

But Sahara had already started to climb down.

'Sahara!' Henri called, perplexed.

Her sister now had her feet planted firmly on the forest floor.

'How are you supposed to scout anything from down there?' Henri said.

'You *know* I hate heights.'

'We don't even have to go that high!' Where Henri now stood wasn't the highest point of the canopy by a long shot. She paused. She could hear Sahara scratching the tree trunk – no, not scratching, *carving*.

Not again ... Sahara had gone through phases of defacing their home with etchings of a single word. It was unusual, unheard of – Henri could never remember what it was, even after all these years ...

'You think that's *not* high?!' Sahara called.

'Well, I can go higher.'

'Don't! What if you fall?'

'I don't fall.'

'Come down from there, you're making me nervous.'

Henri laughed and slid easily down to the forest floor. 'Happy?'

It felt good to tease her sister again. They had been so serious of late; this felt far more natural.

With her back against the tree trunk, Sahara studied her, taking in Henri's near-identical form.

'You should be queen,' Sahara said, shattering all illusions of fun.

'*What?*'

'You're what they want, and what the people need ...'

It sounded as though this was not the first time her sister had considered the subject.

Henri glanced up at the living bridges. They really should get back. They were abandoning their duty. 'Don't be stupid, Sahara. You're the heir,' she said lightly.

'I can't fight —'

'*Won't* – you *won't* fight.'

'It's the same thing.'

'No, it's not.'

'It is. You just can't see it yet. Plus, I have no power.'

'You have plenty of power.'

Sahara shook her head. 'We both know that's not true.'

But Henri hadn't meant magic. Sahara was a force to be reckoned with all on her own.

It wasn't until Sahara pushed off from the tree

trunk that Henri spotted the familiar carving. There, in looped cursive, was one word: *OREMERE*.

'Find someone else for sentry,' Sahara called flippantly over her shoulder.

'Sahara!'

But Sahara kept walking. There was a lightness to her step that Henri hadn't seen in a while. As though some sort of weight had been lifted from her shoulders, and she was, at last, free.

Henri frowned again, starting up the ladder once more. Sahara needed a break. That was all.

When new kindred came to relieve Henri of her duty, they didn't question where Sahara was. Henri left them the remains of the wildberries, and with one last glance at the shifting mist beyond, she took to the living bridges, back towards the keep.

She couldn't understand why Sahara didn't love it up here. *This* was freedom. *This* was what it was to be wild: the wind catching in her hair, leaves rustling across her leathers. Henri's magic murmured against her skin. With a burst of energy, she harnessed it, using it to shift the branches before her with a gentle wave of her hand, bending them to her will. She created an archway for herself, marvelling at the dexterity of the trees and the life brimming within them that bowed to her power. Foliage kissed the crown of her head as she made her way through.

'Have you mastered it without the use of your hands?' said a familiar, cool voice.

Allehra stepped out from one of the bridge offshoots, hands clasped behind her back.

Henri came to a stop before her mother. 'Not yet.'

The branches around them drifted back to their rightful places. Henri shifted from foot to foot, feeling Allehra's magic pulse around her. Her mother's power was different to hers. While Henri was an energy shifter through and through, Allehra had a more ancient sort of magic that didn't manifest in one form. It had always made Henri uneasy, not understanding how it worked.

'Have you been practising?' Allehra asked.

Henri fell into step beside her mother as they walked. 'Yes,' she lied.

If Allehra detected falsehood, she gave no indicator. Instead, she seemed to be contemplating something else entirely.

'I've just seen your sister,' she said finally.

'Oh?'

Allehra nodded. 'She seems more herself this afternoon.'

'More herself?' While Henri knew what Allehra meant, she wasn't about to throw her twin to the wolves. But judging from Allehra's furrowed brow, the heir of Valia wasn't due for another scolding, as such.

'Sahara …' Allehra started, but stopped to mull over her words.

'Sahara what?'

The Queen of Valia sighed and came to a halt at the crossroads of the bridges. 'Sahara has been struggling.'

Slowly, Henri nodded. Part of her was relieved that someone older and wiser was voicing the same concerns.

'Yes,' she allowed. 'Ever since we lost Addi in Havennesse.'

Allehra studied her for a moment, and suddenly the years between mother and daughter felt immense. 'That was years ago, Henri,' she said, with a gentle touch to her shoulder. 'And she's been struggling since long before then.'

Memories washed over Henri in a wave. Sahara always flinching when they called her their 'future queen'. Sahara speaking out against the elders on the mountain, all that time ago. Sahara sailing past the falls during the Crossing, her grip coming loose on the vine …

'You know what I speak of,' Allehra murmured, watching Henri as she emerged from her reverie.

'I …' But what could Henri say? A final image flashed before her: a carving. The same one Sahara had made on the ship back from Havennesse, the same one she'd carved all over Valia …

OREMERE.

Henri swallowed the lump in her throat. 'I'll talk to her.'

. . .

Spirits were high at supper that evening. Petra and Tilly regaled the group with tales of Marvel's dramatic failure as a baker that afternoon, describing her charcoal lump of bread in detail.

'You mean this thing?' Athene said, producing a black, rock-like object from a piece of cloth at her feet. 'I asked the kitchenhand to save it as a memento for you, Marvel.'

It was Sahara who laughed the loudest at this, her cheeks tipped pink and her graphite eyes bright.

Henri grinned. *That* was the Sahara she knew. The rest of the unit seemed to feed off Sahara's good mood, teasing each other mercilessly and passing around a large flagon of wine. Henri's face was flushed and she knew she'd had more than her fair share of the drink, but … Sahara was *back*. She was *happy*. The afternoon off sentry duty had done her the world of good. She was her usual, carefree self again.

When supper was done, their unit, their family, stayed until the moon was bright and high in the night sky.

Athene sighed as she got to her feet and scooped a sleeping Luka up in her arms. 'I'll bid you lot goodnight here,' she said. 'I've got to get this one to bed, and then it's off to sentry duty down by the southern stream.'

Sahara looked up. 'That's where Henri and I were today. There should be a handful of wildberries left by the double oak, before the ladder to the bridges. Luka would love them.'

Henri wasn't the only one who failed to hide her surprise. All around their table, brows shot up and jaws dropped.

Is this a peace offering? Henri stared at her sister in disbelief.

'Thanks.' Athene gave a wary nod. 'I'll keep an eye out.'

By the time Henri and Sahara retired to their rooms, Henri's face hurt from smiling – and so did Sahara's, by the looks of things. Exhausted but happy, the sisters peeled off their leathers and tugged oversized nightshirts over their heads.

'That was a fun night,' Sahara said, running her fingers through her short hair and leaning against the ladder to her bunk.

'It really was,' Henri agreed, at last pulling her sheets back and sliding into bed. For a moment, her drink-addled thoughts took her back to the living bridges with Allehra ... *'I'll talk to her,'* she'd said. The promise echoed in her mind.

Sahara was still standing at the foot of the bed, smile still wide, eyes still bright. 'Night, Henri.' She gave a final grin before climbing up to her bed. Above, the covers rustled and Henri heard her sister settle.

She'd talk to her tomorrow, Henri vowed. 'See you in the morning,' she called up.

There was no response. Her sister must have fallen asleep the moment her head hit the pillow.

Henri's dreams were filled with roiling mist. A thick wall of it coiled at her feet and white feathers of it drifted skyward. Her skin and magic prickled in its presence, entrancing her like some hypnotic creature from the deep. The mist seemed to know her. It whispered strange words in her ear, words she'd heard before but couldn't remember. A tuft of it brushed her fingers. Where was she? What was the place beyond that seemed to call to her?

Her magic thrummed suddenly. She stepped back in shock. Magic filled her entire being, rich and vibrant in a way she'd never experienced before, until —

Her power constricted around her. Its grip tightened to the point of pain, to the point at which she might burst. Magic was choking her, like a viper suffocating its prey —

In the dark and early hours, Henri sat bolt upright, her sister's name on her lips.

'Sahara?' she said again, hauling herself out of bed and peering up into the top bunk.

But the bed was made.

Henri pressed a palm to the pillow, finding the fabric cool beneath it.

An unspeakable fear gripped her. She tugged on her leathers and boots and made for the door.

Something is wrong.

She followed her gut to the keep. What she found there only fuelled her terror.

Allehra, along with her elites, Makena and Quinn, stood by a dying fire, their expressions grave.

'Mother?' Henri said as she reached them, the night air chill on her skin. She couldn't remember the last time she'd called Allehra that. 'What's going on?' she asked. 'I can't find —'

The Queen of Valia's expression fell at the sight of her and she drew her arms across her chest, as though trying to keep herself warm. She took a dazed step toward Henri.

'You had it too …'

Henri couldn't keep the tremor from her voice. 'Had what?'

'The dream.'

A feather of mist flashed in Henri's mind. Fear curled in her stomach. Slowly, she nodded. 'She's not in her bed …' The words were barely a whisper.

'I know.'

Something rustled in the bushes just beyond the keep and Henri's heart soared. They'd been making a fuss for nothing. Sahara had just gone for a night-time wander. Henri mentally prepared all manner of reprimands for her sister for causing so much worry —

But it was Athene who emerged from the trees.

'Your Majesty?' she said. 'You asked for me?'

Henri's heart sank.

'I did. You were stationed for sentry at the southeast post, correct?'

'Yes, Majesty.'

'With whom?'

Athene frowned. 'No one, Majesty. It was a solitary shift this evening.'

Allehra took a fast step forward. 'What?'

'A solitary —'

Henri couldn't breathe as she watched Allehra battle internally with herself.

'There are no solitary shifts, Athene,' the queen said quietly. 'Did you see anything out there?'

'No, Majesty.' Athene swallowed. 'Nothing out of the ordinary.'

'You didn't see Sahara?'

Athene blinked. 'No. I saw no one.'

Henri opened her mouth to start protesting her friend's interrogation – but her breath caught in her throat, snagging on what felt like a lick of fire.

Her magic flared in her veins as an intense, panicked sensation filled her: the feeling of crossing a threshold. Mist danced once more before her eyes and she staggered.

Allehra caught her just before she hit the ground.

Henri gasped, her eyes locking with her mother's. 'Sahara's gone,' she croaked. 'She's not coming back —'

And then, all Henri saw was black.

SAVAGE SEAS

Up on the deck of *The Daybreaker*, the midday sun soaked into Bleak's skin. It warmed her blood in a way that only rays reflected from the sea could. She and Senior grappled with the nets at the stern, hauling them up from the dark waters below. Her arms ached with the effort. Usually there were a few more hands to help, but in low season, particularly *this* low season, it was just Bleak and her guardian. She didn't mind hard work, with the briny breeze kissing her salt-cracked skin and whipping her sun-bleached hair from its tie. She relished the strain of her muscles as the net hit the deck at last.

Empty.

The net was empty, or as good as. Only a handful of bream flapped helplessly against the timber.

Bleak frowned. Even for low season, this was bad.

This catch wasn't even worth a trip to the local markets, let alone Heathton. She raised her brows in Senior's direction, but he was staring blankly at the horizon.

Bleak didn't need to be a mind whisperer to know where his thoughts lay. Her guardian's face, which had always borne a weathered appearance, was now more haggard and wrinkled. Skin hung loose and thin from his cheekbones and his eyes were shadowed with purple. Grief had added another decade to him.

'Not a great catch, hey, Senior?' Bleak said, waving to the empty net.

'What's that?'

'The catch,' Bleak repeated. 'Not what we'd hoped for, is it?'

Senior's gaze slowly took in the half-dozen fish. He shrugged. 'Can't control the seas, can we, Half-Pint?'

'No, but —'

'Get those in a barrel, will you? They'll at least feed us and the Claytons for the next night or so.'

Bleak didn't have the heart to remind him that Mrs Clayton wasn't accepting his fare. That any food left on the Claytons' doorstep either landed in the hands of the town beggar, or off the side of the white-faced cliffs.

Instead, Bleak just nodded. 'At least they're a decent size …'

Senior grunted his agreement.

Bleak sighed and glanced up at the crow's nest. Usually Bren would be up there, looking to the waters ahead. But today, like the days and weeks before, no one manned the lookout.

'When do you think Bren'll come back?' she ventured, scooping the flailing fish into a barrel of water and gathering the soaked net.

'What's that?' Senior said again, his eyes vacant.

Bleak clicked her tongue. 'When do you think Bren will be back on deck?'

'Oh.' Senior looked at his boots. 'I don't know, Half-Pint. Mrs Clayton's forbidden all her boys from working out on the water.'

'But that won't last forever,' Bleak pushed. 'Will it?'

'I don't know,' Senior said again. 'Can you blame her? The seas haven't been kind to their family, eh? Maybe give it a rest for now.'

'But Senior —'

'No buts. That family's been through a lot, ya hear?'

'I know —'

'End of discussion. Now tend to the sails, will ya? We want to get back before dark.'

There was nothing for it. Bleak did as Senior bid and began to reel in the ropes.

They hadn't talked since it had happened, not properly. Out on the water, Senior was gruffer and more blunt that ever, but at home … Back at the cottage, things were different. He barely ate. He'd taken to drinking a particularly harsh amber liquid, often straight from the bottle, while he stared at the fire.

It was nearly sundown when they moored *The Daybreaker*. Upon entering their small cottage, Senior headed straight for that amber bottle. Kicking his dirty boots off, he sank into the worn armchair before the cold hearth without so much as splashing the sea from his face. His thoughts slowly seeped into Bleak's mind: *If only I'd said no to that voyage … Stupid. My fault – poor Nora … Two dead boys … At my hands –*

Bleak had to step away. Senior's thoughts were a dark, vicious cycle of blame and self-loathing. They took up all the air in the room.

'How about some stew?' she called from the kitchen. Her attempt last night had been a far cry from the mouth-watering feasts Mrs Clayton made, but it was edible. Bleak didn't wait for a response. She set the pot to heat on the stove.

As she waited, she tended to the fire, stealing glances at Senior as she layered the kindling and firewood. She'd never truly acknowledged how much he'd done for her until now. Since she was little, he'd cooked their meals, simple but hearty. He'd washed and mended their clothes. He'd cleaned the cottage and looked after her in every respect of the phrase, all while embarking on deep-sea fishing trips and journeys to the capital. Now, the least Bleak could do was feed him.

She placed a steaming bowl of stew on the table by his armchair. 'Eat,' she commanded. She'd learned in recent weeks not to ask. She stood over him while he slurped the food down, making sure he finished the bowl. When he was done, she topped up his glass with the pungent amber liquid, but took the bottle with her.

On the way to her room, she paused in the doorway. 'It wasn't your fault, you know,' she said, as she did every night. But like all the nights before, though his thoughts crashed into her stronger than any wave, Senior said nothing aloud.

The next day, Senior was in no condition to leave the cottage. He hadn't moved from the armchair, except to locate another bottle he'd hidden somewhere. In the harsh light of day, his eyes were bloodshot and his skin sallow. He also couldn't stand. Bleak left him with a flagon of water and some bread. Donning his waxed coat, she set out to the wharves. If they wanted to keep eating, they needed a decent catch, and soon.

The sun hadn't even fully risen when she cast off and set sail. As the wind picked up, she looked to the empty deck and crow's nest. Gods, she missed Bren. She'd barely seen him since Willem and Tobias had died, though not from lack of trying. Mrs Clayton had turned her away several times, and Bren had been working long hours down in Felder's Bay, helping to construct a nobleman's new property.

Bleak felt selfish admitting it, even just to herself, but … she was lonely. She couldn't remember the last time she'd had an extended conversation with someone. One where both people were invested in each other's thoughts and opinions.

Selfish. She was being selfish. Willem and Tobias had *died*. Bren had lost his brothers. Mrs Clayton had lost two sons. And Senior … Senior had lost them *and* himself.

Bleak shook her head, willing the self-pity away, and set to work casting the nets.

That night, having moored *The Daybreaker* and fed Senior, Bleak ventured up the hill towards the town. She needed to be around people, needed to hear a voice other than her own.

She passed the Claytons' on the way and left a small bucket of fish on their doorstep. It felt wrong not to, now. Hopefully Bren would come upon them. He knew how to scale and fillet them, and he did have a way with seasoning.

There was only one place she could go at this time: the Angove Inn, a local alehouse. She entered to find it as it always was: buzzing with patrons, but not too rowdy – yet. She ordered an ale and found her usual table in the corner. There, she sat sipping her drink, studying the people around her. She'd come to learn to scrutinise their words, their body language, before dipping into their thoughts and seeing if they matched. More often than not, they didn't. It was a sad reality of the realm, one Bleak felt intensely as she sat drinking alone.

Someone slid into the seat beside hers.

'Long day?' a light voice said. Maz, the blacksmith's son.

'Long month,' Bleak quipped, taking a long draught, feeling it numb her magic.

'I heard,' he replied, swigging from his own mug.

'Nice bracelet,' Bleak said, eyeing the leather braid around Maz's tanned wrist.

He glanced down at it. 'Thanks. My ma made it for me.'

Bleak knew that Maz's mother had died in the bout of plague that had nearly claimed her own life when she was younger.

'I'm sorry,' she heard herself say. 'About your ma.'

Maz toyed with the bracelet. 'Thanks.' He looked around. 'Who are you here with, anyway?'

'No one. You?'

Maz shrugged. 'No one important. Mind if I stay a while?'

Bleak didn't know why the handsome apprentice was choosing to sit with her rather than the group of friends he'd no doubt come with, but she didn't object. She could use the company.

Over the next few hours, they drank and talked

quietly, just the two of them. They spoke of the town's latest gossip, and of the Eery Brothers' performance (Bleak had heard one or two melodies before Senior had broken the news about the Clayton boys). To Bleak's surprise, she found that she was enjoying herself, and it helped that Maz's thoughts were somehow kept at bay, not intruding on her own mind.

It was past eleven o'clock when they parted at the path down by the cliffs. They agreed to meet again in two nights' time. Bleak felt as though a weight had been lifted.

The next two days followed the same pattern as those preceding. Bleak woke before dawn, left Senior with water and food, and then set sail. She didn't know what to do about Senior, didn't know how to help Bren – or even see him, for that matter. It wasn't until she was on her way to meet Maz that she came upon her friend at the outskirts of the village.

Bren was riding atop an old farm horse. He looked different. Thinner, mostly, his face more hollowed out.

'Bren!' she called, having to stop herself from running up to him and startling the horse.

'Bleak,' he said, swinging a leg over the saddle and dismounting nimbly.

Without thinking, she lunged for him, wrapping her arms tightly around his middle.

After his initial surprise wore off, he returned the embrace, squeezing her firmly.

'How are you?' she said, finally stepping back to look at him. Immediately, she regretted the stupid question. She couldn't take it back now. Instead, she took in his appearance. He was indeed thinner. His usually sun-streaked hair was dull, and his wintry-blue gaze had lost its usual brightness.

Bren ran a calloused hand through his hair and let out a puff of air. 'I don't know,' he told her, his other hand toying with the horse's bridle. 'Between comforting Ma, feeding the others and working in the bay, I've barely had time to think … or feel. And I don't feel their absence like the others do because I'm barely there. I keep thinking they're both just gonna stride through the door one evening, ya know?'

Bleak didn't know. Nor did she know what to say. It must have shown on her face.

'Don't worry,' Bren said with a sad smile. 'There's nothing to be done. Or if there is, yer already doing it. We've been getting the food – thanks. I've made sure Ma's keeping it. We let her rant for a bit, but we eat it all the same.'

Bleak nodded slowly. 'It … it wasn't his fault, Bren.'

Bren met her gaze, and for a moment Bleak waited for the onslaught of accusations. But they didn't come. Instead, his memories of Willem and Tobias flared before her. There were many, spanning from childhood to the very recent. All laced with sorrow and regret.

Bren cleared his throat. 'I know it wasn't,' he said. 'Ma knows it too, deep down. But grief doesn't always follow sense. She'll come round when she can.'

'It's eating away at Senior. Couldn't you talk —'

But Bren was already shaking his head, and Bleak cursed herself for being so insensitive.

'I'm sorry. I didn't mean —'

Bren waved her away. 'I know. There's just only so much I can do right now, eh? Where are you off to now, anyway?'

Bleak hesitated.

'What?'

Bren and Maz had never gotten along, but she couldn't lie – not to Bren. 'I'm meeting Maz.'

'You're what?'

'I'm meeting —'

Bren's eyes narrowed. 'I heard you,' he snapped. 'I just can't believe you'd be so naïve.'

'I'm not! We talked the other night. He was really nice —'

Bren was shaking his head, cheeks suddenly flushed. He started to lead his horse away.

'Bren!'

But Bren didn't turn around. Instead, he called back to her in a steely tone, 'I can't deal with this right now. Go make yer own mistakes then, Bleak.'

Bleak didn't follow him. Chewing her lip, she

wandered slowly towards the alehouse, trying to stop the burning tears from falling.

'Everything alright?' Maz asked, pushing off from the wall he'd been leaning against and opening the door for her.

She nodded.

Maz raised an eyebrow. 'Let's get you a drink.'

They occupied the same table as last time, only this time on the side with the bench. Bleak noticed that Maz was closer to her than before, but it might have simply been because the inn was louder tonight. He pushed a foam-topped mug towards her and lifted his own.

'Here's to new friends,' he said.

'To new friends,' Bleak echoed. She clinked her cup against his and took a long swig of the cold ale. It was just what she needed to steady herself, to get Bren's words out of her head. She drank again. And again.

When the cup was empty, she ordered another and leaned back. With a relieved sigh, she realised she had, at last, started to relax. She listened to Maz talk about his father's workshop, about how unorganised and chaotic it was.

'It's not how I'd run a smithy,' Maz said boldly. 'But if my father ever heard me say that ...'

It was known around town that Maz's father was a bit of a brute. That he had the inclination to take a belt, among other things, to his son more often than not.

'He won't hear it from me,' Bleak said, drawing into the condensation on her mug with her finger.

Senior had never hit her. Had never even come close, even when she'd been younger and more mischievous. In fact, Senior had barely even raised his voice to her. She'd gotten lucky – more than lucky. Maz's father, Bren's … They were a different sort of man.

'Where'd you go, then?' Maz was staring at her.

'What?'

'What were you thinking?'

'Oh.' Bleak drained her drink again and signalled for another. 'Nothing, really.'

'Didn't look like nothing.'

Bleak shrugged and slid a coin to the barman, greedily eyeing the fresh ale before her. It wasn't until she'd downed that tankard that she realised how late it was, and how drunk she was. When she stood, she swayed.

'Oops,' she mumbled as she staggered into the table.

Maz chuckled and pulled her arm over his shoulder. 'Come on,' he said. 'I should get you home —'

But as she stumbled again, she knocked over Maz's half-full tankard. Ale sloshed over his free hand and arm. He cursed loudly and released her, shaking the liquid from his wrist, where the drink had soaked into his bracelet.

Bleak reached for it to inspect the damage. 'Sorry —'

'Don't!' Maz snapped, snatching his wrist away from her.

Bleak froze, a buzzing suddenly sounding in her head. It wasn't from the drink. This was something else – magic. Her magic was thrumming, as though whatever had been keeping it at bay had been —

Bleak's gaze shot to the dripping bracelet, recognising it for what it must be. A talisman. An object treated with magical herbs, designed to protect its wearer from Ashai power.

Maz knew. Or suspected.

As the realisation hit Bleak, so did Maz's thoughts.

Any feelings of drunken merriment evaporated and Bleak's blood went cold. The ale had stripped away the bracelet's protection, and now his mind was open to her, his internal voice echoing loudly in her head.

I can salvage this, he thought. *The charm's still effective – she hasn't said anything. Stupid girl's drunk out of her skull, anyway. I just need to get closer. I nearly had her ... Just one little slip-up and I'll know her power for sure. And once I do ... I can demand a price. Offer her to the highest bidder —*

Bleak schooled her face into drunken neutrality and Maz saw what he wanted to see.

Bastard, she cursed silently. *Fucking bastard.* There

was *no way* she'd ever let him discover her secret. She would protect herself, and Senior, at all costs.

'I think I'm gonna be sick,' she slurred, staggering away from him.

'Here, let me help you.'

'No, thanks —'

But despite her protests, his hands found her waist, and as he led her from the inn, his palm rested on the small of her back. Perhaps she really *would* be sick …

She pulled away, slamming into the side of the building, playing the drunk card. In reality, she now felt stone-cold sober. It had all been a lie. He hadn't wanted to be her friend, hadn't had any interest in her, except to sell her out.

Fucking bastard.

He was still trying to get close to her, forcing his body up against hers, acting the part of the concerned companion, the potential new lover. His hand skimmed the bare skin of her wrist and she shuddered, his thoughts still loud and clear.

A pressure point, she said there was a pressure point, and if I found that —

Bleak had no idea what a pressure point was, or who Maz had been speaking to, but … she was done.

'Get off,' she said.

'What? Bleak, it's alright, I'm just getting you home ...' He looked genuinely baffled. Bleak felt a surge of fury at the nerve of him.

He reached across and tucked a loose strand of

hair behind her ear, his eyes a mask of sympathy. She pushed his hand away and straightened her shoulders.

'Maz?' she said, sounding braver than she felt.

'What is it?' he asked, voice laced with concern.

'You can fuck off now.'

He started. 'What?'

'You heard me.'

She watched and heard the confusion wash over him, and then the realisation. The realisation that he would get *nothing* he wanted that evening. Confusion turned to fury.

'Go fuck yourself, Bleak,' he spat, his mouth curling into a sneer as he strode away. 'You're nothing but a filthy gutter rat.'

She'd known men like this from the taverns in the capital: a kind facade at first, but once spurned, becoming something else entirely.

'I just can't believe you'd be so naïve ...' Bren's words followed Bleak all the way down the path to home.

She swore, palming the tears from her eyes, frustrated and humiliated. Was it naïve to think that someone could enjoy her company? Her conversation? Apparently. She'd fallen for Maz's subtle touches and lingering gaze. Like a prize idiot.

Never again, she vowed, gritting her teeth as she pushed the cottage gate open.

She didn't bother keeping quiet as she entered. Senior was as she'd left him – head tipped to the ceiling, snoring lightly, hand grasped around the neck of the glass bottle. Fresh tears burned her eyes, and this time, she let them fall freely. After all, there was no one there to see.

Bleak's eyes were sore and puffy the next day as she made her way down to the wharves. She was tired. Selfish or not, exhaustion had made her bones heavy.

'Thought I'd find ya here,' a familiar voice sounded from the deck of *The Daybreaker*. There was a soft thud as Bren jumped from ship to marina. His gaze lingered on her red-rimmed eyes, but before he could ask, she blurted:

'You were right.'

A steely rage seemed to settle over her friend. 'What did he do?'

Bleak couldn't tell him even if she wanted to. Only Senior knew of her secret, and even he didn't know the true extent of it. No one could. So now, Bleak swallowed the truth and simply shook her head.

'I took care of it.'

'What —'

'Nothing needs to be done. I'm more than capable of handling it myself, and I have.'

Bren studied her for a moment before nodding. 'Fair enough.'

She let out a breath of relief. 'What are you doing here, anyway?' she asked.

'I'm not here,' he replied.

'Huh?'

'Well, I'm not *supposed* to be ... Not yet.'

'Oh?'

'I spoke to Ma,' he said. 'Last night. Gave her a bit of a talking to, really. I'm still not allowed out on the water.' He gazed at the sapphire waves longingly. 'But things are ... well, you'll see.'

Bleak frowned. 'Alright ...'

Bren winked, looking more like himself than he had in weeks. 'Be seeing ya.'

She watched him go, feeling more *herself* than she had in a long while, too. As she set sail, she found herself smiling.

There was something different about the cottage when she approached the gate at dusk. Warily, Bleak realised that the front door was ajar, and there was a strange clanging noise coming from within.

She had no weapon. Hands trembling, she picked up the largest stick she could find and approached on her tiptoes. Heart hammering, she pushed the door wide.

It was Senior. In the kitchen.

'What ...' she started, dropping her makeshift weapon and stepping inside.

She couldn't believe her eyes. Senior was at the counter, tossing a salad in a large mixing bowl. *What in the realm* ... But then she saw it.

On the kitchen table, displayed proudly on a thick

wooden board, was one of Mrs Clayton's famous palma pies.

'Senior …' Bleak began, stepping closer.

But the sight of Senior's grin caused a thick lump to form in her throat. He strode over to the table, placing the salad bowl next to the pie and straightening the cutlery he'd set out.

'Tomorrow, I'm gonna get us some rainbow trout,' he told her. 'The Claytons are coming over for dinner.'

The bottle of amber liquid was gone, and as Bleak and Senior sat down to eat, she felt something shift back into its rightful place.

She swore it was the best damn palma pie she'd ever tasted.

The next morning, Senior insisted Bleak take the day off.

'I'll come with you,' she argued, already grabbing her coat.

'Nonsense. You've been carrying this family for weeks. I've already asked Jolly Sam and Abner from our Heathton crew to join, anyhow. You take the day. Do whatever it is that young people do.'

Bleak paused in the doorway. She had no idea what people her age did. She'd spent her whole life riding the coastal tides with Bren and Senior, and that was exactly how she liked it. She wanted to go with Senior now. Wanted to tell him that she'd missed him terribly, and that now he was more himself again, she wanted to spend all the time in the world with him. But as Senior shrugged on his waxed coat, she said none of it. They never spoke of such things.

He waved at her from the gate and set out towards the marina. *I'll do better,* she promised herself.

Bleak spent the day doing something very foreign to her: cleaning. She and Senior were generally tidy people, but over the last few weeks, the cottage had started looking worse for wear. And with them expecting company for once, it seemed like the right time to locate the old broom and mop.

Surprisingly, Bleak found that she enjoyed herself. The rhythmic sweep of the broom, the satisfying wipe of a damp rag across a grimy surface – it all kept her from reliving the utter humiliation of the night at the inn. Instead, she focused on how pleased Senior would be when he saw their spotless home.

The relief she had felt upon seeing that palma pie had been immense. Bren's 'talking to' must have been incredibly effective. Bleak hoped that, before long, she'd have her best friend back out on the water with them.

As she cleaned, she couldn't help her mind wandering to the night of the Eery Brothers' performance. She and Bren had *danced*. Together. In a way that had made her chest pound and her hands grow clammy. Things might have gone in a very different direction if … Bleak shook the thought from her head. No one knew what would have happened, what could happen still. All anyone could do was face each day as it came.

It was late afternoon when a knock sounded at the door.

'Bren!' Bleak smiled as she pulled the door inward. 'You're early.'

But there was something wrong. Bren could hardly meet her gaze, his hands shoved into his pockets.

'What is it?' she asked, reaching for him.

He stepped back and his face crumpled. 'I didn't know how … There's no best way … Bleak … I have to tell you …'

'Tell me what?' A dozen possibilities flashed before her. Mrs Clayton had changed her mind – Bren was forbidden from fishing with them ever again. Or worse: they'd lost someone else – another brother?

But before she could focus on the images coursing through Bren's tormented thoughts, she spotted the farm horse at the gate, something large wrapped in canvas lying across its back.

'Bren …' She took a trembling step towards it.

Bren made to grab her arm, but she shook him off. He followed her. 'He washed up in Felder's Bay. Him and Jolly Sam … I was the one who found them. I …'

Bleak stopped listening when she reached the

horse. A strangled cry escaped her and she fell to her knees, not feeling a thing as she slammed onto the stone path.

For peeking out of the greying canvas was a tanned, weathered hand, and the sleeve of Senior's waxed coat.

THE LAST ORDER

The fire in the hearth crackled, warming Swinton's chilled skin as he pushed his boots off and sank into the settee with a contented sigh. Eliza's home, *their* home – for the time being, anyway – was small but cosy. A perfect place to spend the Ellestian winter nights.

A soft hand brushed Swinton's arm and he shuffled back to make room for his wife. She squeezed alongside him and rested her head on his chest. He could feel that she was smiling.

'How was it?' she asked, pulling his arms around her and resting his hands on her firm, round stomach. He ran his palms over the pronounced bump, still in awe that Eliza was growing his son or daughter inside her.

'It was fine,' he told her as his mind traced back through the day. He was overseeing the preparations for the annual King's Tournament in Willowdale. An odious task ordinarily, but this time … This time it meant that Swinton was able to stay with Eliza, in a way that husband and wife had not yet been able to. He sighed again and stroked Eliza's stomach.

'There was some misunderstanding about the dimensions of the king's private tent,' he continued. 'But the mistakes have been rectified. Everything else is going well and according to schedule. I think the king will be pleased.'

'Even though his favourite soldier isn't competing?'

Swinton smiled. 'King Arden knows I don't joust any more …'

'Who said I was talking about you?' Eliza quipped, squeezing his arm.

'Very funny.' Swinton kissed the top of her head. He wished they could stay here forever. Their tiny home was a gardener's cottage at the back of the Carlington family's main house. Here, they could pretend that there weren't such things as noble ranks and duties to the King's Army.

Swinton vowed things would be different soon. He wouldn't have his child born into a life of secrecy, a life where their father wasn't a presence in their early years. Nor could he stand the thought of Eliza left unsupported. He'd been doing his best, but he knew it wasn't enough. Knew his best didn't yet equate to the husband and father he wished to be.

'What do you think of Ameliah?' Eliza was saying, tracing circles on the back of his hand.

'What?'

'For the baby,' she clarified, not missing Swinton's momentary daze.

'Ameliah.' Swinton sounded it out. 'I'm not sure …'

'Well, we need to agree on some options soon. We don't have long now.'

One month. That was all the time they had left before the little one graced them with its presence.

'How can you be so sure it's a girl?' he asked, kissing Eliza's temple absentmindedly.

'Because my morning sickness was so severe, and I'm carrying high … That's what Ma said, anyway.'

Swinton had heard the explanation a dozen times at least, but he couldn't shake the feeling in his gut that their child would be a boy.

'Dimitri?'

'Hmm?'

'Have you told Fi yet?'

Swinton chewed the inside of his cheek. Fi knew he and Eliza had been courting – had been the one to encourage it, in fact – but he knew nought of their wedding, nor of their expanding family.

'You haven't,' Eliza answered for him. 'I'm beginning to feel as though you're ashamed of me, my love.'

Swinton drew back, horrified that such a thought would cross her mind. Eliza turned to look at him, and he took her face in his hands. '*Never*,' he said fiercely.

'Then why?'

Swinton didn't know why – not exactly. He knew he didn't want to burst their little private bubble of happiness. He selfishly wanted Eliza just to himself. But there had been setbacks, too … Lennox's return, the king's somewhat public shaming of Swinton, Fi's increasing number of journeys back to Battalon … But these were no excuses, and Eliza saw right through each and every one.

'You're afraid,' she said quietly.

She was right. More than anything, he was afraid of how Sir Caleb Swinton would react. He couldn't bear the thought of Eliza being humiliated and disrespected as she had been during her last visit to the Swinton Estate. And worse, he couldn't stand the thought that his child might be born into a family who wouldn't acknowledge it.

'I know,' he said finally.

Eliza didn't push him. She was patient like that, one of the many reasons Swinton knew she'd make a wonderful mother. She was still tracing circles on his arm and he felt his eyelids droop. They would figure it all out, he vowed silently. They would figure it all out together.

The next morning was cold and crisp. Swinton left Eliza in bed as he set out to see Stefan, who had been left to supervise the squires' horsemanship training. Though the sun was high over the Willowdale stable grounds, its warmth was just out of reach. Between barking orders from the fence at the squires in the corral, Stefan cupped his hands to his mouth and blew hot air into his palms. The young soldier didn't take his eyes off his trainees, calling out instructions to one of the lagging squires as Swinton approached. Swinton felt a surge of pride. It wasn't all that long ago that Stefan had been in their boots. Running a finger along the jagged scar down his chin, Swinton recalled the youngster's heroic actions in Battalon. Were it not for Stefan, he wouldn't have made it home to Ellest …

'Commander.' Stefan bowed his head in greeting.

'Stefan. How are they progressing this morning?'

Stefan tugged his cloak more tightly around him. 'Well enough, Commander. We've been at it since dawn.'

'Good. They need to be ready for the display at the tournament.' Even the squires needed to demonstrate their skills to the king.

'We won't let you down, sir.'

'How many times must I tell you, Stefan? I'm not a sir.'

His eager disciple winked. 'Not yet.'

Swinton shook his head. He'd never met someone who had such blind faith in a rumour. All the same, Swinton was grateful. Sometimes, a little blind faith was nice.

'Dimi!' boomed a deep, melodic voice. There was no mistaking who it was. Captain Fiore Murphadias strode into view. Wrapped in thick black palma furs, he seemed larger than life – even more so than usual.

'Morning, Stefan,' Fi said cheerfully, clapping a strong hand to the young man's shoulder.

'Good to see you, Captain,' Stefan replied with a grin.

Swinton turned to his friend. 'What brings you here, Fi? Aren't you meant to be supervising the remaining work on His Majesty's tent?'

'I thought you'd be happy to see me, old friend,' Fi said with a laugh. 'But worry not, Dimi. All is finished. I came to ask you about lunch plans.'

Swinton cocked a brow. 'It's not yet noon.'

Fi shrugged, eyes bright with mischief. 'A man's got to eat, no?'

'I have lunch plans.'

Fi beamed. 'Excellent, because I had none. I'll join you. Where are we dining?'

Before Swinton knew it, Fi was following him through the paddocks towards the Carlingtons' house, where Swinton had arranged to join Eliza's parents for the midday meal.

'Kind of them to host you, eh, old friend?' Fi said as they walked.

'What?'

'Don't tell me you've been staying in Grayside, Dimi. Haven't seen you there in a week.'

'I —'

'Have paid for a room, I know. Damn waste of coin if you ask me.'

'I *didn't* ask you,' Swinton muttered as the Carlingtons' modest home came into view.

Fi huffed a laugh. 'You're your usual cranky self today, aren't you? Do the Carlingtons know you're staying with their daughter?'

Swinton considered denying it, but realised immediately that there was no point. 'They know,' he allowed, pushing the small gate open and starting down the gravel path to the house.

'Dimitri!' a warm voice greeted him from the front garden. Eliza's mother was crouched over the small herb patch, a handful of freshly picked sage grasped between her fingers.

'Sorry I'm early, Dorothy,' Swinton said. 'My friend Fi here apparently hasn't eaten for a week and invited himself along. If it's a bother I'll send him right on his way —'

The comment earned Swinton a rough elbow to the ribs from Fi.

'Nonsense.' Dorothy waved the concern away. 'Emmett always makes enough for an army anyway. We'd be delighted to have you, Captain.'

Fi stepped forward and took Dorothy's hand, planting a brief kiss on the back of it. 'Then please, call me Fi.'

Swinton watched the exchange with a sort of terrified pleasure. If he did away with all the secrets, this was what things would be like. Fi would fit seamlessly into his new life – wouldn't he?

'Fi!' a soft voice called.

Fi's face broke into a wide smile at the side of Eliza pushing through the gate, a basket of bread hanging from the crook of her elbow. To Swinton's relief, she was wearing a thick coat, which hid her growing belly from sight.

'Eliza,' Fi said warmly. 'Lovely to see you.'

'And you.'

Swinton cleared his throat. 'I didn't know you were coming for lunch.'

Eliza raised her eyebrows. 'Surely it's not that unusual for a daughter to break bread with her own parents?'

'I only meant —'

'But you're right,' she said with a playful smirk. 'I'm only dropping these off. There's a horse in labour back at the stables that needs my assistance.'

'What?' Swinton stepped forward to protest. They'd had many a disagreement about Eliza working with unpredictable horses in her current state. But she knew he couldn't say anything. Not in front of Fi.

'Best be off,' she said, flashing another grin as she handed him the basket, her eyes inviting a challenge.

Filled with a conflicting swirl of pride and frustration, Swinton grit his teeth. His wife was a stubborn woman.

. . .

Swinton's afternoon was spent in the arena, overseeing the final touches to the tournament's opening ceremony, due to start that evening. The usually sleepy village of Willowdale was bustling, with a tent city sprawling across the nearby paddocks beyond the arena. Nobles from all over the realm were arriving by the minute, shouting orders at their servants and trying to locate their accommodations.

Swinton wasn't made aware of the king's arrival until he was summoned to his tent. While Arden and the royal family were to stay in one of the many royal estates, on-site quarters were still required for them to retire to amidst the revelry.

As Swinton made his way across the grounds, he silently thanked the gods he'd had Fi ensure the tent's readiness that morning. The king's quarters were sectioned off away from the rest, under full guard as instructed. Swinton reached the entrance, pausing at the threshold upon hearing voices within. He cleared his throat.

'Your Majesty?' he called.

'Come in, Commander, come in,' came King Arden's voice.

Inside, the king's tent was adorned with tapestries and fine furnishings. Goblets and decanters of wine, remnants of the previous meeting, lay scattered on the long table. But there was no one else here.

'Commander,' the king greeted Swinton, his face slightly flushed.

'You asked to see me, my king?' Swinton stepped

forward, suppressing the urge to wring his hands. Their last encounter had not been pleasant.

'Sit.' King Arden waved a ringed hand towards a chair.

Jaw clenched, Swinton did as he was told and waited, his palms growing clammy as he gripped the armrests.

King Arden paced the carpets, his gaze flicking to a canvas bag by the tent's entrance.

'I have a task for you, Commander,' he said slowly. 'Should you complete it, it will see you earn the title you have so desperately sought all these years.'

A great thrill rushed through Swinton, and his mind began to race. His future wasn't lost! He had been right to be patient for all this time! At last, his moment was here.

'I am at your disposal, Your Majesty,' he said, fighting to keep his voice steady. 'What must I do?'

The king considered Swinton, scanning his uniform and the battleaxes strapped to his back. 'You are to go to Valia Forest with a package of immense value. You will deliver it as per a very specific set of instructions.'

'Of course.'

'You will leave today.'

'To-today, my king?' He swallowed. Eliza would be furious. 'What of the tournament?'

'Your captain will take over for you. And in any case, you no longer compete, do you?'

Swinton flushed. 'No, Your Majesty.'

'A shame. But you're available to attend to far more important matters.' He pointed to the canvas bag. 'That is your cargo. Treat it with the utmost care. If it is broken, the consequences will be … unimaginable.'

'Yes, Your Majesty.'

King Arden nodded, motioning for Swinton to stand. Swinton did and moved towards the bag.

'Commander?'

'Yes, my king?'

'Tell no one where you're going. Discretion is paramount to the success of this task. You'll find detailed instructions inside the bag. Do not open it until you reach the Valia River. Do I make myself clear?'

'Yes, Your Majesty,' Swinton said, reaching for the bag. 'I live to serve you.'

'One last thing.'

Swinton waited.

'Remove your axes before you set out. In those parts of Ellest, it may prove prudent to not be so easily recognised.'

'As you wish, my king.'

King Arden brushed past him, nodding to the two guards stationed outside the tent. 'You are to leave at once, Commander Swinton. Good luck.'

Before Swinton could respond, the king's thick cloak was trailing through the mud, a set of guards on his heels.

Swinton glanced at the canvas bag now in his

hand. He couldn't open it here – or at all, not until the Valia River, if King Arden's orders were to be followed.

And of course he would follow them.

'What do you mean you have to leave?' Eliza's voice rose as she stood firmly before the cottage door, barring Swinton's exit.

'I told you,' Swinton said gently. 'I have orders from the king. There is something I must do for him.'

Eliza gaped. 'Now? Amidst the biggest event of the year? What has he asked you to do, Dimitri?'

'I cannot say.'

Eliza folded her arms across her chest. 'I'm your *wife*.'

'He's my *king*, Eliza. I've been ordered not to disclose any information.'

'Do you even *have* any information? Do you even know what he's asking of you?' She fired the questions mercilessly at him, but her words were laced with worry. Swinton faltered – and Eliza pounced. 'Dimitri, how can you follow someone so blindly?'

Swinton threw his hands up. 'Do you expect me to disobey our king? What then? What would that mean for our family? *Eliza*,' he implored. 'If I do this, I can take care of us. If I —'

But Eliza was shaking her head. 'This is about knighthood again, isn't it?'

Swinton was quiet. He watched Eliza's body slump and she stepped aside, holding the door open for him.

'You are chasing something we don't need,' she told him, her eyes lined with tears. 'But if it will make you happy …' She put a hand to her swollen belly. 'We won't stand in your way.'

He stepped forward, folding her into his arms. 'Eliza … I'm sorry —'

'Do not miss the birth of your daughter,' she said into his chest.

He hugged her tightly, savouring the warmth and comfort of her body against his. 'I won't,' he murmured. 'I love you. This will help us, I swear it. Let me do this for our family?'

Eliza nodded sadly within his embrace. 'Come home to us. Quickly.'

Fi insisted on riding as far as the Angove River with Swinton. It was already dark when they set out, tension thick between them. Swinton ground his teeth as they rode through the crisp night air. He wasn't sure he could handle the lecture his friend was sure to deliver, not after saying goodbye to Eliza like that. His chest hurt at the thought of it. He wished there was some way he could prove to her that he was trying to do right by her, right by their child.

He adjusted his grip on the reins. He was already doing the only thing he could do.

After a time, he chanced a glimpse at Fi riding beside him. 'You're not going to say anything?' he asked his friend, the silence getting the better of him.

Fi shrugged. 'What is there to say, old friend?'

'What do you mean?'

A loud sigh sounded. 'You know this feels all wrong, no?'

'I'm doing as my king commands.'

'Doesn't mean it's not wrong, Dimi.'

'You don't even know what it is.'

'Neither do you.'

Swinton took a deep breath before he said something he would regret. He was saved by the sudden sound of rushing water. They had reached the Angove River.

'It's here I leave you, old friend,' Fi said, bringing his horse to a halt and looking at Swinton, a glint of sadness in his eyes.

Swinton forced a smile. 'I'll see you in a few days.'

Fi merely nodded. 'Be careful, Dimi.'

'I'm always careful.'

'That's what I thought, until now.'

'Fi —'

But Fi had already turned his horse around. He didn't look back as he rode towards Willowdale once more.

Swinton pushed on, towards the roar of the river, and towards his future.

. . .

It had been a long time since Swinton had made an extended journey alone. Since Fi's arrival in Heathton, the Battalonian had accompanied him on every ride, which meant there had never been a dull moment. Now, his journey across the moonlit plains of the East Farmlands was different. Quiet but for the drum of his horse's hooves upon the earth. No one to laugh at Swinton's seriousness, or tell embellished tales of the festivals in Battalon.

Swinton found the silence disconcerting, and his thoughts became too loud. Eliza's tear-lined gaze appeared before him, the disappointment on her face more crushing than any blow.

Never again, he vowed. Never again would he be the cause of that look.

He rode hard the next day, across vast fields of wheat and sugarcane, only stopping to water his horse twice. He thought only of home. He daydreamed about the kind of life he'd be able to offer his family upon his return. Hope spurred him on, and it wasn't long before he reached the foot of the Hawthorne Ranges.

In their shadow, he paused, marvelling at the sheer size of them – their forest-covered peaks disappearing beyond the clouds. It was rumoured that the mountains before him paled in comparison to the Hamasaand Ranges and Kildaholm Alps of Havennesse. Perhaps one day he'd see them for himself.

Swinton rubbed the goosebumps from his arms,

his eyes scanning the slopes and treetops. In their presence, his skin prickled uncomfortably.

Magic.

Folk believed that it still ran wild and unchecked in Valian territory, and although the ranges weren't technically part of Valia, he knew the kindred paid that minor detail no heed.

There's magic here, alright, Swinton thought. The most ancient and powerful kind. He'd never met a magic wielder, or Ashai, as some people called them. He hoped he never would. Magic brought nothing but trouble, from what he'd heard.

At last, exhaustion gripped him. Resigned to spending the evening at the foot of the mountains, he brought his horse beneath the shelter of the trees to set up camp. Tomorrow they would reach the Valia River, but for now, they needed rest.

Swinton tried to walk off his saddle-stiffness as he chewed on a hard piece of bread. It was a clear evening, the stars brilliant in their thousands against the midnight-blue canvas. Filled with a sense of awe, Swinton sighed. He'd right everything with Eliza. And he'd be home in time to greet their little one with the life she and her mother deserved.

He drifted off to sleep beside the crackling campfire, a smile on his face.

A scream pierced Swinton's dreams.

A scream of terror, a sound so deeply primal it

wrenched him back into consciousness. He bolted upright and whirled around, scanning the trees in the dim light of the dying fire. His gaze went to his horse – she was calm. The mare was exactly where he'd left her. She stared blankly at him as she chewed a mouthful of grass.

What in the name of all the gods …?

It had been in his dream, then, he concluded. Though the sound of it was still ringing in his ears. It had seemed so real …

Suddenly, he was cold. An icy shiver shot down his spine as the trees around him quivered in the wind.

Swinton's skin prickled again —

'Stop!' Eliza's voice trembled.

She stood in one of the empty stalls at the stables, rake in hand, facing five men who blocked the gate.

'No can do, sweetheart,' one said menacingly.

'There is nothing for you here. The best horses are at the tournament —'

'We ain't fussy. And besides, that don't mean there's nothin' here for us, does it lads?' The man stepped into the stall.

Eliza's knuckles were white as she gripped the rake, holding it before her like a weapon. Fear poured off her. She backed into the wall, but the man lunged, grabbing her arm in a bruising grip. Her coat fell away, revealing her pregnant belly.

The man's lip curled. 'Shouldn't be here all alone, should you?'

Eyes wide, Eliza looked from him to the others leering from the gate. She took a deep breath, and screamed –

Swinton couldn't breathe.

It was *real*. It was happening. Or about to happen. There was something deep within him that knew.

He was already swinging his pack onto his shoulders and mounting his startled horse. He didn't know what sort of magic lurked in these woods, or what magic had been awoken in *him*, but what he'd seen … It had been a *vision*.

He had to get back to Willowdale, now.

His heart hammered as hard as his horse's hooves. They galloped across the county at breakneck pace. Swinton didn't care if he damn near killed his mount. Eliza needed him. He should never have left.

Fear like he'd never known rose in Swinton's throat. He rode through the dark and then the light with sweat coating his skin, unable to shake the gut-wrenching sound of Eliza's cry from his mind.

The journey was a blur. He didn't know how long they'd ridden for, only that it was dark again when he finally reached the Willowdale stables. He jumped down from his sweat-slicked horse and burst inside.

Eerie quiet settled around him. Once again, he couldn't breathe. Forcing one foot in front of the other, Swinton made his way to the southern wing.

His shirt was soaked with perspiration and his head was filled with an ominous humming.

Then he smelled it. An unmistakable scent to anyone who'd been on a battlefield. A scent that lingered, days after …

Blood.

Swinton began to shake uncontrollably as he reached the stall he was looking for.

He fell to his knees. The hay within was in disarray – and spattered with violent red. The walls, too.

A strangled sob escaped him. He looked around, eyes wild.

Eliza … She wasn't there.

With a desperate gasp for air, Swinton hauled himself to his feet and launched himself through the stables once more, boots pounding the cobblestone and then the earth as he raced towards the Carlingtons' cottage across the paddocks.

Candlelight flickered within.

He reached the door, panting, and flung it open, praying that he'd find the Carlingtons having a late supper, that Dorothy would dish out a stern warning for his bad manners.

But that wasn't what he found.

Eliza lay on the dining table. A white sheet, stained red at her middle, covered her still body.

Swinton didn't remember crossing the room. All he knew was that he was now beside his wife, her skin cool to his touch, her eyes closed and her long lashes resting against her colourless cheeks.

An icy fist gripped his heart, and the cold spread outwards through his veins.

He stared at her, studying her face, so different in death than it had been in life. His eyes travelled down to the bloody patch at her stomach.

He gulped for air, not able to inhale deeply enough —

Their baby —

His hands shook so badly he couldn't grip the sheet. And he knew that some part of him didn't want to see what lay beneath. But the fabric – it didn't rise in the right place … It was too flat —

'Dimitri.'

The voice was no more than a whisper, but to Swinton his name was the loudest thing he'd ever heard. He tore his gaze away from Eliza and found Dorothy standing in the hallway.

Words wouldn't form on his tongue. His mouth was dry. And he still couldn't breathe.

'Dimitri.' Dorothy said his name like a command this time, and he latched onto it, as though it were all he had left.

Eliza's mother came forward. Her warm hand gripped his arm and her voice trembled as she said, 'She's gone.'

Eliza. She was – she couldn't be – how – what had —

Swinton searched Dorothy's bloodshot eyes and

there, he found the truth. A mother's eyes could say more than any reality placed before him could.

Eliza was dead.

Swinton's face was wet. He hadn't realised he'd been crying.

'Our daughter?' he croaked.

'Son.'

Emmett, eyes hollow and face bone-white, appeared in the doorway, a bundle cradled carefully in his arms. 'You have a son.'

Swinton took a single step forward before his legs gave out.

He didn't try to stop the fall. He let himself crash to the floor. He felt no pain where his knees slammed into the ground. Felt no stinging scrape against his face as he screamed into the stone. The only thing he knew was the agony of his chest ripping open, of his soul splitting into a thousand pieces.

He screamed and screamed as his whole world caught alight.

When Swinton opened his eyes it was as though a hundred years had passed. He was weary to his very bones and his head ached horribly. He heard the soft crackle of the fire and sat up to find himself on the Carlingtons' settee, a heavy blanket draped over him.

He whirled around to face the dining table. There was nothing on it.

It was just a nightmare —

But he knew in his heart that that wasn't true. The world held less life – he could feel it in his very being, could see it in the dullness of the colours around him.

He knew she was gone.

He stood, unsteady on his feet, feeling weaker than he ever had before. But he couldn't sit, couldn't stay here —

'Dimitri.'

Dorothy's voice sliced through him like a knife, his name on her lips reminding him instantly of Eliza. He couldn't be here. He stumbled towards the door.

Dorothy stopped him, eyes blazing, her grip on his arm surprisingly strong. 'Dimitri, you *will* meet your son. Now.'

An order. Orders were simple. Orders were what he knew.

Numb, he followed Dorothy up the short hallway, to the room he knew used to be Eliza's as a child. Morning light streamed through the window, making shadows dance across a wicker basket on the bed. The blankets within it stirred.

Swinton let out a shaky breath and a gentle hand at his back pushed him forward.

A dark head of hair peeked out from beneath the soft fabrics, and a pair of dark, curious eyes.

'This is Zachary, Dimitri,' Dorothy said, her voice breaking.

'Zachary?' Swinton heard himself ask, not taking his eyes from the bundle before him.

'A few days … before … we told her to choose a boy's name, just in case. She was so sure it was going to be a girl, but I had this … *feeling*. I *knew* he would be a boy. Knew it in my bones.'

Swinton reached out, but withdrew his hand just as quickly. 'Zachary?'

Dorothy stepped up to the infant and with an effortless motion, scooped him up into her arms. It forced Swinton to look at both her and the child. *His* child.

'Zachary Caleb,' Dorothy said, offering the bundle to Swinton.

Terrified, he stepped back.

'She bet three bronze coins we wouldn't need the name.'

Hot tears stung Swinton's eyes at that and Dorothy seized the moment, pressing the baby into his arms. Swinton let her, suddenly mesmerised by the dark eyes staring up at him. His son blinked, seeming to take in his features. It was impossible, but it was as though he recognised Swinton. His gaze seemed to say, *I know you*.

Swinton stared back, in awe of the little life he now held in his hands. Together, he and Eliza had made this tiny person —

But then thick panic filled Swinton's throat. He pushed his son back into Dorothy's arms and ran from the room, shoving past Emmett at the front door.

Grief and terror raking his insides, Swinton

turned back and grabbed a fistful of his father-in-law's shirt. 'I can't do it,' he cried desperately. 'I can't do *this.* Not without her. I can't —'

And he ran.

He ran and ran, all the way back to where he'd left his horse the night before. Someone had tended to the mare, but she eyed him warily as he approached.

'I have a task for you, Commander.'

The king's words rang out in Swinton's mind, clear as the day before him. He thought of the cargo he had abandoned near Valia, the half-completed task King Arden had given him. He thought of what it had cost.

Swinton mounted his horse. He didn't look back at the stables. He couldn't. The very sight of the place would kill him.

But orders … orders were simple. Orders were what he knew.

INTERLUDE

DAWN OF MIST

To the known realm, the mist had always been there. It lingered in the dark pockets of outer territories: a whisper, a dare, a quiet threat. But for all its uncounted years of existence, it remained dormant, as though happily contained to its own self-imposed borders.

Until something changed.

Amidst the secrets, the grief and the greed of the world, there had been a shift. A hooded man, cloaked in sorrow and shame, had followed the orders he'd been given. And now, little by little, the mist began to creep forward, searching.

In eerie silence, it roiled slowly across deserted lands, unknown to those who would yet be at its mercy. It yearned for magic – magic to feed its insatiable hunger.

Once inert, it now gathered strength, as though a formidable purpose had stirred within it. As though a sleeping beast had at last opened an eye.

DASH

Far from the creeping walls of mist, beyond the stretches of forests, farmlands and rivers, the stable master's son awoke.

Five-year-old Dash Carlington was too excited to sleep. It was not yet dawn, but he could hear his pa and the stable hand, Alfred, already packing the carts for their journey. He kicked the quilt off his legs and ran to the window, his stuffed bear, Bryson, tucked under his arm. On his tiptoes, he peered out across the front garden. Sure enough, Pa was tying a thick rope across their belongings while Alfred harnessed the horses.

'Master Dash,' his mama's voice sounded from the doorway. 'If you insist on being up this early, quit your spying and come help.'

Grinning, Dash made to bound past her. Today

was the day! He and Bryson Bear were off to the capital!

But Mama blocked his path, hands on hips. 'How many gentlemen you know go about town in their nightclothes, eh?'

He looked down at the oversized nightshirt that hung to his calves. 'Sorry, Mama.'

Mama's face was stern, but as always, there was a glint of a smile in her eyes. 'Get dressed, then come have some breakfast. We can't have you packing carts with no sustenance.'

Dash nodded vigorously. He was *starving*.

As he dressed and scoffed down the porridge Mama had made, Dash daydreamed of the journey ahead. Pa had been summoned to work in the *royal* stables in Heathton, which meant all three of them, and Bryson, were to move to the capital, where all manner of adventures awaited. Heathton was where all the knights and ladies lived – where *the king* himself lived! Dash had been waiting *weeks* to leave the sleepy town of Willowdale and start their quest.

The front door groaned as Pa walked inside, dusting his hands on his trousers.

'You nearly ready, Dash?'

Dash nodded, showing Pa his empty bowl.

'Good boy. You go wash that up for your mama. Then we'll see how well you've packed up your room ... You've got everything you need?'

Dash nodded, waving Bryson Bear at Pa.

Pa gave an amused sigh. 'Well, as long as you've got him, I suppose.'

They were on the road just after dawn, gold and rose hues sprawling outwards from the horizon. They had two carts filled with their belongings, and a number of horses and stable hands in tow.

Dash looked back at their entourage. The older boy, Alfred, rode Mama's favourite mare, Silver, keeping the rest of the horses in line. Several belonged to the king, but the one Dash liked best was the black stallion that belonged to the Commander of the King's Army. *Xander is a real beauty,* Pa would say as they worked the horses around the corrals. He'd been boarded at Willowdale since he was a foal, but now he was old enough to ride, he was coming with them to Heathton.

'What are you doing, Dash? You'll fall off the wagon craning your neck like that,' Pa chastised him.

Sitting up front beside Pa, Dash faced the road once more, but couldn't wipe the smile from his face. He'd never been outside of Willowdale. The furthest he'd been was the outer grounds of the stables, where Ma sometimes took him to visit her favourite tree. She was odd like that. Dash didn't know why anyone would want to visit a tree. Not when there was a whole big realm out there to explore.

The excitement of the adventure ahead soon wore off as the monotony of the long, slow journey sank in. There was no one to play with except Bryson Bear, and games were limited sitting beside Pa, who kept sighing heavily. Pa didn't seem happy about their move to the capital. Dash had heard him and Mama arguing a few times about it when he was supposed to be sleeping.

As they travelled, Dash tried not to frustrate Pa with questions. He sat quietly, munching on an apple, recalling stories Mama had told him of mythical beasts that had once prowled the lands. Mama was a wonderful storyteller. Maybe tomorrow he'd ride with her instead.

That night, they camped beneath the stars. Dash was giddy with excitement once more. He'd never camped before. Had never eaten by a fire, with the brilliant moonlight shining down upon him. This really *was* an adventure. *This* was the sort of thing knights and warriors did all the time.

He slurped his soup, gazing around the campsite in awe. Mama and Pa were sharing a flask of something that eased the crease between Pa's brows, and Alfred was lying on his bedroll, humming a melody out of tune.

The country air was sweet, despite the smoke from the fire, and Dash needed no instruction from Mama to find his own bedroll. Holding Bryson Bear tight against his chest, he lay down, eyes heavy, and was soon dreaming of swordfights and creatures of legend.

The next day, the paddocks and rows of crops either side of the dirt road became fewer and further between. They passed a number of other travellers, who all smiled when Dash waved at them. One man even handed Dash a plum after Pa gave him directions to the river.

On they rode, barely stopping to water the horses. Pa was eager to reach the capital well before nightfall. Dash rode with Mama this time, Bryson Bear tucked between them as she entertained them with stories of a warrior queen from a distant territory who travelled the realm, training for war.

But then Mama stopped mid-story. Dash looked up to find her staring ahead, her eyes glazed over.

'Look …' she said, more quietly than before.

For upon the horizon was the shadow of the great city of Heathton.

'That's Heathton?' asked Dash.

'That's Heathton. See the castle atop the cliffs?'

Squinting into the distance, Dash's heart soared. Mama was right – he could make out the outline of the sturdy walls and the castle beyond, looking out over the lands.

'Whoa …' he breathed.

Mama squeezed his knee before clicking her tongue and urging their horses onward.

Dash squirmed in his seat for the rest of the

journey. It felt like forever until they reached the city gates, but at last they were there. Dash stared in awe at the guards who stopped their carts. He recognised the symbol on their uniforms: two mighty axes and a fiery crown. The royal crest.

Pa handed them a piece of weathered parchment. Dash could see the king's wax seal on it.

'Very good, stable master. Welcome to Heathton,' said one of the guards, handing the parchment back.

The first thing Dash noticed as their entourage entered the city was the smell. Unlike the sweet open air of the countryside, the air within the city walls was damp and rotten. Dash wrinkled his nose and looked up at Mama. Her expression mirrored his.

They followed the main road into the town centre. Dash had never seen anything like it. Men stumbled out of inns, cursing with words he'd never heard. Ladies stood beneath unlit streetlamps, smoking pipes and inching their skirts up their legs.

'Eyes forward, Master Dash,' Mama said with a frown.

He did as he was told – and gasped. Now he could see the castle walls much more clearly, looming over the city. The castle sat atop great cliffs, with a waterfall cascading down into the river below.

'That's Heathton Falls,' Mama told him, following his gaze. 'And *that* is Heathton Castle.' She pointed to where watchtowers and turrets peeked out from behind the immense stone walls.

Dash squirmed in his seat again, a thrill rushing through him. 'Are we there?'

Mama gave a knowing smile. 'Not long now ...'

The final leg of the journey was the hardest. By the time they reached the castle gates, the horses were sweating and panting. As they pulled into the courtyard, they drew to a sharp halt. A *royal* carriage was passing.

Dash gaped openly as guards opened the carriage door. Queen Vera stepped down, followed by her young daughter, Princess Olena. Dash had never seen clothes so fine. The gowns they wore had so much fabric they could make twenty dresses! No wonder they needed help.

Their carriage was led away, and the queen and princess started up the steps.

Mama hopped down from their cart, leading the horses by hand into the courtyard, averting her gaze from the royals. But the young princess, a few years Dash's senior, reached the top of the stairs and turned to face the gates, her gaze falling upon Dash's cart.

Thrilled, Dash waved at her, Bryson Bear flapping in his other arm.

The princess stared right at him. But Dash's heart sank as she took a breath and turned back to the castle.

'Princesses don't wave to stable boys,' Alfred sniped as he jumped down from the cart behind.

'Why?'

But Alfred merely scoffed and went to take the reins from Mama.

Dash looked up to the castle to see the train of the princess' gown disappear into the grand entrance. He didn't know why she wouldn't wave to him. It seemed like she needed a friend.

Their cottage was located on the outer castle grounds, not far from the royal stables. It was smaller than their home in Willowdale, but it had a great hearth, perfect for telling stories by. Mama said that if Dash was good, she'd tell him one of his favourite tales after dinner.

The afternoon grew late as Mama and Pa unloaded the carts, Dash hovering nearby.

'Dash, stay in the corner over there, you're getting underfoot.'

'But Mama —'

'Master Dash, what have I told you about backchatting?'

'Can I go exploring then?'

Mama clicked her tongue, exasperated. 'Do you —'

'Dore,' Pa stepped in. 'Let him go. It's his home now, and he's been cooped up on the cart for two days.'

Mama looked from Pa to Dash, a slight crease between her brows. She sighed. 'Very well, but be careful. And be sure to be back here before sundown or there'll be trouble.'

Dash couldn't believe his luck. He snatched Bryson Bear from the bench and made to race out the door.

'Forgetting something, Zachary?' his father's voice sounded. Dash knew he'd made a mistake when Pa used his proper name.

He turned back to his parents. 'Thank you, Mama.'

'Off with you,' she replied with a smile.

Grinning, Dash bolted from the cottage, Bryson Bear in tow. Across the vast green paddocks, he ran and ran. He was in Heathton! Here, he could be a real knight – just like in the storybooks Mama had read to him.

In the near distance, he saw the royal stables, and Alfred tending to Xander and the king's horses. Dash shook his head – there would be plenty of time for the stables. Now, he wanted to explore the castle.

He wandered the great structure's perimeter in awe, gazing up at the thick stone towers and at the bustle of servants and guards who paid him no heed. He watched as a cart, piled high with food, was brought in from a side gate. Kitchenhands emerged from a small wooden door and began to unload the crates of fruit and vegetables with great efficiency. Dash spotted why: a pinched set of eyes oversaw the proceedings. By the spotless apron and muscular arms folded across her chest, Dash guessed the woman was the castle cook.

Getting the distinct feeling he was about to get 'underfoot', as Mama said, he left the kitchenhands to their tasks and continued his exploration.

He was about halfway around the castle when he heard a shout, and the sharp sound of sticks hitting sticks. Were there other boys playing nearby? Rushing towards the noise, eager to make new friends, he reached a private courtyard.

There, he saw what he'd only dreamed about. Squires in training.

Dash's mouth hung open as he watched two older boys spar with wooden practice swords. The taller boy was advancing on the shorter one, using his size to his advantage. Dash clutched Bryson tightly as he watched in suspense, noting the way the smaller boy's feet moved like a dance. He did what Mama had explained was a feint – and went on the attack! It was everything Dash had imagined. He watched in utter awe, chest bursting —

Until a pair of dark eyes fell upon him from across the courtyard.

The gaze shifted from his dark mop of hair to the toy bear in his arms —

'You there.' The Commander of the King's Army crossed the yard in what seemed like a single stride. Dash gaped up at him, the warrior's battleaxes gleaming across his back. It was the closest Dash had ever been to the famous leader. Mama and Pa always sent him off with a task when Commander Swinton visited Willowdale.

Now, something flashed across the warrior's face when he looked down at Dash. 'Get out of here, stable boy,' he said.

Dash didn't need telling twice. He raced from the courtyard, grinning like a wolf.

For the next week, whenever he had the chance, Dash returned to watch the squires train. He found that if he left Bryson Bear at home, he could climb one of the trees on the outside of the wall and peer into the courtyard, hidden among the branches. He would watch in wonder as the older boys parried and struck. Commander Swinton watched them too, sometimes calling out instructions or a critique of what he called 'footwork'. But the commander would also often gaze at the spot where he'd discovered Dash, an odd expression on his face.

One afternoon, on his way back to help Pa in the stables, Dash detoured through the gardens. He wasn't *supposed* to, not really, but he liked the fresh smell of the flowers and all the bright colours of the petals.

'Honestly, Thomas, just tell me —' The voice of a young girl.

'It's blue, Your Highness. Just like every other day,' said the resigned voice of an older man.

Dash turned a corner to find himself facing Princess Olena and two of her guards. She was sitting on a stone bench, her face tipped to the sky.

'What are you doing here?' one of the guards demanded.

Dash froze. 'I …'

'Shoo!'

The princess' eyebrows shot up. 'Thomas, who are you shooing?'

Dash frowned. Why was she asking that? He was standing right in front of her!

'Just one of the stable boys, Your Highness.'

'Well, that's rather rude.'

'Your Highness –'

Dash took a tentative step forward. This close to the princess, he saw that there was something different about her eyes. They were cloudy. And although they looked in his general direction, they didn't quite settle on him.

'Why can't you see?' Dash blurted.

He felt a swift cuff about his ear. 'You little –' the guard called Thomas started.

But the princess laughed. 'It's alright, Thomas. What's your name? We can't have you called *stable boy.*' The princess patted the space on the bench beside her.

Dash sat next to her, ignoring the incredulous looks from the guards.

'I'm Dash,' he said, offering his hand as Pa had

shown him. Realising the princess couldn't see, he took her hand in his and shook it.

Thomas started forward, outraged. But Princess Olena laughed again.

'I'm Olena. Pleased to meet you, Dash. And I don't know why I can't see. I was born blind.'

'Oh.' Dash couldn't imagine what it would be like to be unable to see the world around him: the colours, the landscapes, the swordfights ... He looked up at the sparse clouds. 'The sky is big and open today,' he heard himself say. 'Like a giant yawn.' He flushed. 'Is that silly?'

Olena shook her head. 'That's perfect.'

Dash saw the guards exchange amused glances, but they said nothing.

'I can see it in my mind ...' Olena's eyes were closed and her face was tipped once more to the sky.

'Then I should be your eyes!'

Olena smiled. 'I'd like that.'

Dash beamed back at her.

That night in the new cottage, Dash told Mama and Pa about meeting Olena.

'*Princess* Olena,' Pa scolded. 'You must address her formally, Dash. As a show of respect.'

Dash frowned. 'Why? She told me to call her Olena.'

'Gods help us,' Mama muttered into her plate. 'You shouldn't bother the princess, Dash.'

'I wasn't. I was —'

'We don't play with the royal family, Dash,' Pa said gently, rubbing his temples.

'Why not?'

Mama laughed and rested a hand on Pa's arm. 'Perhaps that's a battle for another time, Emmett?'

Pa nodded, looking relieved.

Over the next week, Dash spent his days watching the squires and helping Pa in the stables. He didn't mind the work, not even mucking out the stalls if it meant he got to lead the horses around the corrals. He loved working with Silver, which was lucky because Pa didn't like handling her for some reason.

It was while Dash was brushing Silver's coat one day that a servant appeared at the stall's gate. 'Princess Olena requests your presence in the gardens,' he called to Dash.

Dash beamed and wiped his palms on his trousers as he'd seen Pa do so many times. He started after the attendant.

'You can't go dressed like that!' the older boy said, horrified.

'How come?'

'You ... you just can't.'

That didn't seem like a good reason to Dash. Besides, despite her flouncy dresses, he didn't think Olena would care about the type of shirt he was wearing. Ignoring the attendant's protests, he made his way to the gardens. He was proud that he remembered the right path.

Upon hearing his footsteps from where she sat on the stone bench, Olena's face lit up. 'I can tell it's you, Dash,' she said. 'You don't sound like a giant ogre when you walk!'

The guards exchanged irritated looks. But Dash laughed, delighted. He sat down beside her.

'I hope I didn't interrupt your day too much with my request to join me,' the princess said.

'I was just grooming Silver.'

'Silver?'

Dash nodded. 'One of our horses from home. We brought her with us.'

'Do you work a lot in the stables?' Olena asked thoughtfully.

'Yep. Every day. Pa lets me warm up the horses. When I'm bigger I'll be able to help saddle them and clean their tack. He says I'm too small now.'

'Well, he's probably right. Saddles are heavy things, aren't they?'

'Not for strong men,' he retorted. 'Or strong ladies,' he added quickly.

Olena smiled at that. 'Do you take lessons?'

Dash started to fidget. 'Just letters and numbers with Mama. Mama says everyone should be able to read.'

'She's right.' Olena nodded. 'You can learn a great many things from books.'

Dash frowned. 'But how can you read?'

'There are special books for people like me …' She trailed off.

Dash waited, but the princess didn't continue. So he looked around the gardens, spotting the towering green hedges of the castle maze. Mama and Pa had expressly forbidden him to go near it.

'Have you ever gone inside the maze?' Dash asked Olena, gazing at it longingly.

'I'm not allowed,' she said, frowning slightly.

'Me either. It looks like an adventure, though …'

'How do you mean?'

'It moves in the breeze. It's like it's waving at us to come inside.'

Dash nearly jumped when Olena slid her hand into his. He looked down at their fingers entwined. Hers were soft and clean. His were rough and lined with dirt.

'I like having you as my eyes,' Olena said quietly, smiling.

The next morning, Dash heard Mama and Pa talking in hushed voices in the kitchen.

'— strike you as strange?' Pa was saying.

'Of course it does, Emmett. But what are we to do? It's an order. And an opportunity for him …'

'But *how*, Dore? How has she got this past the king and queen? She's only a little girl herself.'

Dash lingered in the hallway, peering out from the shadows. He saw Mama nod to herself. 'That's the thing about young girls ... Everyone tends to underestimate them.'

'But Dore –'

'I have a good feeling about this, Emmett. It'll be the finest education in the entire realm. I will not deny him that. Nor the chance at friendship.'

Dash entered the kitchen, still clutching Bryson Bear. He spotted the piece of parchment his father held. 'What happened?' he asked.

Mama smiled widely. 'You, Master Dash, are to have lessons with Princess Olena.'

Mama made him wear his best shirt and trousers, and insisted he run her comb through his hair one hundred times. Dash practically bolted from the cottage when she at last gave her nod of approval. Gripping the princess' letter in his small hands, he raced through the grounds and the courtyard, stopping short at the castle's entrance stairs. He was allowed to *go inside!* He would see the great halls, the tapestries of battles on the stone walls, the guards and the nobles – maybe he'd even see the king!

He started up the stairs, chest bursting with excitement. It felt like his name day. His legs couldn't move fast enough. He was going to see the princess – he was going to see her every day! And in the *castle*. Mama and Pa weren't even allowed in the castle –

Dash barrelled straight into a towering figure.

'You ...' a deep voice rumbled, and a pair of firm

hands gripped him by the shoulders. The Commander of the King's Army.

'What are you doing here?' the commander hissed, looking around worriedly.

Dash stared up at him, eyes catching on the jagged scar that cut through the commander's dark shadow of a beard. *Did he get that in a battle?*

'Za— *Boy*.' The commander cleared his throat. 'I asked, what are you doing here?'

Dash thrust the parchment forward.

Eyes narrowed, the commander took it, examining the princess' royal seal and the instructions within. He ran his thumb over the scar on his chin and Dash could have sworn the warrior smiled for a moment before he passed the parchment back.

'Go on then,' the commander said. 'Follow the corridor until you reach the end, then turn left. It's the third door on the right. You can't keep the princess waiting.'

'Yes, sir.'

'I'm not a sir,' the commander said quietly, but Dash was already moving. He could feel the commander watching him as he bolted down the passageway.

Finally, Dash found the right door and knocked.

'Come in, come in!'

He pushed the door open to find a thin, older woman standing by a chalkboard at the front of the room, Princess Olena sitting at a desk before her.

'Sit here,' Olena said, patting the empty chair beside her.

Dash grinned and went to her. Olena pointed to the front. 'That's Mrs Milner.'

The woman smiled. 'I'm assuming this is your young friend?'

'I hope so, or I've got things terribly wrong.'

Mrs Milner laughed and turned to Dash. 'Do you have writing materials?'

Dash bit his lip and shook his head. Did that mean he couldn't do the lessons?

'No matter. Here …' Mrs Milner put a piece of parchment, a quill and a pot of ink in front of him.

Olena elbowed him.

'Thank you,' he spluttered.

Mrs Milner nodded before turning to her chalkboard. 'Now, today,' she said, 'we're going to be learning history. More specifically, the Battle of Heathton —'

Dash's ears pricked up. Battles? They were going to be learning about *heroes* and *fights*?

'— and how Ellest came to gain its most famous knight.'

Dash's heart soared. He wanted to know everything there was to know about knights. He was going to be one, one day.

ACKNOWLEDGEMENTS

An author is a different person by the time they finish writing a book. Let alone a series. It's been months, even years, since they wrote that first sentence, dreamed up that first character … It's even more of a surreal experience when an author comes back to a finished body of work, only to write narratives that pre-date the original plot …

What I'm trying to say is that writing books is a messy, befuddling business, and as always, I need to thank those who have helped me along the way.

First, to the mist dwellers – the original and the new. The bloggers, reviewers and street team members from all over the world who took a chance on *The Oremere Chronicles*. This book is for you.

Special mentions to Jen from A Bookish Peach, Jodie from the AU review, Stacy from Book Series

Recaps, Sarah from The Book Tweeter, Sofia from The Literary Casanova and Shealea from Shut Up Shealea.

Next, to Claire Bradshaw. Editor and friend extraordinaire. Through hair-pulling timelines, title debacles and every scerrik of doubt I had, you were there cheering me on. And we did it. We made it through a whole series +1, in one piece. Thank you.

To my fellow Talem Press authors, Bronwyn Eley and Bonnie Wynne – your books have provided me with much inspiration and escape from the harder times working on the *Oremere* titles, so thank you for the amazing worlds you've created.

Thanks are also due to my partner, Gary, who listens to me ramble about these characters and their story arcs with no end in sight, and asks insightful questions that no doubt make me a better writer. But the most important thanks here are for encouraging me to leave my office and experience the world. And always in the best possible ways.

A big thank you to Eva, for her fantastic advice on making this cover just a little different from the rest. And to Alissa, who executed our vision so well.

To all my family and friends, thank you for your support throughout this whole series: the launch parties, waiting for rankings to come through and forcing my books onto random strangers.

And finally, as always, thank you to YOU, my dear readers. Thank you for loving this series, thank you for requesting more of these short stories, thank you for supporting this little indie author who's trying to make her way in the world.

Until next time,

Helen

ABOUT THE AUTHOR

Helen Scheuerer is a YA fantasy author from Sydney, Australia. Her debut novel, *Heart of Mist,* was the bestselling first instalment in her trilogy, *The Oremere Chronicles*.

After writing literary fiction for a number of years, Helen was inspired to return to her childhood love of fantasy by reading the work of Sabaa Tahir, V.E. Schwab and Sarah J. Maas.

Helen holds a Bachelor of Creative Arts, majoring in Creative Writing, and a Master of Publishing. She is also the Founding Editor of Writer's Edit (www.writersedit.com), one of the world's largest online learning platforms for emerging writers.

She is now a full-time author living amidst the mountains in New Zealand.

www.helenscheuerer.com

DID YOU ENJOY THIS BOOK?

You can make a difference.

Reviews are one of the most powerful tools for an author. They help bring books to the attention of new readers.

If you enjoyed this book, the author would be incredibly grateful if you could spend a few minutes leaving a review on the Amazon page for *Dawn of Mist*.

Printed in Dunstable, United Kingdom

81608146R00201